ACROSS THE
CHEYENNE RIVER

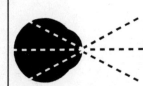

ACROSS THE
CHEYENNE RIVER

JOHN D. NESBITT

THORNDIKE PRESS
A part of Gale, Cengage Learning

GALE
CENGAGE Learning·

Farmington Hills, Mich • San Francisco • New York • Waterville, Maine
Meriden, Conn • Mason, Ohio • Chicago

GALE
CENGAGE Learning®

Copyright © 2014 by John D. Nesbitt.
Thorndike Press, a part of Gale, Cengage Learning.

Thorndike Press® Large Print Western.
The text of this Large Print edition is unabridged.
Other aspects of the book may vary from the original edition.
Set in 16 pt. Plantin.

LIBRARY OF CONGRESS CATALOGING-IN-PUBLICATION DATA

Nesbitt, John D.
  Across the Cheyenne River / by John D. Nesbitt. — Large print edition.
    pages ; cm. — (Thorndike Press large print western)
    ISBN 978-1-4104-7235-9 (hardcover) — ISBN 1-4104-7235-3 (hardcover)
    1. Murder—Investigation—Fiction. 2. Large type books. I. Title.
PS3564.E76A64 2014b
813'.54—dc23   2014018449

Published in 2014 by arrangement with Cherry Weiner Literary Agency

Printed in Mexico
2 3 4 5 6 7 18 17 16 15 14

For Dennis Ward and Doug Canadas

CHAPTER ONE

Archer nudged his horse over the top of the ridge and drew rein. After several miles of climbing through grassy hills with the warmth of the sun on his back, he welcomed a rest. Here at the top, a light breeze moved. Archer tipped back his hat and enjoyed the cooling air on his sweaty forehead and temples. He took a drink from his canteen and lifted his head to see what lay ahead. All along the north side of the ridge and down into the folds of the small canyons on the right, trees and bushes made a dark cover. A little ways ahead as the trail went down, a grove of pine trees stood as if waiting. The shade was inviting, and the fresh green had an aura of comfort.

He touched a spur to the horse and moved downhill. To the left of the trail, the hillside was mostly rocks and grass, with a lone tree here and there. The sun had crossed the high point of the day, so the shadows were

7

moving to the right. When Archer came to the grove of pines, he found a spot off the trail a ways where the ground did not slope too much and where there was room for him and the horse without fighting branches. He dismounted, patted the smoke-colored horse on the neck, and led him to the shade. Once there, he turned the animal around and loosened the cinch.

Archer sat on a thin layer of pine needles and let the reins droop through his fingers onto his lap. From here he couldn't see much of the country around him, but he could picture what he had seen — broad stretches in every direction, with rolling grassland, hills, bluffs, buttes, and long ridges such as this one. It was big country, and lots of it. A man could ride for days and see more of the same, always more. There was no center unless a person drove a stake in the ground, or four stakes. He was nowhere near that yet, but the idea of having his own land was always with him. He tipped back his hat and took another drink of water. By calculation he was not yet halfway to the Bar M Ranch, and it was someone else's place.

The air did not move where he sat, and the scent of pine trees was faint. Archer picked up a twig, broke it with his thumb and two fingers, and sniffed. The pine smell was closer now. Pine and dust. No telling if there would be trees at the Bar M or whether it was country where men dug as much as they built.

A black ant crawled onto his lap, and he brushed it away. Ants were builders. Some of them amassed large domed nests of grass and twigs, and some of them built broad, peaked anthills out of grains of rock. Now that he thought of it, they were diggers, too.

The horse over his shoulder gave a snuffle and a whinny. Archer came to his feet and laid his hand across the top of the horse's nose. He thought he heard hoofbeats in the earth.

A minute later, a horse and rider came over the ridge and stopped. Archer held still. The rider shook his reins, and the sorrel started down the slope. The scuffle of saddle leather blended with the clop of horse hooves as the man leaned back and swayed with the sorrel's movements. When he came to the spot where Archer had left the trail, he stopped and waved.

Archer raised his head in greeting. "Good afternoon."

"Looks like you've got the right idea. Hope I don't crowd you if I do the same."

"Go ahead."

The rider swung down and led his horse to the shade. He was a young fellow of average height and build, sandy hair, and blue eyes. He wore a light-colored hat, a pale blue bandana, and a brown vest. His shirt was a drab grey, and his trousers were of faded denim. He had an easygoing air about him, and Archer took him to be about his own age and station in life.

The young man took off his hat and dragged his cuff across his forehead. "Take advantage of the shade when you can find it."

"Goin' far?"

"Maybe another ten miles." The sandy-haired fellow raised his hat and set it cocked on his head.

"About the same for me," said Archer.

"Oh. Uh-huh. You work up that way?"

"Lookin' for work."

"Huh. Me, too." The young man turned to his horse and tipped his head to each side as he loosened the cinch.

"Goin' any place in particular?"

The easygoing stranger turned to face Archer. He wore a light expression. "I'm goin' to a place called the Bar M. Folks in town said the fella was lookin' for help."

"That's what they told me," said Archer. "We're going to the same place." He frowned. "I hope that doesn't bother you."

"Not me. There ought to be room for everyone — if not there, then somewhere else." The young man shrugged. "If you come right down to it, you were a little bit ahead of me to begin with. We can ride in together, if you don't mind, and if the boss has got room for just one hand, why, I can move on to the next place."

"Well, I don't —"

"Nothin' to worry about. It won't be the first job or the last one that I rode on past. And even if he's got work for the both of us, nothin' lasts forever."

"Isn't that the truth?"

"Yep." The young man's eyebrows went up, and he gave a close-mouthed smile. With his hat still cocked on his head, he had a good-natured appearance. He put out his hand and said, "My name's Boot Beckett."

"Mine's Russ Archer. Glad to meet you." The two of them shook.

Beckett let out a breath and glanced around. "They said we'd come to a pine ridge, and they were right. I guess it's just grass where we're goin'."

"I don't know."

"What they said. Trees are nice, but you don't need 'em all the time. I'm more interested in how the fella treats his help,

11

what kind of work he's got, and what the grub is like. Aren't you?"

"I suppose."

"No profit in worryin' too much ahead of time, though. Find out sooner or later." Beckett drew the makings out of his vest pocket and held the little cloth sack forward.

Archer shook his head.

"Don't smoke much myself," said the other. "A sack of Deuce lasts me a while." He peeled out a tan paper and troughed it. "Worked on other places around here?"

"Not much. I came here last year. Worked for an outfit over east, but they wouldn't give me anything better than night wrangler again this year, so I came this way."

"Where'd you come from?" Beckett shook out a mound of tobacco, then pulled the drawstring with his teeth.

Archer was surprised at the bluntness of the question, but he answered it straight. "Kansas."

"I'm from Colorado. Down by Peblo."

"Pueblo?"

"Yeah." Beckett licked the seam and patted it down. "Got kin there. Yours in Kansas?"

"Don't have much kin."

"Oh. Didn't mean to ask too many questions. Just somethin' to talk about." He lit the cigarette and shook out the match.

"No harm. Just not much to mention. I grew up without folks of my own."

Beckett moved his head up and down as he turned. "How old's your horse?"

"About eight."

"That's what I'd guess." Beckett took a slow drag as he gave the smoke-colored horse a looking over. "Mine's about twelve. That's what they said."

"Had him long?"

"I traded for him less than a week ago. He's all right." Beckett glanced at his sorrel and back to Archer. "You trade?"

"Not much."

"It's somethin' to do." He took a puff on the cigarette.

"Well, I've never had much, and what I've had, I've kept until I was done with it."

"Not a bad way to be. I've got a brother like that. He's had the same pocket knife for ten years. Lives on the home place, drinks his coffee out of the same cup every day. I don't know about you, but half the time I drink my coffee out of a can." Beckett made a spitting sound as if he was getting rid of a fleck of tobacco.

"So do I, sometimes. But if I had a place where it wouldn't get broken, I might keep a crockery mug."

13

"Nothin' wrong with that. Them's good. My grandpa had one like that, and then it was my pa's, until one day he dropped it. Like I said, nothin' lasts forever." Beckett raised his eyebrows. "And it wasn't all bad. When it broke, you got to see what a double-walled cup looks like. Hollow, you know."

"That's what I thought."

Beckett took another long, slow drag, and with a good half-inch left, he dropped the butt on the ground and crushed it with his bootheel. "Well, I suppose we should be movin' along, don't you think?"

"Might as well." Archer reached for the cinch and gave it a pull. "See what this Bar M has to offer."

Archer and his new friend led their horses out onto the trail, mounted up, and headed down the slope. Their road took them northward. As they left the pine ridge behind, the country opened up into a valley of good grassland. The trail ran through the middle of the valley as hills rose on either side at a distance of half a mile or more. The grass was thick and tall, holding the green of late spring, and a couple of fenced-in, weathered stacks showed that it was good hay country.

The two young men rode on, coming to an area of washes and draws, breaks, and an occasional pine ridge smaller than the first one they had crossed. The country leveled out for a while into pastureland of good grass and a scattering of sagebrush. Through two creek bottoms with cottonwoods in full leaf, the trail wound and came out into sparser country. The grass was still thick but shorter and of a paler green, and the landscape was broken with rocky outcroppings.

From a hillside, a buck and a doe antelope watched the two men ride by. The country was climbing again, with more uphill than down. About a mile past the first pair of antelope, Archer saw a buck with two does. They stood in the open grassland about two hundred yards off the trail, the does behind the buck and all three at broadside. The sun shone on their tan sides and white bellies as the animals held still and watched. When the riders came even with them, the antelope flashed to their left and ran away at an angle.

The afternoon had become dry and hot as the sun reflected off the rising ground. When the land leveled out again, Beckett pointed at a layout of rocks on the ground on the right side of the trail up ahead.

"That might be what we're lookin' for," he said.

As they rode toward the rocks, none of them larger than a small melon, Archer made out the shape of a large "M" with a horizontal bar above it. A trail led off into the hills on the right.

With the sun at their backs, the two riders followed the path across the empty land. The grass, though not tall, made a thick carpet. Not much cactus had gotten hold here, and the sagebrush was sparse as well. Up ahead, a ridge grew out of the surrounding plain like the back of a dinosaur Archer had seen in pictures. Rocks along the spine looked like scales or barnacles.

Archer led the way around the south end of the ridge. The shadows had lengthened, and it took him a few seconds to pick out the weathered buildings that sat in the lee of the hump of earth.

"This must be it," he said.

Beckett rode up alongside. "Looks like it."

They turned north and rode the quarter mile upslope into the ranch yard. On Archer's left, closest to the rising ground, sat a one-story ranch house, a plain building of clapboards with a pyramid-shaped roof. Next to it sat a smaller building that Archer took to be a cook shack, and after that a barn and stable ran perpendicular to the other two structures like the long leg of a letter "L" rotated a hundred and eighty degrees.

Archer let his gaze wander beyond the buildings to the east, where the land sloped upwards to a rocky hillside. The late afternoon cast a combination of glow and shadow. For a split second he saw motion, about a mile away, as if a man on horseback had gone behind a rock. When he focused his eyes and bore down, he did not see any more movement.

He turned his attention to the ranch yard ahead of him. The place remained quiet except for the clip-clop of the two horses. The ranch house lay in shadow, and the front windows were as expressionless as lidded eyes. As Archer drew rein and reached for the saddle horn to dismount, the door of the house opened. A man of indistinct shape appeared in the shadowed doorway.

"Help you?"

Archer straightened in the saddle. "Lookin' for a Mister Lidge Mercer, at the Bar M Ranch."

"That's me," said the man. He stepped forward into better light. "You boys can pile off and rest if you like."

Archer took him in at a glance. Lidge Mercer was somewhere in middle age, filling out above and below the waistline. He had a salt-and-pepper beard and a full, shiny face above it. He wore a dull brown hat with a narrow brim, a dusky grey shirt, a charcoal-colored vest, and dark denim trousers. He did not wear a gunbelt, and in Archer's view of him, he could just as well have stepped out onto the porch of a farm implement store.

Archer swung down, as did his fellow traveler. They tied their horses to the rail and faced the ranch owner, who had not come down from the doorstep.

"My name's Russ Archer, and this here is Boot Beckett. We heard in town that you might be hirin'."

Mercer's dark brown eyes moved from Archer to Beckett and back. "You boys come through the Hat Creek Breaks?"

"Yes, sir."

The eyes moved again, and Mercer's voice was smooth. "I don't know how many men I need. I hired a man ahead of you two. You boys aren't afraid to work, are you?"

"Not at all," said Beckett.

Mercer's eyes narrowed. "Some of these cowboys, if they can't do it from horseback, they don't want to." He waved outward. "I don't have much stock yet. I'm building up. That means holes to dig, lumber to cut, anything that needs to be done."

Beckett spit to one side. "If I can't do it, I'll learn how."

"You're not brothers, are you?"

"Oh, no," said Archer. "We just met back on the trail. Rode in together."

Mercer's chest went up as he took a breath. "Go ahead and put your gear in the barn. Put your horses in the corral. I'll see if I can use both of you, at least for a while. Bring your bedrolls to the shack there when you're done."

Neither of the boys had more than a pair of blankets, so they were not carrying much when they knocked on the door of the cook shack.

A coarser voice than Mercer's called, "Come in. Door's open."

Archer pushed the door inward and stepped inside the small building.

"You can leave it open," said Mercer. He was sitting at a table with two other men, and the light from the door lit up the middle of the room where they sat.

The shack was all one room, about twelve feet by twenty, with the cookstove on the left and bunks on the right. Archer counted three beds, and figuring the boss slept in the ranch house, he could see someone was going to sleep on the floor. He sat his bedroll in the corner, and Beckett did like-wise.

"Well, boys," said Mercer, "meet the rest of the crew. This here's Oscar, the cook, and this is Whitmore, the other hired man."

"Whitmore?" asked Beckett.

"Yeah." The man was a slender type in loose-fitting clothes. He had brown hair running to grey, a stubbled face, and muddy brown eyes. When he spoke, a dark area showed where he was missing a bottom tooth. "They named me Willard, but I don't care for it. I go by my last name."

"I knew some folks back home by the name of Whitmore."

"Oh, they're all over. At one time, some of 'em were Whitemore, some of 'em were Wetmore, and half of 'em couldn't read or write."

"This was down by Peblo. They had a shippin' business."

Whitmore shook his head. "Wouldn't know 'em."

Oscar spoke up in the voice Archer had heard a couple of minutes earlier when he knocked at the door. "If I'd known you were comin', I'd have had you pick me up a few things."

Archer assumed the comment was a light joke from an old hand to a youngster. He took a full glance at the cook. Oscar was a short, lean, bald man who didn't look as if he got much sun.

"Maybe next time," Archer said.

"Sure." The cook's face wrinkled as he smiled. "I'll tell you, we're gonna eat in a little bit, so you boys can wash off some of the dust if you want. Throw your water out the back door. You'll see where I've got a spud patch."

"I'll get some firewood," said Whitmore. He put on an old tan hat with an upturned brim and left the back door open as he went out.

Archer did not see a wash basin, so he did not move right away.

Beckett, however, stepped forward. "Shall I get some water?" he asked.

"Sure," said Oscar. "Here's a bucket. The basin's on the wall there in back of you." He turned to Archer as Beckett left the room. "Here, sit down. No one's in a hurry. What's your name, anyway?"

"Russ Archer."

"Russ, like Russell?"

"That's right." Archer took one of the two empty chairs.

"Better to go by the short version. We don't use that other word around here. Ha-ha-ha."

Archer made a "heh-heh" sound, and Lidge Mercer put on a smile.

"Don't mind me," Oscar said. "I'm just the old man that pisses in the bread dough. Ha-ha. Not really."

"Have you always been a cook?" Archer asked.

"Oh, no. I tried barbering, but it got to my back. Then I had a tobacco store, and I got tired of all the loafers. I decided not to work in a whorehouse because I knew only one tune on the piano, so I took to rollin' biscuits and boilin' beans. Hazin' dried apples."

"That aim to be pies," said Mercer, with a smile.

"That's right. And if you bring me a bucket of lard the next time you go to town, I'll fry up a batch of doughnuts."

"I'll try to remember."

"I'll give you a list. I know you boys. You go to town, and you forget about ever' thing except wettin' your whistle and dippin' your wick."

Archer glanced at Mercer, who gave an automatic smile. Archer figured the cook was trying to make a humorous first expression, so he said, "I don't know Boot that well yet."

Whitmore came in with an armload of

sticks and dropped them next to the stove. Without saying anything he pulled back the remaining empty chair and settled into it. He drew a bag of makings out of his trousers pocket, as he wore no vest, and hiked one leg over the other. His rough hands went to work at rolling a cigarette.

"Here's what," said Oscar. "There's only one bunk, and I don't think it's big enough for you two boys."

"I'll sleep on the floor. It doesn't bother me."

"What I'm sayin' is, you don't have to. Not on the bare floor, anyway. You can get a sheet of canvas and some gunny sacks from the barn and make up a tick for yourself. During the day, you shove it under your pal's bunk. What do you think of that, Lidge?"

"Sounds fine to me."

" 'Course, it won't be that way for long," Oscar said. "We're gonna build a bunk-house, aren't we, Lidge?"

"That's right." Mercer smiled again, in a way that suggested that he wanted people to like him.

Whitmore shook out the match he had just used to light his cigarette. "From the ground up. Are you boys ready to dig a foundation?"

"Oh, sure. We're not afraid of work."

"Ha-ha," said Oscar. "This is a good day for you, Whitmore. This boy likes to work."

Beckett came in with a pail of water and set it down.

Oscar said, "Do you like to work, too?"

"I 'magine."

"Well, that's good. What's your name, any-way?"

"Boot Beckett."

"Beckett with the bucket?"

"Somethin' like that."

"Hah. Looks like we'll get along just fine. Isn't that right, Lidge?"

"It sure is. We need to find a crate for a fifth chair, and when the carpenter gets here, we'll make a bigger table and some benches. We'll need 'em later on anyway." The boss turned to Archer. "Meanwhile, it'll just cost you a little work to put together a bed."

"That doesn't bother me either. I believe in working for what I get."

A faint smile appeared on the boss's face, and this time he tipped his head in a gesture of appraisal. "That's a good way to be," he said.

After supper, when the boys went out to the barn to get the sacks and canvas for a bed,

Archer took a long glance at the spot where he thought he had seen a man earlier. Dusk was falling, and the landscape lay still and shadowy. Maybe it had been a deer, or maybe he had seen nothing at all. There was no telling now, at this lonesome time of evening when the land stretched away in silence and a fellow was sure there wasn't another soul for miles.

CHAPTER TWO

Archer kept his left hand on the sorrel horse's shoulder as he brushed the animal's coat with his right. The sorrel was not a tall horse, just a little over fifteen hands, but he was deep-chested and round-muscled. He had a neat appearance, with a narrow white blaze and a pair of white socks in back. His hair was soft, and he was all done with spring shedding. Archer did not know what to expect in the saddle, but the boss had told him to ride the horse, so he was getting it ready.

He put on a double blanket, then the saddle. Rather than pull the cinches tight, he left them snug until he got the bridle on. He led the horse into the yard, made a half-circle, and stopped. The sorrel came to attention and put his front feet together. He seemed like a well-mannered horse.

Archer pulled the front latigo and buckled it at the point where he could put two fingers between the cotton web of the cinch and the horse's brisket. He left the rear cinch as it was, touching the belly but not cutting in.

When he turned the stirrup out to mount up, the horse started backing up, so Archer stuck his left boot into the stirrup. The horse stopped, and Archer swung aboard, settling into the seat and catching the right stirrup with the toe of his boot. But before he could nudge the horse to walk forward, the animal started bucking.

It began with a rocking-horse buck, not very forceful, and Archer stayed with it. He saw the swirling red mane and muscular withers rise and fall beneath him. He reached his right hand across his left and grabbed the slack of his reins in front of the saddle horn. The horse began to buck harder now, raising its reddish-brown head in silhouette against the sky, plunging, and raising even higher. Archer thought the horse might go over backwards, so he leaned forward. The animal pitched down in front and up in back, giving Archer a pop. Archer lost his left stirrup, but still he hung on with one leg loose. Then he felt his right foot slip free, and as the horse came up in front again, Archer lost his seat and slid to the side. When the horse went back down and kicked up its hindquarters, Archer was thrown free. He hit the ground with his left hip and broke his fall with his hand and forearm. As he began to scramble away, the horse's hind end went up again and over him, kicking high in the air with the sun shining on the round hips and horn-colored hooves.

The horse landed and took off forward in a half-dozen plunging leaps until it came to a stop some fifty yards away. Archer pushed himself up to his feet. He felt roughed up, but he could stand and walk. He went forward and approached the horse, which stood with the reins touching the ground at his feet. As Archer took hold of the reins, he noted that the rear cinch had loosened. The horse was breathing hard, but it did not resist as Archer led it back to the center of the yard.

Boot Beckett stood waiting with his thumbs in his trouser pockets. "Hardly a vacation from digging postholes, huh?"

"For you." Archer glanced toward the shade of the barn, where Lidge Mercer stood watching.

"What do you think you'll do?" asked Boot.

"I think I'm supposed to get back on."

"That's what they say. I don't know if

anyone would blame you if you didn't, though. He bucked pretty hard."

Archer ran his eyes over the animal. The brute power had been incredible. "I don't know," he said. He looked across the yard at Mercer and called, "Do you want me to try again?"

The boss walked toward him from shadow into sunlight. "Not today," he said. He had a smile on his face as he came up to Archer and put his hand on his shoulder. "You did real good, though. It was somethin' to remember. You didn't even lose your hat."

Archer reached up and touched it. "I guess I didn't."

Mercer gave another, smaller, smile. "You can go ahead and put him away, and go back to what you were doing yesterday."

A little while later, when Archer and Beckett were digging postholes, Whitmore came by.

"That was a good try you gave," he said. His face wrinkled with his smile.

"I don't know much about it. Boot said I could have held him in a little tighter, but I think he would have bucked me off anyway."

"Well, you stayed on longer than Lidge did. He went flyin' off after the first couple of hops."

"Oh, so he tried to ride it before?" Archer

29

let the knowledge sink in for a second. "Do you think he wanted to see how hard the horse would buck, or how long I could stay on?"

Whitmore shrugged. "I don't know. But we got to see both."

"I guess so." As Archer went back to digging, he felt proud at having done what he was supposed to do, but he wondered if he was cut out for riding other men's rough horses.

Archer was saddling his smoke-colored horse when the boss came out of the ranch house and crossed the yard.

"This should all be pretty easy," Mercer said.

"Sure," said Archer. "Get the things on Oscar's list, send word to the carpenter, and come home tomorrow."

"That's right. And you don't need to get the supplies until you're ready to leave town."

"More or less what I thought." Archer tugged for another hole on the cinch.

"You boys enjoy yourselves."

"We won't get in any trouble."

"I wasn't worried that you would." Mercer lowered his voice as he said, "But there's one thing."

"What's that?"

"I don't know what Oscar might have told you, but don't bring back anything to drink."

Archer paused as he moved to the rear cinch. "He didn't say anything to me about that."

"Good. I'm trying to get those two dried out." The boss's voice was smooth and calm. "I don't drink myself, but that's just my choice. Somebody else wants to, I don't have anything against it. Like you boys. You want to have a drink or two, that's up to you. Just don't bring any back to the ranch. We don't need burnt beans and cross words, or someone layin' around sick as a dog."

"Sure. I'll tell Boot, soon as we get on our way."

Beckett came out of the stable carrying a bridle and went about slipping it onto his horse's head.

Mercer raised his voice to normal. "That's fine, then. You boys have a safe trip, and we'll see you back here tomorrow."

"Thanks."

Archer took the bridle off the saddle horn and worked the bit into his horse's mouth. He pushed the headstall over the horse's ears and buckled the throat latch. After separating the reins he loosened the neck rope, coiled it, and tied it to his saddle. Boot Beckett was mounted and pacing his sorrel back and forth.

Archer led the smoke-colored horse out into the open and swung aboard. It was a relief to be riding his own horse. He caught up with Beckett, and the two of them left the ranch yard on a fast walk.

Boot had his head turned down as he watched his horse's feet. "Gets impatient, this one does. Doesn't want to stand still."

"Trade him."

"I might, but not because I don't like him. He's all right. After all, this is the first day we've rode since we came out here." He smiled. "Our own horses, that is."

A quarter of a mile out, Archer spoke. "Did Oscar say anything to you about bringing him back something from town?"

"No, why?"

"The boss thought he might. Said he didn't want us to bring back anything to drink. He wants to keep those two dried out."

"Just as well. Long as he don't think I'm some kind of a Methodist or Presbyterian."

Archer laughed. "No, he made that clear. He doesn't expect us to be teetotalers. Just stay out of trouble."

"I can usually do that, unless I get pushed

into a corner by a pair of big tits."

"The boss didn't say anything about that kind of danger."

"Well, we won't bring any of them back, either. Just flour and beans and canned tomatoes. What else? A pail of lard?"

"It's all on the list."

The boys rode on with only the sound of hooves breaking the silence of the morning. By habit, Archer scanned the hills to the east. Since that first day, be it morning or midday or evening, he had never seen anything but rocks.

Archer and Beckett rode down the main street of Ashton in the early afternoon. Buggies and ranch wagons were scattered along both sides of the street, and saddle horses stood hipshot at the hitching rails. Two men with tongs were unloading shiny blocks of ice from a covered wagon in front of the butcher shop.

"Shall we go to a café?" asked Archer.

"They serve food in the Drover. That way we can have a glass of beer. It's not every day we get to town."

"We could. If we're going to do that, we should put the horses up. Then we won't have anything to tend to until we get ready to leave in the morning."

"Well, you think ahead, don't you?"

"Sometimes."

The inside of the Drover was shadowy and cool. The front and back doors were open, and a faint motion of air made the place comfortable. Archer and Beckett sat at a table and ordered the daily special, which was beef stew, plus beer from the tap.

The beer was cold, at least in comparison with the day outside. The young men drank two each as they had one bowl of stew and then another.

"I suppose we should get checked into a room," said Archer. "Get cleaned up, send the boss's message to the carpenter."

"Somethin' to do. I don't think we want to stay in here all afternoon. Be stumblin' drunk by sundown."

"Get to bed early that way."

"And miss out on the danger of gettin' cornered."

By nightfall they were back in the Drover. A few patrons had come in, and the lamps were lit. Archer felt rested and clear-headed, and he had no urge to drink fast. He was glad to see that his pal took it slow as well.

The beer did not taste as cold as it did in the afternoon. Archer figured it was a matter of comparison, as they had had the earlier beer in the heat of the day.

"Do you know those two?" asked Beckett. With his eyes he motioned down the bar to his right.

Archer followed with a glance. Two men who looked like ranch hands stood each with a foot on the rail. One was a little taller and darker than the other, and they both had the common look of men who did rough work and came in straight from the trail. Archer felt a tinge of dislike, but he brushed it away.

"Don't recall seein' 'em from before," he said. "May have, though."

"They seem to be lookin' us over."

"Ah, let 'em. Everyone does that." Archer turned so that he wouldn't see the men.

A minute later, as he glanced to his left, he caught a sight that gave a much more agreeable sensation. Down the bar, a young woman with light brown hair and a prominent bosom tossed her head and gave a high laugh.

The man she was talking to was a portly fellow in a broadcloth suit. He seemed to be telling a story and was using his hands as accompaniment. A cigar in his left hand came into view and disappeared. The girl laughed again, and the man wagged his right index finger. His voice rose, but Archer couldn't make out the words. The girl gave

35

one more airy laugh, patted the man on the arm, and stepped away.

Her eyes met Archer's, and she moved in his direction. She had an attractive figure, and she showed it to advantage as she walked. Archer looked over his shoulder at her, then turned halfway as she came closer.

She had brown eyes and a face a little longer than in perfect proportion, but she had a friendly expression. "How are you?" she began.

"Just fine, and getting better."

"That's good. Did you just come into town?" Her teeth were not straight, but they were clean and none seemed to be missing.

"We rode in a little earlier in the day. We work on a ranch north of town."

"Oh, then you're not just passing through. That's better. You can come in every week."

Archer smiled as he took another glance at her figure. "I don't know how often. It's not always up to me."

"Of course not." She gave him a soft look with her brown eyes. "What's your name?"

"Russ. Russ Archer. And yours?"

"Rosanna."

"That's a pretty name."

"Thank you."

Archer felt the conversation stall, but she picked it up.

"What do you do when you come into town?"

"Deliver messages, pick up supplies."

She raised her eyebrows and gave him a teasing smile. "You're not doing that tonight, are you?"

"Not right now. Already did the first part, plan to do the rest in the morning."

"Well, you're free as a bird, then." She laid her hand on his forearm.

"In a manner of speaking, I suppose."

She put on a look of concern and pouted her lips. "You're not tied down?"

"Oh, no. Nothing like that. I just have to remember that I've got work to go back to."

"When I said you were free as a bird, I just meant for right now. That's all that matters. As far as the rest goes, I don't care for men who don't work."

"Cigar store loafers."

She lifted her eyebrows again. "Well, them, too. I was thinking of the kind that live off their wits, or think they do."

"Oh, yeah. They're always trying to get the best of someone."

"You're not that way, I can tell." Her eyes seemed to rove past him for a second.

"I work for what I get, and I pay my own way." As soon as he said it, he realized how blunt it sounded.

She passed it over by asking, "Are you in town for just one night?"

"Yes."

"You shouldn't miss the opportunity, then." Her voice was lower, and she pressed her hand on his arm. "A little relaxation of the right kind."

Boot Beckett's voice came from over his shoulder. "I'm goin' to watch this card game for a little while."

"All right."

Rosanna still had her fingertips on his arm, and she gave a light touch. "Did the two of you come in together?" she asked.

"That's right." His eyes met hers again. He felt light and cool. He imagined lying next to her by a pool of water.

With her voice soft and low, she said, "You're even freer than before." She moved so that her bosom pressed against his arm, above where her hand touched him.

A boldness stirred in him, and his heart was beating in his throat. He swallowed and with a husky voice said, "For a little while."

"No hurry," she whispered. "You can take your time." She moved her hand down his arm and took his hand. "You'd like that, wouldn't you?"

Her voice and her hand and the swirling sensation gave him a vision of cool water, shadow and fern, light mists. He felt the tightness in his throat, and he heard his own voice, still husky, say, "Yes. I'd like that."

At the bar once again, Archer drank from a fresh glass of beer. It was cool, not cold, but it hit bottom and spread a feeling of contentment. Next to him, Boot Beckett rolled a cigarette in his untroubled way.

"It would take a lot of ice to keep this beer cold," Archer said. "I saw them unloading ice earlier, but I think that was at the butcher shop. They probably don't use it for the beer."

Beckett nodded as he paid attention to his work. "I think they cool it with water. Works all right."

"Seems to. Did you learn anything from the card game?"

"I don't think so, but it didn't cost me anything. You learn anything?" Beckett licked the edge of the paper.

"I don't know. It might be like riding horses. At some point you realize you're better at it than you used to be."

Beckett gave a sly smile as he tapped the seam of his cigarette. "That's why you like to ride every day, when you get a chance."

"Tell that to Lidge."

"Oh, he's all right. He don't smoke, and

he don't drink, and he don't seem like a fool for women. But he's straight with us. I've got no gripe."

Archer shrugged. "Me neither. Even if he doesn't do those things, he's got no objection to us doin' 'em. He's not like some old flint that would have us come back the same day."

Beckett lit his smoke and stood for a few seconds without saying anything. He turned his head to the right, and Archer followed his glance.

The two men Beckett had pointed out earlier were walking in their direction. Each one had a whiskey glass in his hand.

They stopped where Archer and Beckett stood at the bar, and the two young men turned.

"Evenin', boys," said the taller one.

Archer said, "Good evening," and Beckett said, "How-do."

"Thought we'd come down and be neighborly," said the man.

"Sure," said Archer. He took a quick glance. In the shadow of a dull black hat, the man had a rough complexion, red-rimmed eyes, and a straight, prominent nose. His coarse hair had a powdery, black color like the dust that settles by the grindstone in a blacksmith shop.

"You boys new in town?"

"We work on a ranch north of here," Archer said.

"Which one?"

Archer hesitated. The stranger was a little more inquisitive than Archer cared for, but it was a harmless question, at least on the surface. "A place called the Bar M," Archer said. "About fifteen miles north."

"I think I've heard of it." The man turned his eyes to Beckett. "How do you like it there?"

"Suits me all right." Beckett took a drag on his smoke and glanced at the man's partner. Then he said to the taller one, "You fellas lookin' for work?"

"Oh, no. We've got work."

"Oh."

The man seemed to resent the implied question. He raised his head and looked down at Beckett, who just flicked his eyebrows and took another drag on his cigarette.

Archer took the moment to get a better look at the stranger. He was tall with a broad spread of shoulders, long arms, and thick wrists. He wore a grey wool shirt with pockets, and he did not wear a vest, so the expanse of grey, along with the red-rimmed eyes and long nose, gave the impression of a

41

large, powerful rat.

"Who runs that ranch now?"

Beckett tipped the ash of his cigarette. "Fella named Lidge Mercer."

"Good to work for?"

Beckett gave a light shrug. "We got no complaints. In fact, we were just talkin' about that. No complaints at all."

"How long have you worked there?"

"Can't remember." Beckett turned his cigarette as if he was inspecting the ash. "What would you say, Russ?"

"A little over a week."

The muttering died down around them, and the singing voice of a woman came from the front of the saloon.

He was only just a cowboy,
But his heart was kind and true.
For he learned to love a maiden
Whose eyes were heavenly blue.

The stranger tossed an irritated look across his shoulder. "I get sick of that song."

"That's 'Cowboy Jack,' " said Beckett.

"I know what it's called. They sing it every night in here. You'd think they'd learn something original." The man took a sip of his whiskey. "What are you boys' names, anyway?"

42

"Boot Beckett."

"Russ Archer. What's yours?"

"Peavey."

"And your friend?" Archer motioned with his head to take in the man at Peavey's side.

Peavey moved back half a step and laid his hand on the other man's shoulder. "This is Wyse. Mister Milward Wyse."

Wyse was a man of medium height and stocky build, with blond hair sticking out beneath his brown hat. He raised his head to show a flushed face and bulging blue eyes. "Just call me Wyse," he said in a gravelly voice. "I don't use the Milward very much." He put on the relaxed smile of a man who had had a few drinks.

"I know a fella," said Beckett, "his name is Willard. He doesn't use it much, either."

"How many names does a man need," said Peavey, with no intonation of a question.

"Three, if you're Henry Wadsworth Longfellow, and no short ones." Boot ran his tongue along his lower lip and raised his cigarette.

"Don't know him."

"He's a poet," said Archer. "He wrote 'The Village Blacksmith' and 'Paul Revere's Ride.' "

"Must've thought a lot of himself."

43

"Others used three names as well. John Greenleaf Whittier, Oliver Wendell Holmes. Just the style of the times, I guess."

"You a schoolteacher?" asked Wyse. His teeth showed as he smiled.

"No," said Archer, "I just went to school for a while."

"No harm in that," said Wyse, his voice still gravelly. "A fella can get caught up later."

"That's right," said Peavey. "Lots of things in this world, they take you a minute to learn and the rest of your life to forget."

Wyse lifted his head again. "Other things, they take you too long to learn, and they're over in a minute." His bulging eyes had a leer to them as he stared at Archer and gave a close-mouthed smile.

Peavey gazed at the wall in back of the bar as if he was trying to ignore the comment.

Archer ran a glance over the two men. Wyse, in a dull white shirt and tan vest, made a contrast with his taller, darker companion, and they seemed to play off of each other as the would-be comic and the grouch. But they had something in common, a coarseness that settled on them as if they were cut from the same cloth. And one other thing: they both wore gunbelts. Wyse had a white-handled revolver in a sorrel-colored holster, while Peavey carried a black-handled pistol in a dark, oiled holster.

The woman's voice carried as she came to the chorus of "Cowboy Jack."

Your sweetheart waits for you, Jack,
Your sweetheart waits for you,
Out on the lonely prairie,
Where the skies are always blue.

Boot Beckett was the next to speak. "Where do you fellas work?"

Peavey drew in an audible breath through his nose, showing no hurry to answer. "We've been workin' for a man named Scott, south of here."

"How is it there?"

"It's work."

Wyse added, "You don't have to like it. That's why they call it work." He smiled as if he was satisfied with his own humor.

Boot took a last pull on his cigarette, dropped the stub, and stepped on it. "Either of you fellas want to buy a watch?"

"What kind?" asked Wyse.

"Good one." Beckett reached into his pants pocket and pulled out a silver watch on a chain. He clicked the stem, and the watch opened to show a face with Roman numerals.

Peavey shook his head.

"Not right now," said Wyse.

"Do you fellas trade?"

"Not watches."

"Well, I'm always interested in trading."

Wyse reached into his own pocket and drew out a tobacco pouch. He opened the flap and pinched a wad of dark, stringy stuff, which he lifted to his mouth. After he got it shifted into place, he said, "I don't trade small things, usually. In fact, I buy and sell more for straight cash than I trade. But I've got some horses back in Nebraska I should bring out here. Good saddle horses."

Beckett's voice was light. "You bet. If you do, let me know."

"Thing is, I've got no place to keep 'em here, and I do there. Got a little place, you know."

"Sure." Beckett slipped the watch back into his pocket.

"Good horses, got 'em pastured on good grass. I've thought of bringin' 'em out here, though."

"What part of Nebraska?" asked Archer.

"The middle part."

"Is that where the grass starts getting longer?"

"Oh, um, well, not so much. I'd say that's

a little farther." Wyse leaned toward the spittoon and shot a stream.

The woman at the front end of the saloon was singing a livelier song now as the piano tinkled a polka rhythm.

You should see me dance with Charley
    When he comes home from sea.
He's a strong and handsome sailor,
    And he loves to dance with me.

Peavey scowled as he took out a sack of Bull Durham and began to build a cigarette. With his head lowered, he raised his eyebrows and said, "You from Nebraska?"

"Kansas," said Archer.

"You like it better out here?"

"I like it all right so far."

Peavey shifted his gaze to Beckett. "You from Kansas, too?"

"Coloradda. Down by Peblo."

Peavey finished rolling his cigarette. He lit it, dropped the match, and stepped on the dying flame. He held the cigarette away from his mouth and looked at it as if he didn't like it. His eyes settled on Beckett again. "Does your boss let you trade horses? What's his name again?"

"Lidge Mercer. Actually, we haven't talked about it."

"Lots of these cattlemen, you know, they don't like their hired men to have stock of their own. End up with three or four kevs to a cow. As for horses, a man's still dealin' in his own stock when he's supposed to be lookin' out for someone else's."

Beckett answered with a light tone. "As far as that goes, he doesn't have many cattle yet. But I can see the point. Fact, I've heard it before."

"Oh, yeah. I didn't think it was news." Peavey gave another critical look at his cigarette. "Is he just gettin' started?"

"Came here less than a year ago, as I understand it."

"How much land has he got?"

Archer thought Peavey was asking a lot of questions, but Beckett seemed unfazed.

"Says he's got title to thirty-two hundred acres."

"And as much grass as he can steal after that."

Beckett showed a hint of resistance when he said, "There's a lot of open range."

"Oh, I just said that without knowin'. Every cattleman I've known, and sheepman too, takes as much grass as he can get."

"I suppose." Beckett glanced off toward the woman who was singing.

Peavey took a drag on his cigarette and

came back to Archer. "You don't talk much."

"I don't know much."

"Neither do I." Peavey raised his chin.

Wyse's voice cut in. "I was wonderin' why you asked me about Nebraska." In spite of his rough voice, it sounded as if he was making an effort to seem neighborly.

"Tryin' to learn."

"Thought maybe you'd been there."

Archer met the other man's eyes long enough to be polite. "Not yet," he said.

"You'll like it." Wyse's teeth showed as he smiled.

The singer's voice carried again.

When Charley's home from sailing,
  He takes me out to dine.
He orders heaps of codfish
  And jugs of sweet red wine.

Boot Beckett was tapping his foot and swaying his beer glass.

Peavey wrinkled his nose as he dropped his half-smoked cigarette and stepped on it. He finished his drink and set his glass on the bar. "Well," he said, "we should be movin' on. It's good visitin' with you boys. We'll leave you to your enjoyment."

"And there's some here," said Wyse with

his leer. "They say that woman who's singing does it all right." When his comment got no response, he added, "So long."

"Pleased to meet you," said Archer.

Beckett lowered his glass and said, "Same here."

Peavey and Wyse went out the back door of the saloon. When Archer could see that they were gone, he said, "Always nice to make new friends."

Beckett put on a simple, open expression. "Can't wait to see the horses from Nebraska."

The piano player was hammering on the keys, and the woman's voice was louder:

My Charley's never naughty,
  He minds his *p*'s and *q*'s
Whenever he tickles bloomers,
  But never ask me whose.

A roar of laughter broke out, with banging on the bar and stamping of feet. Archer glanced around to see if Rosanna was anywhere to be seen. She was standing by the bar where Peavey and Wyse had been earlier, and she was talking to a well-dressed man in a frock coat and matching hat.

Archer felt a tinge of resentment. The man was older, better off, and smooth in his ways. He moved his hand as he talked to the girl, then touched her on the shoulder. A minute later, he tapped her with the back of his fingers. Archer looked away. He had no claim there, or right to think he had — no more than the last man did before she stopped to talk to Archer.

CHAPTER THREE

Archer swung the pick downward and broke loose a chunk of cream-colored clay. He kept his mouth closed to keep out particles that chipped up from the impact. After blinking his eyes, he raised the pick, shifted his hand, and slid it down the handle as he drove the point of the pick into the hard earth again. Another shower of brittle pieces flew up in a spray. Archer rested the head of the pick in the bottom of the foundation, rubbed the dust and sweat from his face, and lifted his hat for ventilation.

In the trench that ran perpendicular to Archer's, Boot Beckett set aside his pick and lifted out a dirt-encrusted rock the size of a sheep's head. He tossed it to the outside of the building area and stood up straight. When he caught Archer's glance, he shook his head.

"Make a big strong boy out of you," said Archer. "Like Charley the sailor."

"You'd think after a week of diggin' postholes, this would be easier."

"At least there's an end to it. We've got only one of these foundations to do. And think of how it would be if he hadn't hired us both."

Beckett widened his eyes. "Bein' a man of my word, I would have let you have this job. I think it would have been all yours."

"Even without you knowin' what you were givin' up."

"I might have gone on to get the kind of job some people have." Beckett motioned with his head.

Across the ranch yard in the shade of the barn, Whitmore was holding the end of the cloth tape measure for Middleton, the carpenter.

Archer said, "Maybe your turn will come."

Beckett shrugged. "It's all right. I said I'd do whatever work came up. I've seen where they just lay a few rocks on top of the ground and put the floor beams on that, but if the builder says this is the right way to do it, then I guess that's it."

"He looks like he knows what he's doing. Measures everything twice, makes his cuts nice and careful."

"Oh, yeah," said Beckett. "That bench is a lot better than sittin' on a crate."

Across the yard, Middleton picked up the plank from the sawhorses and turned it end to end. Whitmore moved position and leaned on the board as the carpenter picked up his saw. Archer wondered how a man got to be precise and patient, whether he was born that way or grew into it with time. At any rate, it was a good bet that the planks for the tabletop would come out neat and even.

Archer wiped his face again and settled his hat into place. As he balanced the pick handle in his hands, he caught motion at the corner of his left eye. Lidge Mercer had come out of the ranch house and was headed for the shack, probably to chin with the cook and have a late-morning cup of coffee. The boss didn't do much physical work that Archer noticed, but at least he didn't come around and meddle. Even from a distance, though, he took his impressions, and he did have a word of praise now and then. Just the evening before, he had said, "I'm glad I hired you boys."

Archer put his weight into the downward swing of the pick and drove the polished tip into the clay. Bits of earth spit at him, and he spit back. But he was glad to be able to do this kind of work. If his time came and he ever had a place of his own, he would be proud to do his own labor.

Oscar had hot biscuits to go with the bacon and beans at noon dinner. "Have at it," he said. "One good thing about workin' right at the ranch. You get three hot meals a day."

"Suits me," said Beckett.

" 'Course, we go through the grub a lot faster that way, especially with six men workin' on it."

"That's all right," said Mercer in his smooth voice. "Don't anyone worry on that account." He smiled. "Not that you would." After a second he said, "We'll get more when we need it. Are you going into town any time soon, Theo?"

The carpenter rested his spoon. "Wasn't plannin' on it."

"It's just as well. We can send the boys when it looks like you can do without 'em for a day." The boss's eyes came around to Archer for a couple of seconds. "Go in, come back the same day. Take a third horse to pack the supplies."

"That's fine," said Archer. "Whatever we need." He glanced at the others around the small table. Whitmore and Oscar seemed to pay no attention, although the mention of a trip to town probably meant something to each of them, just as it did to Archer. As for

Middleton, going to town would be going home, and he had come here to work. He had mentioned a wife and two little ones, but he seemed accustomed to "working out," as he called it. He had come in a canvas-covered wagon carrying his tools and his bed, and at night after smoking his pipe he went out to his wagon and slept.

Mercer reached for a biscuit. "Mortar should get here in a couple of days," he said. "These boys finish diggin', they can go out to gather rocks."

"It'll take more than it looks like," said the carpenter. "Always does."

"We'll get plenty. The second load of lumber should be here a day or two after the mortar."

Middleton had a thoughtful expression on his face. "We can cut lumber for a few days while the foundation sets up. That might be a time for you to send the boys in for grub."

Mercer gave a short, automatic smile. "That should work all right. As long as you don't lose any time for yourself."

"Oh, I'll move right along, as long as I've got materials."

"Don't rule out a day or two of rain," said Oscar. "This country's so dry it don't look like you get enough to wet the bottom of a tin cup, but you can get a pretty good rain this time of year. Isn't that right?" He bobbed his chin at Whitmore, who sat next to him at the corner of the table.

"That's right," said the older hand. "You get a shower or two at other times, but now, and maybe the beginning of October, you get enough that the roads are all gumbo. Good luck gettin' a wagon through then."

"We'll be all right," said the boss. "Nothin' we can't deal with."

Archer and Beckett worked through the hot afternoon, following the lines that Middleton had laid out. The first few inches had gone all right until they hit the white clay, and now it looked as if the job was going to take at least one more day. Archer rested his pick and straightened up. With the sun at his back, he tipped up his hat and wiped his face.

The sound of hammering came from the shade of the ranch house, where Middleton and Whitmore had carried the cut lumber. The only other sound was the crunch of Boot Beckett's shovel. Archer opened and closed his hands a couple of times and went back to work.

After supper that evening, Beckett and Whitmore rolled cigarettes while Middleton brought out his pipe and got it going. During the day the carpenter wore a battered, short-brimmed hat, but in the evening when he hung it on a peg, he looked younger in his full head of dark brown hair. He didn't talk much, and he didn't seem bothered by Oscar's prattle.

"Wherever you boys go, you want to be careful about gettin' the clap. The worst place is where the girls have been around soldiers, because them fellas pick it up and carry it all over."

"Oh, the girls do, too," said Whitmore.

"Sure they do. That's why you can catch it right here in town, though you stand a better chance if you're at a hog ranch next to an army post."

Beckett paused before lighting his cigarette. "How do you keep from gettin' it?"

Oscar gave him a direct look. "If you don't know, it's time you did. You save a little whiskey in the bottom of the bottle, and you use it to douse the little feller when you're done."

"And that works?"

"Haven't known it to fail. But you drink the last drop of whiskey and don't have any for that, and you might find out otherwise."

Middleton laid his index finger against his long thin nose and moved his eyes in Mercer's direction.

Oscar waved his hand. "Oh, Lidge don't mind this kind of talk. He's heard it before. Isn't that right?"

The boss rubbed his salt-and-pepper beard and gave a little laugh. "Don't worry about me. Oscar likes to talk. But when it comes to goin' off with the girls, he knows as well as I do that all that's for young men."

"Ha-ha. That's right. And that's why I'm warnin' 'em, so they won't come back all doubled up and can't do their work."

"Well, there's plenty of work to do," said Mercer.

Silence hung in the air for a minute until Boot shifted on his bench and brought out his silver watch. He clicked it open and showed it to Middleton.

"That's nice," said the carpenter.

"You bet it is. All silver. Keeps perfect time. You could be a railroad conductor with this one."

"Uh-huh."

"Thing is, I got a nickel-plated watch that keeps good time. I'd like to see this one in the hands of someone who could use it."

Middleton puffed on his straight-stem pipe. "Is it an heirloom?"

"No, I traded for it."

"So you want to sell it or trade it to

59

someone else."

Beckett shrugged. "If someone wanted to."

"Well, it's a handsome watch, but I've got no need for another one right now." The carpenter puffed another cloud.

"That's fine. Never any harm, though."

"Oh, no."

Beckett leaned back to put the watch in his pocket, and Whitmore spoke.

"You say it keeps good time?"

Beckett relaxed and sat forward. "Oh, perfect. You could use it the rest of your life, or you could sell it anywhere. Like money in the bank."

Whitmore pushed out his lower lip. "I don't have any spare money right now."

Beckett's eyebrows went up. "I'm always interested in a trade."

"Can I see it?"

"Sure." Beckett handed over the watch.

Whitmore opened and closed the case, wound the stem, and held the watch up to his ear. Then he opened it and looked at it again.

"If it doesn't keep good time for you, I'll take it back. Hundred percent."

Whitmore's eyebrows went up as he continued to study the watch. "How much is it worth?"

"What have you got?"

Whitmore let out a breath. "I've got a pair of spurs I've been hangin' onto. There's as much silver in the rowels as there is in this whole watch."

"Do you have 'em here?"

Whitmore rose and handed back the watch. "I'll go get 'em."

He came back in a minute with a ditty bag made out of a trouser leg. He set the bag on the table and drew out a pair of shiny spurs, which he handed across to Beckett.

"These are nice." Beckett spun the rowel on each one. "These are made out of silver dollars, aren't they? The rest of this is nickel-plated."

"I think so. But they're good as new."

"I can see that." Beckett handed the spurs back to Whitmore. "Pretty close. But if you had a little somethin' else to throw in, I might think it was more even."

Whitmore peeked inside the bag and said, "What would you think of a hoof knife? It's like new, also."

"We can look at it."

Whitmore reached in and took out the knife. The handle was clean, and the blade with its curled tip was shiny. Whitmore held it up, but Beckett did not reach for it.

"Anything else?" he asked.

"I think that's all." Whitmore set the hoof knife on the table.

"Oh, I don't know," said Beckett. "This is a better kind of watch. Don't you have anything else?"

"Just a ring."

Beckett perked up. "A ring? Like for a girl?"

"No, a cinch ring." Whitmore looked around the table. "Don't laugh. It's never been in the fire. Never been used for anything." He sat up straight, lifted the end of the bag, and shook out a three-inch iron ring that clinked on the table.

Beckett twisted his mouth. "I guess it's good for somethin'."

"Rings and hooks and chains have a lot of use," said Middleton.

"That's true," said Beckett. "I hadn't thought of it. You could use this at the end of a chain on a wolf trap."

"Well, that's all I've got," said Whitmore. "It was the last thing I had to offer."

"Oh, that's good enough, I guess." Beckett held out the watch, accepted the spurs in return, and then took the knife and ring.

Oscar pointed at Middleton. "See there? You could have bought that watch and sold it later to some swell."

The carpenter puffed on his pipe. "I just

stick to my work, and I don't expect to get rich."

"No harm in that," said Oscar. "And I didn't mean you'd get rich buyin' and sellin' trinkets. No offense, Boot."

"None at all. It's just somethin' to do."

Mercer had been silent all this time. "Seeing that watch reminds me," he said. "The next time you boys go to town, one of you could set your watch by the clock at the train station. Then when you get back, I can set my clock to yours. Mine tends to pick up a minute or two over a period of a couple of months. If I don't reset it every once in a while, I'm half an hour off when the shortest days of the year come around."

"I'll do it," said Beckett. "My nickelplated watch keeps good time."

"Either of you," said Mercer.

"I'll do it," Beckett said again. "I should use that watch anyway."

Beckett climbed onto the wagon seat next to Archer. "Can you believe that?" he asked. "Last rock of the day. Now home?"

Archer glanced at his pal, who was holding his vest out by the bottom hem. The fabric was torn in an irregular curve, and a flap of it hung down.

"How did you do that?"

"One of them rocks. Pinched it against the sideboard, and she ripped."

"Too bad," said Archer. "Now you'll have to sew it up."

Beckett shook his head. "Not me. I don't even have a needle and thread."

"I do. I'll lend 'em to you."

"Nah, that's all right. I'll get someone to do it. Cost me two bits." Beckett gave a disapproving look at the tear in his vest.

Archer motioned with his elbow. "Maybe you can give her that ring. Find a seamstress with fingers three inches thick."

"Or one who's got a fella that's a cinch-ring artist."

Archer slapped the reins, and the wagon started toward the ranch. Beckett took out the makings and began to build a cigarette.

"The way I've got it figured," he said, "we'll handle every one of these rocks at least three times. And between the diggin' and the haulin' and then the settin' in place, this foundation's goin' to take at least a week."

"Well, it's work. And you never know how some of this might be useful to know in the future."

"That's true." Beckett moved with the rocking of the wagon as he shook tobacco into the paper. "But I wouldn't want to get

64

so educated at it that this would be the kind of work I do from now on."

Archer looked ahead as he handled the reins. "You remember what Lidge said the first day we got here. Some of these punchers don't want to do anything if they can't do it sittin' on the back of a horse. Well, they come and go. The way I see it, the more a fella knows how to do, the more days out of the year he's going to have work. Especially on a ranch. No matter what comes up, somebody's got to do it, and you can't just send downtown for it."

Boot held out his torn vest and looked at it again. "Well, some things."

"Oh," said Archer, still looking ahead, "if you don't want to do that sort of thing yourself, you get yourself a little woman. Next thing you know, you've got clean clothes, hot meals —"

"I'm not sure if I'd want to move her in with the rest of you."

Archer turned to him. "I was thinking past the Bar M. Don't you?"

"One thing at a time. I've got to get this vest sewed up, and then I want to get a six-gun."

"Of course. But can you see yourself the age of Oscar or Whitmore, still living in a bunkhouse and working for poor wages?"

Beckett paused in rolling his cigarette as the wagon rocked. "I try not to think that far ahead. You know me, I take things as they come."

"Well, you have to, to a certain extent. But I hope I'm not doing the same thing twenty years from now, working for day wages and living in a boar's nest."

"Ah, hell, you can walk away from it any time." Beckett went back to rolling his cigarette.

"Sure. And go to another place just like it. That's all right when you're young. But I want to be building on something, and I don't mean someone else's bunkhouse." He hesitated and then said, "Growing up as I did, I never had a thing of my own. I didn't even feel like I owned the clothes I wore. And all the time, I thought someday I'd like to have something to call my own."

"So you want to have your own place."

"That's right. One of these days when the chance comes up, when they open up another tract of land for claims, I want to file. Have my own piece of land."

Beckett raised his eyebrows as he licked the edge of the cigarette paper. "And have a little woman to wash your clothes and keep a milk cow."

Archer smiled. "That was for you. I don't

need someone to take care of me. I've learned to do everything for myself. But if I don't want to spend the rest of my life living among other men, a woman's a pretty good alternative." He leaned with the wagon as it rolled over a hump. "I thought everyone wanted something like that — a place of his own, and someone to pull together with. Didn't you always assume it?"

"I suppose." Beckett lit his smoke. "Don't know that everyone else does, though."

"Maybe you're right. It seems like some fellas tried and didn't make it, but as time goes by and I see more, I wonder if some didn't want it to begin with."

"Or didn't want it bad enough."

Archer tipped his head in consideration. "That could be. No doubt there's more to some people's stories than meets the eye."

"Yep."

"Like why a woman with fingers three inches thick would have a cinch-ring artist for a sweetheart."

Beckett blew away a cloud of smoke. "Maybe he just looked for someone who fit what he had."

Archer laughed. "Or she did."

Neither of them spoke for the next several minutes as the wagon rolled on toward the ranch. Beckett smoked his cigarette down to a stub and ground it out on the floor-board. Archer alternated between looking at the surrounding country and keeping an eye on the horses as they pulled the wagon.

As the wagon jostled down the last half-mile slope toward the ranch headquarters, an object caught Archer's eye. A horse and rider were leaving the yard and setting out onto the trail for town. The man was dressed in dark grey clothes and a dull black hat. He rode hunched in the saddle, and his pointed nose was visible at a distance. The horse was a large, brown animal that matched the rider with its drab tone.

"Looks like someone leaving," said Archer.

Beckett yawned. "Sure does."

"You know who it looks like to me?"

"Who?"

"That fellow Peavey."

Beckett sat up and paid attention. "Oh, yeah. I think you might be right."

Lidge did not come out of the house while the boys were unloading the rocks, and he did not show up for supper until everyone else had sat down. An uneasiness seemed to hover in the cook shack. The boss made furtive glances during the meal but did not speak to anyone. Oscar made small talk with Whitmore and Middleton, while Archer and Beckett kept to themselves. Mercer got up from the table as soon as he finished eating, and after the usual comment of "Good grub, Oscar," he picked his hat off the peg and went back to his own quarters.

The atmosphere was more relaxed now, but no one mentioned the afternoon's visitor. Left to his own thoughts, Archer wondered about Peavey's line of questions that night in the saloon. The man had acted as if he didn't know Lidge Mercer, but the apparent effect of his visit gave Archer some doubt. Peavey had also said he was not looking for work out this way. Archer believed it then and still believed it now.

Archer led the smoke-colored horse away from the hitching rail. He set his reins, put his foot in the stirrup, and swung aboard. Boot Beckett was mounted and waiting on the sorrel, shifting with the horse as it fidgeted. Whitmore handed Archer the lead rope to the packhorse, a short-coupled bay. Archer checked to see that the panniers were in place, snugged up with the light load of newspapers and burlap sacks for packing the supplies.

"So long, boys," said Whitmore. "Have a good trip."

"Thanks. We should be home by dark." Archer nudged his horse, and the group left the ranch yard at a fast walk. Beckett let his horse run out ahead and then stopped it at the end of the ridge that resembled a dinosaur's back. He was walking it in circles when Archer caught up.

"Did Lidge say anything about the liquor this time?"

Archer shook his head. "Nah. He didn't have much to say. But I figured he knew that I knew that he didn't want us to bring any back."

"I imagine." After a couple of seconds Beckett said, "Did it seem to you that he was actin' kinda fidgety ever since Peavey dropped by?"

"It sure did. But I didn't see where it was my place to say anything."

"Oh, no. If there's anythin' to it, it's between them."

"Well, I hope so," said Archer. "I don't care much for Peavey."

"Neither do I."

They rode on for a minute without speaking until Archer said, "On the lighter side, though, Oscar had his warning for me."

"Oh, yeah," said Beckett. "He told me, too. Said you could catch it in the daytime just as easy as at night. Good thing is, there's none to be caught at the ranch, so he doesn't need any whiskey to kill the germs."

They rode down out of the hard grass country, across two creek bottoms, through pasture land and breaks and the valley of lush grass. At the foot of the pine ridge they watered the horses at a small green pond that Archer preferred not to drink from. After a rest, they climbed the ridge, crossed the grassy hills, and rode down into the town of Ashton.

When they hit the main street, Beckett said he was going to look for a place where he could get his vest mended.

"Did you bring along your ring?" Archer asked.

"Didn't care to. Not the kind of thing I like to carry when I'm ridin' past other people's cattle. Not as bad as havin' a runnin' iron underneath your saddle skirt, but not polite all the same."

"Well, good luck findin' someone. I'll see you a little later. Don't forget to set your watch by the station clock."

"That's the first thing I'll do."

Archer rode along leading the packhorse until he came to the general store. He turned in to the hitch rack and dismounted, holding the lead rope clear. He loosened his saddle cinch with one hand and then tied the horses to the rail.

Up on the sidewalk, he crossed into the shade of the awning. After a stretch in the country, he noticed simple objects of everyday town life, like the barrel with brooms and mops sticking out like a shock of corn. He walked past the display, opened the door, and heard the tinkling of the bell as he stepped into the cool interior.

Fenton the storekeeper was standing behind the counter. Dressed in his white shirt and collar, black bow tie, and green apron, he held a scoop at chest level and was trickling beans onto the scale. He had his head lifted and his mouth open as he peered through his glasses at the balance needle. A broad woman in a full dress and small hat watched.

Fenton tipped up the scoop and said, "That's two pounds."

The woman moved her head down and up in slow motion.

"Be with you in a minute," said the storekeeper.

Archer stood with his thumbs in his pockets as Fenton wrapped up the woman's order and wrote the sale on her account. When the woman with her shopping bag turned away, Archer stepped forward.

Fenton's voice rang out. "Yes, sir, and how

can I help you today?"

Archer wondered at anyone calling him "sir," even when it was the artificial manner of the ready businessman. From the storekeeper's blank stare, Archer could tell that Fenton cared no more about him than about any other common working man.

"Here's a list for the Bar M."

"Mercer, uh-huh." Fenton took the half-sheet of paper and studied it.

Archer waited, and with nothing else to do he observed the storekeeper. The man had a hard, pale face with a bristly mustache. His dark hair was parted in the middle and combed back to the sides, slick as with a pomade. He filled out his shirt and apron, and his abdomen swelled and receded with each breath.

"You've got fifty pounds of beans here. Do you want it in two twenty-fives?"

"That would be fine."

"Same with the flour. Two twenties?"

"Sure."

The grocer's mouth went out like a flower and came back. "I can get them. I'll see about some help with the canned goods." In a louder voice he called, "Kate!"

A dark-haired girl came out from behind one of the aisles. She was wearing a grey apron and had her hair pinned up, but

Archer saw enough to appreciate. Her hair was a rich dark brown that matched her eyes. She wore a high collar and a long-sleeved dress, and her figure was shapely.

"Yes?"

"Get a dozen cans of tomatoes and a half-dozen of peaches."

"Yes, sir." The girl turned to leave, but her boss's voice stopped her.

"That's not all. Get us a pail of lard."

Archer's jaws tightened at the condescending tone, and he shifted his eyes to catch a glimpse of Fenton. The storekeeper was taking a full and obvious look at the girl's figure as she walked away.

Fenton turned to Archer with no apparent awareness of having been caught gawking. "And fifty pounds of potatoes. I'll get them as well. They come in twenties and fifties. I'll give you the fifty in one sack, and you can divvy the weight if you want. I see you brought a packhorse."

"That's right. I've got some grain sacks. We'll double-bag the flour."

"Always a good idea. Coffee, too. I see it's on here."

"Uh-huh."

"This is quite a list. That horse'll have a heavy load."

"I can carry some of it on the back of my

saddle, and my partner can do the same."

"Oh, you've got someone with you. I didn't see him."

"He'll be along. Same fella that was with me last time."

"Of course."

As Fenton stacked the items on the counter and marked them on the bill, Archer carried them out to the panniers. On one trip, he met the girl, Kate, who stood inside the door with the six cans of peaches.

"Thanks," he said as she began to hand them to him one by one. Although his hand did not touch hers, he was conscious of touching each can while she did.

Her dark eyes met his as she said, "You're welcome."

He made himself speak before the moment passed. "Did I hear your name is Kate?"

"That's right."

He held three cans of peaches with one arm as he took off his hat. "My name's Russ. Russ Archer."

"Nice to meet you."

"The pleasure's all mine."

She smiled, almost a wince of shyness.

"So you work here," he said, anxious not to let the conversation die.

"Yes."

"And you live in town, I imagine." He had a vision of standing on a porch, waiting for her to come to the door.

"Yes, I do. I have a room in the house that's in back of the store here."

A sinking feeling went through him. "Oh, are you, um, part of the family?"

"No, but I room with them and I help out."

Fenton's voice sounded. "What have you got there?"

"Peaches," she called back.

"Did you mark 'em down?"

"Yes, I did." Her eyes came back to Archer as she handed him the last two cans together.

He took his chance. "I'd like to see you again some time."

Her eyes were shining and her voice was soft as she said, "I'm always here."

"Here," said Fenton, in a loud echo. "Five pounds of raisins."

"I'll see you later," said Archer. "Thanks for your help."

"You're welcome." Her words were quick as she ducked away.

He did not see her again as he finished loading the supplies. He had the coffee and raisins tied across the back of his saddle and a sack of rice balanced on the seat when

Boot Beckett showed up. He raised his chin as he gave the pannier lashes a looking over.

Archer said, "Let's get this tied onto yours, and we can start back."

Beckett gave a slow tip of the head. "Did you forget about eating?"

"I guess I did. Looks like you got your vest mended."

"Oh, yeah. First-rate." Beckett swung down from his horse.

"No comments about who did it?"

"Not today."

Archer gave his best imitation of a girl's voice. "Let me throw a stitch in that for you, honey."

"Ah, come on. Let's get this tied on and go eat."

CHAPTER FOUR

Archer waited with a fork in his hand as Oscar set a platter of flapjacks on the table.

"Here's grub," said the cook. He went back to the cookstove as the men dug in.

Light fell from the kerosene lamp overhead, and Archer was relaxed as he ate. With all the beds except Oscar's moved to the new bunkhouse, the cook shack had an ample feel to it. Archer did not have to hunch his shoulders or hold his elbows in, and Boot Beckett had set his hat on the bench between them. Across the table, Whitmore and Mercer had plenty of room as well.

Oscar came back to the table with the coffeepot. "I don't know if you can still smell it, but there was a skunk underneath here in the middle of the night."

"You didn't shoot at it, did you?" asked Mercer.

"Next time I might. So don't be surprised

if you hear a shot in the night."

The boss took the molasses jug that Whitmore handed him. "Like Middleton said, that's a good thing about having a solid foundation. You don't get anything crawling under the building. Not just skunks, but other things that get under there and die. You get a dead coon or possum, now that's a smell."

Boot Beckett crinkled his nose and set down his fork.

"Sorry," said Mercer. "Not the best thing to talk about at mealtime."

Oscar sat down at the end of the table and scooted his chair in under him. "I wish we could do the same here. Close it up all the way around."

"Lot of work," said Whitmore.

"I'm the one that has to sleep here. And as far as that goes, we all eat here."

Mercer set down his coffee cup. "We might be able to do something. There's some of that mortar mix left, and we can plaster the rest with mud. You boys know where to find more rocks, don't you?"

"There's no shortage of 'em," said Archer. "We won't have to dig a footing, will we?"

"Hardly at all. Just enough to settle the rocks in, and we'll fill up the chinks. What's the matter, Boot?"

"Oh, nothin'."

"He ripped his vest loading rocks last time."

"I remember," said Mercer. "Well, that can be avoided. Just take it off when we get out there."

"You goin', too?" Oscar's voice had a note of surprise.

"It'll do me good to get out and look around." Mercer dug into his hotcakes.

Something in the boss's tone of voice made Archer reflect. He had noticed that Mercer hardly ever left the immediate area of the ranch headquarters. When he did venture out, it was on foot or in the wagon, and he did not go alone.

"We'll be careful not to rip your clothes," said Beckett.

The boss spoke without looking up. "What do you boys do for snakes?"

Beckett answered. "We stay away from 'em. Sometimes get one with a rock."

Mercer glanced each way. "Neither of you has a side-gun, eh?"

"Not yet," Beckett said. "I plan to get one, though. I think Russ does as well."

"Bring along a rifle," said Oscar. "In case you get a chance at some game meat."

Beckett perked up. "That would be all right. I wouldn't mind takin' a pop at one."

Mercer took another sip of coffee. "If we see one, we'll let you take the shot."

As Archer expected, the boss let his two hired hands lift all the weight. He stood by and watched, rubbing his beard once in a while and passing judgment on the size of the rocks. The boys passed up boulders that they would have loaded for the foundation of the bunkhouse.

"Nothin' bigger than a watermelon," said Mercer in his smooth voice.

Boot Beckett, who had ridden a ranch horse alongside as Archer and the boss rode on the wagon seat, had his vest tied onto the saddle. He wore leather gloves and picked up rocks of various sizes.

Archer did the same. When he had a piece that he needed both hands to lift, he held it away from himself as he hefted it over the side of the wagon. Before long he began to perspire. The day had started out cool but it had warmed up, and working near bluffs and outcroppings was always warmer than out in the open.

The heap in the wagon box was growing. Archer lifted a rock about the size of a man's head and set it on the edge of the pile inside the wagon. As he was rubbing the grains and dust from his gloves, he heard Mercer's voice.

"I wonder who this is."

Archer walked to the front of the wagon and stood by the boss. Two riders were angling down the slope from the southeast. Archer took off his gloves and wiped his shirtsleeve across his forehead.

"They don't look familiar to me," said Mercer. "Do they to you?"

"No." Archer drew his brows together. The men and horses were common looking, with nothing bright or flashy, and they seemed in no hurry.

Rocks clattered in the wagon, and Boot Beckett came alongside Archer. "Looks like company," he said.

The riders picked their way down the slope and drew rein about twenty yards away on higher ground. They did not dismount, so Archer assumed they were not going to stay long.

"Good morning," said Mercer. "Not quite afternoon yet."

"Afternoon," said the man on the right. His dark hat shaded a tight face with small, deep-set eyes, a pug nose, and a chin pushed up to his mouth. He was a tall man who sat slumped in the saddle and hung out a little around the belt. He wore a brown vest, dark-blue wool shirt, and leather chaps. His spurs had rowels smaller than a dime.

Silence hung for a few seconds until the boss spoke again. "My name's Lidge Mercer. I own the Bar M, which is where we are right now. And yourself?"

"Name's Jenks. And this is Crowell." The man tipped his head toward his partner.

Crowell was a pimple-faced fellow with a weak chin and crooked teeth. He had wavy blond hair and a dark brown hat with a flat brim. The blue bandana around his neck could use a wash.

Mercer broke the silence again. "What can I help you with?"

Jenks drew himself up straight. "Thought you should know you're off your range."

Mercer gave a forced laugh. "Well, friend, I think you might be mistaken. I've got title to this land, and I've got a pretty good idea of where it begins and ends."

"Anyone can make a mistake," said Jenks, "so just count this as a friendly warning." He lowered his right hand out of sight to where his gun and holster would be.

No sound came from Mercer. He had an uncertain expression on his face as his eyes roved in the direction of the two strangers.

Archer spoke up. "Do you work for someone around here?"

Jenks's small eyes bored down on him. "Who are you?"

"My name's Archer. I work for the Bar M."

"Pickin' up rocks."

Archer felt his blood rise. "At the moment."

"Pretendin' to be a cowpuncher. You ought to be punchin' holes in cheese."

"That's for me to decide."

"You look like a puncher."

"I might be."

Jenks's eyes flickered and came back to Archer. "Are you the tough one out of your bunch?"

"Depends on who wants to find out." Archer made his hands keep still as he held them by his sides. He took a full breath and kept his eyes on the other man.

Jenks looked at Crowell. "You want him?"

Crowell showed his crooked teeth as he said, "Go ahead."

Jenks stepped down from his horse. "I'm a sportin' kind. I see none of you is packin' a gun." He unbuckled his gunbelt, took it off, buckled it again, and hung it on his saddle horn. "One on one. You make it more, and you'll wish you hadn't." He took off his hat to reveal a bulbous, bald head. He hung the hat on the horn with his gunbelt and handed the reins to Crowell, who had also swung down and now stood with his thumb on his belt.

Archer took off his hat and set it on the wagon seat. He caught a glance at the rifle lying on the floorboard in its scabbard, and he hoped no one would have a need for it. He cast a glance at Mercer, who had stepped back and assumed the role of spectator. Boot Beckett stood in the same place as before and had his face drawn tight.

Archer put up his fists and moved forward. Jenks waited. Archer took another step, and a fist came out of nowhere and slammed him on the right cheekbone. He went off balance to the left, and Jenks rushed him. Flecks of saliva hit him in the face, and he smelled the rank sweat of the man. As he tried to focus, Jenks caught him with hard knuckles on the left jaw.

Archer went down to his right, staggered, and came up. Jenks caught him one-two with a left and a right, and Archer hit the ground. He rolled and scrambled, keeping away from the bigger man, until he got to his feet again. Jenks stood in front of him, weaving, with his fists up.

The side of Archer's head throbbed, and his cheekbone stung. He knew he had swung at least twice, but the other man had the reach on him. Archer led with his left foot, jabbed high, and came in under Jenks's fists. He gave three short punches, as powerful as he could make them, into the man's midsection. He heard a whoosh of breath and punched again.

Jenks stepped backward, his mouth open and his eyes dull. Archer jabbed at the man's guard, then double-jabbed and caught him on the jaw. Jenks's fists lowered, and Archer came across with a right punch that connected on the cheekbone. Jenks stepped back further, wavering as he sucked in a breath.

Archer drove in close again and gave him two more in the stomach. Jenks heaved an ugly breath and sagged, then brought his forearms up as if by instinct. He threw a weak jab that bounced off of Archer's head. Still close, he wrapped an arm around Archer's neck, but Archer pushed free. As Jenks moved forward to get his balance, Archer hammered him with a left and a right to the head. Jenks stepped back, Archer punched him in the mouth, and Jenks hit the ground.

Archer stood back with his fists doubled as Jenks came up on all fours. The man made raspy, gagging sounds that sounded as if he was about to vomit. The punches to the gut had made the difference.

"Had enough?" Archer asked. He pulled in a deep breath, feeling it in the bottom of his stomach.

Jenks waved him away with his left hand and raised his bald head. His eyes were watering, and his mouth hung open like a drunk man's. Crowell stepped in front of him and helped him up.

"One on one," said Archer, breathing through his open mouth and tasting dirt. "I hope that's enough for today."

Crowell gave a sideways look with a lump of chewing tobacco in his cheek. "Maybe today. But this won't be the last."

Mercer seemed to have gotten up the nerve to speak. "I don't know what for," he said, with a quaver to his voice. "This is my land, and I can show you the papers I've got."

Jenks stood hunched. He raised his bulbous head, took a deep breath, and said, "We know who you are." With his back to the Bar M men, he walked to his horse and put on his hat. He left the gunbelt slung on the saddle horn as he mounted up. With his back still turned, he neck-reined the horse and set out in the direction he had come from. Crowell followed.

Archer moistened his lips and let out a

long breath. "I wonder what all that was about."

"I don't know," said Mercer. His dark brown eyes shifted.

Archer cast a glance in the direction of the two strangers. Dust rose as their horses picked up a trot. Archer went to the wagon, got his hat, and put it on. The rifle was right where it should be. He rejoined Mercer and Beckett, who were watching the two men ride away.

"Seems like more than a misunderstanding," said Archer.

Worry showed in Mercer's eyes, which were still unsteady. "I have no idea," he said.

Archer's chest rose and fell, and his hands still had a shake. He was sure that whether Jenks and Crowell came back or not, there was something behind their visit. Archer recalled the figure he had seen in the rocks the first day, and he found it easy to believe Jenks had been there. Then he recalled the image of Peavey riding away from the ranch on the drab-colored horse. He wondered if there was a connection. His thoughts came back to the tangle he had just had with Jenks, and he imagined that Lidge Mercer was glad, once again, to have hired him.

Archer lay on the bed with his hands locked

behind his head. Tired of staring at the ceiling of the hotel room, he let his eyes travel again to the six-gun and holster that sat on the cane-bottom chair near his elbow. It was something to get used to, this new presence. The stained wooden grip, the blued metal, the oiled leather — they conveyed seriousness and status. He could smell the oil and new leather, could see the perfect line of stitching. He rehearsed to himself what he had said out loud several times: he would have gotten one anyway.

Boot Beckett had already put away his gun and holster. His saddlebags were draped across the second wooden chair in the room. Beckett stood at the mirror, brushing his shirt and vest with his fingers. Archer wondered if owning a six-gun had given Beckett a higher sense of his public presence. Most of the time, his appearance struck Archer as being rather casual.

Archer rolled to his left and sat up. He reached for the gun and holster, and the object felt heavier than he remembered. He pulled the revolver out, held it free, and slipped it back in. He could feel the oil on his fingers, smell the leather anew. This was the real thing, like owning his own horse but more compact, more intense. The man who had sold them the guns was well versed and enthusiastic about names and models and calibers, but the details did not impress Archer. He had gotten what he wanted, a Colt .45 and a holster to carry it in.

He stood up, lifted his saddlebags from the floor, and stowed this new, important piece of equipment. He set the saddlebags on the seat of the chair, not wanting them to have the chance of slipping off the curved back.

"Shall we get something to eat?" he asked.

"Might as well," said Beckett.

They left the room key at the desk and went across the street to the Drover. Archer wondered if the special of the day was always beef stew, but he ordered it and was glad to get it.

As he and Beckett were taking their time with a second glass of beer, an unexpected pair walked in and took a seat at the farthest table. Archer recognized Fenton the storekeeper first, and within a few seconds he placed the second man on the basis of his dark-brown frock coat and matching hat. It was the man who had been making light talk with Rosanna and touching her while the crowd was whooping it up over the song about Charley the sailor.

At present, the two men had a business-like air about them as they spoke in low tones. After they sat down, the waiter brought them two glasses of beer. Archer did not see the waiter take their order, so he imagined the men were regular customers.

Beckett finished his beer and said, "Let's take care of the bill. There's somethin' I want to go look at."

"By yourself?"

"I doubt that you'd be interested."

Archer had a picture of Beckett, in his unhurried way, haggling over a saddle or a set of traps. "Just don't get anything too heavy to pack," said Archer. "We've got a full list, you know."

"Don't worry. I'll go light on this trip."

Out on the sidewalk, Beckett turned south to go on his errand while Archer lingered and then went north. Two doors past the first cross street, he turned left into the shadowed doorway of the general store. With Fenton having an afternoon drink, the time seemed optimum.

The bell tinkled as Archer stepped inside the store. The air was cooler than it was outside. He did not see or hear anyone as he walked forward, his bootheels sounding on the wood floor and his spurs making a light clinking sound.

Archer's pulse jumped as the girl came

out of the back area and appeared at the counter. He said her name to himself. *Kate.* Her hair was pinned up, and she was dressed as before in a high-collared, long-sleeved dress covered by a grey apron.

Her dark eyes met his. "Well, hello. It's you."

"Sure is." He took off his hat.

"Do you have an order for today?"

"Actually, I think we'll do that in the morning. I just dropped in to say good afternoon."

She gave her shy smile. "Thank you. That's, um, courteous of you."

He fidgeted with his hat brim. "You said you were always here, so I thought there was no harm."

"None at all." Her dark eyes had a shine.

"I don't suppose you have time to visit at the moment."

"Well, I do have work, and Mr. Fenton will probably be back pretty soon." Her smile was more open now. "He makes sure I don't loiter."

Archer laughed. "I've noticed." His eyes met hers, roved, and came back. "Do you think it would be possible to visit later on, after your workday's done?"

She drew her brows together for a couple of seconds. "Maybe for a little while. There's a porch at the back of the house, and sometimes I go out there to sit in the cool of the evening."

"After eight, then?"

"Yes, at about that time, but before dark."

"Of course. There won't be any trouble for you?"

"I don't think so. I'm supposed to have a little time for myself, and that's when I usually take it."

"That sounds fine. I'll come by at that time. Meanwhile, I'll leave you to your work, not get you caught loitering."

She gave a light laugh. "I don't do much of that."

Archer left Boot Beckett staring at the ceiling of the hotel room as he went out into the cool evening. The town of Ashton had few trees or bushes taller than a person, but the shadows of the buildings had stretched out, and most of the dust from horses and wagons during the day had settled. Archer had a light, happy feeling as he walked along the board sidewalk. Above the sound of his bootheels and spurs, the trilling whir of a locust carried on the evening air. He wondered when the first locust, or cicada, had sung this year, and he tried to remember how many days it was supposed to be from then until frost. Gone. He had heard it, but he couldn't remember. Sixty? Ninety? Forty? Not ninety. Earlier in the day, on the way into town, he had seen the first reddening leaves on a chokecherry bush. It had been up on a flat spot, and the taller bushes in the bottom of the draw were still full green.

His steps took him north to the cross street, west to the alleyway, and south to where he expected to find the back of the store. Ashes and rubbish heaps lay on each side of the alley, and the hollyhocks were blooming at the tops of the stalks. The earlier, lower blossoms had all gone to seed — dry-husked, button-like heads, some of which had parted to show the thin black wafers that were seeds.

His heartbeat thumped in his throat as he looked up and saw an image on the porch directly on his left.

Kate sat in a wooden chair with a book in her lap. She was wearing the same dress as during the day, and her hair was still pinned up.

The porch was a foot above ground level and not enclosed. Archer paused at the step, took off his hat, and said, "Good evening."

"Good evening to you. It's rather nice, isn't it? Calm and quiet."

"Yes, it is." He glanced at the book in her lap. "Have you been reading?"

"A little." She touched the spine of the book. "I refresh my memory of poems."

"Oh, I see. Favorite ones?"

"Yes."

Archer reflected for a second. "So you recite some of them?"

"Not with much of an audience. Sometimes with the children, but not all the poems are for them. Some are."

"Nursery rhymes?"

"Oh, everyone knows a few of those. But I was thinking of others. Longfellow, for instance. They'll listen to 'The Village Blacksmith' and 'Paul Revere's Ride,' but they don't care for *Evangeline.*"

"Really? Do you recite the whole of it? That's a long one."

"Oh, no, not yet. I just have the first nineteen lines. But I really find them stirring."

Archer motioned with his hat, which he still held in his hand. "I'd like to hear you say them sometime."

Her bosom rose and fell as she took a breath. "I would have to practice a little more before I tried it out on you." She smiled. "Anyway, it's a good pastime."

"I'm sure."

"It doesn't cost much. A book or two of poems, and a dictionary, can last a long time."

"Have you got other pieces memorized?"

She brightened. "Oh, I can do all of Gray's 'Elegy.' All hundred and twenty-eight lines."

"Really?"

"Yes."

"Let's hear it. Or part of it."

"Oh, no."

"Please. Just the first stanza or two."

"You'll embarrass me."

"Not at all. I'll be . . . enthralled." He waved with his hat.

"I'll feel like a show-off."

He gave her a smile and a teasing look. "You don't want me to leave disappointed, do you?"

"Well, no."

With his hat at his chest, he put a foot on the step of the porch. "How could you not?"

"I hardly know you."

"It's the third time we've met. And I'm just a plain old fellow. Russ Archer of the Bar M."

"Just a plain fellow. Well, I'm not going to stand up. That's the proper way, you know, but I think it would be too much."

"However you wish."

"Here it goes, then." She put her hands together on the book and in a soft, steady voice she began her recitation.

The curfew tolls the knell of parting day,
   The lowing herd wind slowly o'er the lea,
The plowman homeward plods his weary
   way,
   And leaves the world to darkness and to
   me.

Now fades the glimmering landscape on
   the sight,
   And all the air a solemn stillness holds,
Save where the beetle wheels his droning
   flight,
   And drowsy tinklings lull the distant folds;

Save that from yonder ivy-mantled tow'r
   The moping owl does to the moon
   complain
Of such, as wandering near her secret
   bow'r,
   Molest her ancient solitary reign.

"Oh, that's enough," she said. "It's a beautiful poem, but it's so melancholy. And the line that says, 'The paths of glory lead but to the grave.' It seems so true. But it will have to wait for another day. It seems so, *moping* now."

"It seems perfect to me," said Archer. "With the evening coming in like this, and the sound of our own insects. Crickets and locusts."

"Yes, it is. But I'll do something lighter and shorter, now that you've got me started. I have another one by the same poet. Do you know Gray's 'Ode on the Death of a Favourite Cat, Drowned in a Tub of Goldfishes'?"

Archer widened his eyes. "Can't say that I do."

"Maybe you'll like it." She shifted and sat up straight, took a breath, and said, "I'll have to stand for this." She rose from her chair, and with the book in her left hand, she moved her right in accompaniment to the meter of the poem.

'Twas on a lofty vase's side,
Where China's gayest art had dyed
  The azure flowers that blow;
Demurest of the tabby kind,
The pensive Selima, reclined,
  Gazed on the lake below.

She went on through the poem, narrating how the cat saw herself in the reflection, saw the goldfish, reached, fell in, called for help, and received none. With the cat drowned, Kate finished with the moral that was expressed in the last stanza.

From hence, ye beauties, undeceived,
Know, one false step is ne'er retrieved,
　　And be with caution bold.
Not all that tempts your wandering eyes
And heedless hearts, is lawful prize;
　　Nor all that glisters, gold.

"Bravo!" Archer clapped his hands.

"Shhh!" Kate said.

"That was wonderful."

"I'm afraid I'm blushing."

He took an appreciative look at her. "Maybe a little, but it becomes you."

A voice called from within the house.

Kate answered, "Yes, ma'am. In a minute."

"Oh, I'm sorry," said Archer. "I shouldn't have made so much noise."

Kate held the book against her waist. "I would have had to go in pretty soon anyway. This is the time she puts the children to bed."

He looked at the ground and then up at her. "I suppose I should move along, then."

"I'm glad you came by."

Archer hesitated, trying to linger as he

said, "So am I. Maybe I'll see you tomorrow."

"If you're buying beans and peaches."

He laughed. "That sounds like a song."

"Oh, I guess it does."

"Good evening, Kate. Don't forget about me."

Her voice lifted. "Oh, I shan't." It returned to normal as she said, "Good evening."

Archer and Beckett stood at the bar in the Drover saloon. Darkness lay beyond the open doors in front and back, and men drifted in from the night. Peavey and Wyse had one drink and stopped long enough to say good evening to Archer and Beckett. In his usual noncommittal manner, Peavey gave no indication that he had crossed paths with the Bar M boys in any way since the first time they had met. Like before, Peavey and his pal did not make any gestures toward shaking hands. In a minute they were gone out the back door.

Before the night had worn on very much, the man in the brown hat and frock coat came in through the front door. He stood by himself at the bar, and the bartender poured him a glass of whiskey. The man took a sip and left the glass on the bar as he turned around to survey the crowd.

Archer shifted so that he could not see the man. He let his gaze go vacant as he played the tune of "Cowboy Jack" in his head. The woman had not yet come in to sing, but the melody lingered from before.

A voice brought him out of his reverie.

"Well, good evening, fellas."

It was the man in the hat and coat of matching color. Up close, he was clean and well-groomed, with trimmed brown hair and a white shirt. He held his whiskey glass in one hand, and the other hung at his side not far from where the tip of his holster showed below the coat.

Archer and Beckett returned the greeting.

"Don't know that I've met you boys, but I think I've seen you."

"Probably so. I'm Russ Archer, and this is my pal Boot Beckett."

"My name's Jim Tuesday." He shook hands with each of them. His grip was firm, but his hands were not weathered or roughened. "Where do you boys work?"

"At the Bar M," said Beckett. "Up north."

"Oh, yes. That's not too far from where I am. My place is over the ridge to the east of you, and then a ways south."

Archer perked up. "Do you know a couple of riders named Jenks and Crowell?"

Tuesday gave a quick, thoughtful expression. "Sure don't. But there's lots of men in this country I haven't met yet."

"Same with us. It takes a while." Archer drank the last of his beer.

"Here," said Tuesday. "Let me buy you boys a drink." He waved to the bartender.

"Much obliged," said Beckett. He tossed off the last of his own.

The bartender set down two new glasses of beer. Archer and Beckett each lifted one, and the three men clicked drinks.

Tuesday had steady blue eyes. "Here's to good luck," he said. "It's a good country here, lots of opportunity. Especially for young, hard-workin' men. Who's your boss, by the way?"

Archer lowered his glass. "A fellow named Lidge Mercer."

"I think I've heard his name, but I can't say I've met him."

"Good man to work for." Archer felt as if he said it out of obligation even though he meant it.

"That's good. No sense wasting your life working for a skinflint." Tuesday turned toward Beckett. "Who's his foreman?"

"Oh, he doesn't have one yet. He's just gettin' started, as far as cattle are concerned. We've mostly been buildin' at the ranch."

"I see. What kind of building?"

Beckett raised his head. "A little of everything. Carpentry, rock work."

"Then you boys are pretty handy."

Beckett turned down the corners of his mouth and gave a light shrug. "We get by."

"It's good to know how to do a few different things."

"That's the way we figure it."

Archer thought Beckett was about to sell the man a pair of spurs, but the conversation died.

After a moment, Tuesday spoke. "Well, I'll leave you boys to your devices. I'm sure I'll see you again. And if you're ever lookin' for work, don't be shy. I've got more work than you can shake a stick at."

"We'll remember that," said Beckett. "And thanks for the drink."

"Same here," said Archer. "Thanks for the drink."

"My pleasure, boys." Tuesday shook hands with each of them and went back to where he had been standing earlier.

"Nice enough fella," said Beckett.

"Did you notice his hands?"

"Yes, I did. They look like the kind that get into other people's pockets."

"They might be."

Beckett gave his clever smile. "That doesn't mean you can't do business with him, though."

Kate was nowhere in sight when Archer and Beckett went for the supplies the next morning. Fenton worked his way through the list with full courtesy and finished by sending his best regards to Lidge Mercer. Archer left with an empty feeling, while Beckett seemed as untroubled as usual.

When they had the panniers lashed tight and the rest of the supplies tied on behind their saddles, Beckett put his gun and holster onto his belt.

Archer stood holding the lead rope of the packhorse. "Are you expecting Indians?"

"Nope," said Beckett. "I just want to see how it fits for the ride. You could do the same."

"I'll have plenty of time."

They mounted up, and Beckett led the way. Rather than go north on the main street, he went two blocks to the east and then turned north. In the middle of the block, a plain-looking young woman with dull blond hair appeared on the doorstep of a house on the right. She waved to Beckett, and he waved back.

After they turned at the next corner, Archer rode up alongside Beckett. "Who was that?"

"Her name's Sadie."

"How do you meet a girl like that?"

"She's a good hand with a needle and thread."

"I should have known." Archer rode on and kept the rest to himself. If he had thought a girl was going to come out and wave goodbye to him, he might have put on his new gun and holster as well.

CHAPTER FIVE

Archer poked at the coals until he got a glow of orange. Leaning forward, he tossed on some wisps of dry grass and blew on the embers to make them brighter. As the grass caught fire, he laid on twigs of sagebrush. The flame grew in the center of the pile, and he added thin branches. A cloud of smoke formed, so he blew at the heart of the fire again. A flame rose, and the smoke cleared. He put on branches as big around as his thumb. Now the fire caught strong, and the flames were nearly invisible. He set the tin coffee pot at the edge of the fire and stood up.

Down the hill about two hundred yards, the cattle were scattered around the water-hole, their dark forms visible in the grey light of morning. Some were still bedded down, a couple were drinking, and the rest were grazing the close grass. Archer repeated the count to himself — thirty-seven head.

That was it for a two-day gather, some from as far north as the Cheyenne River.

Whitmore and Beckett were rolling up their blankets. A ways out from the campsite, the six horses grazed on their pickets. Archer stood for a moment and surveyed the broad country. He had seen good grassland from here to the river, some twenty miles of rolling plains with broad, flat pastures a mile or so across. Off to the west and northwest, the ground lay in tighter folds, a land of breaks and ravines. Whitmore said it was not bad for cattle, that a couple of outfits ran a few thousand head each.

By comparison, Mercer's holdings were small potatoes. He had land in his own name plus access to open range, but he had no herd to speak of. He had bought a ranch that never came back from the bad winter of 1886–87, and once he took it over, he did not go out and look after it. Only now, by sending his men to haze his stock back to his own range, was he getting an idea of how many cattle he had. It was not a great number, even counting dry cows, and Archer doubted there would be fifty steers to ship. Even at that, Archer felt that the work was important. Mercer had put him in charge of this small detail of men and horses, and they were bringing in some cattle. As Archer stood on the hillside in the midst of a great wide country at dawn, he had the sense that he mattered. He was helping Mercer pull his ranch together.

Mercer was a lucky man, as Archer saw it. Even if he had a rundown ranch and a straggling herd, he had land. To a person like Archer who had never had anything, land seemed valuable, important. Yet Mercer seemed to take it for granted. He knew which property was his, and the ownership was important to him, but he didn't seem to have much feeling for the land itself. That was the boss man's business, Archer figured. For his own part, he couldn't imagine losing the wonder of it all. He took one last look at the crimson sky in the east and returned to his camp chores.

Beckett and Whitmore were crouched by the fire by the time Archer had his blankets rolled and wrapped in his slicker.

"Just startin' to boil," said Beckett.

Whitmore tossed his cigarette butt into the fire and stood up. "I'll get the grub."

After a breakfast of cold biscuits and bitter coffee, the three men saddled their horses. The sun cleared the horizon as they took a last look around the camp, and each of them led two horses down the hill to drink.

The waterhole was a small pond, some twenty yards by thirty. Several years earlier, someone had mounded a dam on the lower end of this small bowl in the earth. Archer could see where the water used to flow in a curve between two slopes, but it had been some years since, for the mounded earth was now grassed over.

Archer counted the cattle as the horses drank. Whitmore smoked another cigarette. Beckett fussed with his saddle and retied his bedroll. The cattle were beginning to wander, and the sun had jumped in the sky when Archer pulled his horses away from the water.

"We'd better get going," he said. He handed the spare horse to Whitmore and mounted up.

Beckett did the same, and the two of them began to gather the cattle. Whitmore let the horses graze until the other two riders had the small herd in motion, and he fell in behind. Archer took a backward glance at the hillside with its rocks and cedar trees, the pond as it reflected in the morning sun, and the vast rolling country beyond. He fixed the place in his mind. It was public land, not something to covet, but it would be a good place to remember. He would be on the lookout for a piece of land like it.

Archer sighted the pistol at eye level and squeezed the trigger. The bottle flew apart in a spray of clear, shiny bits.

"Good one," said Beckett.

"Three out of four." Archer lowered his gun. "Go ahead. Your turn."

Beckett picked up three bottles from their collection and carried them to the dirt bank. He set them up about two feet apart and came striding back.

Archer took a couple of steps backwards and began reloading his pistol as Beckett got into position.

Whitmore's voice came from behind them. "Remember, now, don't jerk the trigger."

"I know, I know." Beckett drew his revolver, raised it, and took aim. The pistol jumped with the first shot, and all three bottles remained standing. Beckett aimed again, and the shot crashed as the bottle on the left shattered into bits. He missed the next shot and the one after that. He lowered the gun, took a deep breath, and raised the gun again. He blew the second bottle to smithereens. Still intent, he demolished the third bottle with his next shot.

"Three for six." He shifted the gun to his

left hand and opened the wheel.

"You're gettin' better," said Oscar. "Both of ya."

Beckett wrinkled his nose. "We've burned up enough ammunition."

"Takes practice," said Whitmore. "But you're gettin' it."

"Gettin' the practice, or gettin' the hang of it?"

"Both."

Archer glanced at the rubbish heap. "We're just about out of bottles, too."

"Cans last longer," said Whitmore. "Let me go get one." He went to the heap, rummaged for a minute, and came back with a rusted one-gallon can. "Let's put this on a fence post," he said.

The group of four walked to the other side of the cook shack, where a four-wire fence made one side of the horse pasture. Several of the posts were twisted and had uneven tops, but Whitmore found one that was sawed straight across. He set the can on top and came walking back at a fast stride.

"Now, you get where you can hit that at fifty feet," he said. "Don't seem like much until you start throwin' lead at it."

"You go first," said Beckett. "It's your turn."

Archer walked toward the post, moved to

his left, and took another step forward. "This is about fifty feet." With the toe of his boot, he scratched a line in the dirt. He scanned the pasture to make sure no horses stood beyond his target, and he raised his pistol. When he had it lined up, he squeezed the trigger. The can jumped off the post.

"Damn good," said Whitmore.

"Just lucky."

"Well, hold your fire, and I'll go set it up so you can try again."

Archer held the six-gun by his side until the target was ready and Whitmore was in back of him again. He fired twice and missed each time. Then he made himself bear down, and he knocked the can off the post.

"Ha-ha-ha!" said Oscar. "That's hittin' 'em."

Whitmore raised his hand. "Hold your fire. We'll let Boot try next."

After each of them had taken two turns with the can on the post, Archer said, "What next?"

Whitmore's eyes were shining beneath the brim of his battered hat. "You want to try something a little harder?"

Archer shrugged. "What have you got in mind?"

"Each of you saddles a horse, and you try

hittin' it as you ride by."

Archer looked at Beckett. "I don't know. What do you think?"

It was Beckett's turn to shrug. "I guess we could give it a try."

Archer picked out the gentlest horse in his small string, a pale roan that didn't have much spark. Beckett went for a spotted horse he called Pokey. When they had the horses saddled, they led them out back of the cook shack.

Whitmore was all ready. He had the can set up and another in reserve. "Russ, you go first," he said.

Archer paused. "Why don't we flip a coin?"

"Just go ahead," said Whitmore. "The worst you can do is miss."

"Well, no, I can get thrown on my head or break an arm." Archer put his toe in the stirrup and pulled himself aboard. He adjusted his reins and put the horse into a trot. After the first turn he touched the roan's flank with his spur. They loped back and forth within thirty feet of the post, and after the turn, Archer drew his pistol. As the horse took him past the can, he held the gun up and fired.

The roan jumped with its rear end, crow-hopping. Archer got the horse settled down and turned around. As he loped back across, he saw the can still on the fencepost. He made the next turn, raised his gun, and made his shot as he rode by. This time the horse broke into a dead run, and Archer had to pull slack on his reins with the hand that held the pistol. When he came back to the middle, the can was lying on its side in the pasture.

"By God, that's the way to do it," said Whitmore. "Let me set up this other one, and we'll let Boot try his luck."

Archer dismounted and held the reins as Beckett led out the spotted horse and got mounted. Pokey would not cooperate, though. He kept turning one way and the other until Boot got him out on the far end and turned around. Still he tried to turn aside, and Boot spurred him and hollered, "Yahh!" The spotted horse took off, and Boot had to draw fast. The gunfire blasted, and when the horse and rider had charged by, Archer saw the can rolling to a stop. Meanwhile Beckett was pulling on the reins to get the galloping horse slowed down.

Oscar and Whitmore were cheering. Beckett got his horse under control and came back at a fast walk.

"That was some fun," he said. "But I think once is enough for these horses today."

"That's fine with me." Archer patted the roan's pale neck. "Do you want to do anything else? I think I'm good for the day."

"I am, too," said Beckett as he dismounted.

"Hah," said Oscar. "Why don't you give it a try, Whit?"

"Oh, I don't know. It's been a long time since I fired anything."

"You can use that rifle in the cook shack. There's a box of cartridges not doin' anything."

"Sure," said Beckett. "Go ahead. We've had our fun."

"Oh, I guess so. How many bottles have we got left?"

"Four," said Archer.

"All right, then, we'll set 'em up."

Archer and Beckett made short work of putting away the horses. As they stood in the yard, Whitmore went into the barn and brought out one of the two sawhorses Middleton had made for the building project. Oscar came out of the cook shack with the rifle in one hand and a box of shells in the other.

Archer had seen the gun standing in the corner with a sock over its muzzle. It was a .25-caliber lever-action carbine, the kind of saddle gun that a fellow would use when he checked his trapline. Oscar would have liked to get a skunk with it, but so far as Archer knew, he hadn't gotten a crack at one.

Whitmore settled the sawhorse into place on a level spot and put the four bottles on it, about a foot apart. Without looking at either of the younger men, he walked straight to Oscar and took the rifle that the cook held out.

"Is it loaded?"

"I keep a few in it." Oscar, bareheaded and pale, squinted in the sunlight.

"Let's see." Whitmore knelt, took off his hat, and tipped the rifle. He ejected four shiny, compact shells into the hat. He gathered them up and put on his hat. "Give me two more," he said. "I'll put in six."

When he had the gun loaded, he stood up and held it with both hands. He took two long breaths and gave a sidelong glance at the row of bottles. He raised his eyebrows, lowered them, and walked up to within thirty feet of the sawhorse.

Archer frowned. This was like shooting ducks in a barrel. He waited for Whitmore to raise the rifle to his shoulder, but the man didn't do it.

Holding the rifle at hip level, Whitmore worked his right hand and levered in a shell. The gun barked, and the first bottle disintegrated. Whitmore shifted and fired twice more. The second bottle vanished. He moved again and smashed the third bottle, a green one that became a spray of fragments. With his fifth shot he blew away the last bottle, a clear, flat pint that jumped into nothingness.

Archer let out his breath. "That was something," he said as Whitmore turned around.

"I used to be pretty good at it." The older man seemed to be taking careful steps as he took the rifle to Oscar. After he handed it over, he dropped his hands to his sides and stepped back. He was breathing through his open mouth, and as he drew the makings out of his trousers pocket, his hand shook. His tongue touched his upper lip, and he kept his eyes downward as he began to build a cigarette. "I try not to think about it, but I could sure use a drink right now."

Archer stood by the creek as the horses drank. The cottonwoods and box elders had all gone yellow, and half the leaves had fallen to the ground. Even at midday the sun did not feel warm in the mottled shade. The recent rain had left the air clear, just as it had helped bring down the leaves. It had been a slow, cold rain, and it had left the ground dark where there were no trees. Things did not warm up fast, even in the open. Archer pressed his boot sole on a gathering of yellow leaves. Softened by the rain, they made no noise, and a thought stirred in his memory. This was a good time to sneak up on deer, when a man could take quiet steps.

Downstream to the right, Boot Beckett had his head tipped as he rolled a cigarette. Beyond him, Whitmore already had one lit. Broken sunlight came through the trees and fell on the men, the horses, the yellow leaves, and the green grass. A breeze passed through, rustling the cottonwoods overhead and causing Archer to hunch his shoulders. Before long, he was going to need a real coat and not just a jacket.

Beckett yawned out loud. "Don't know why we couldn't have stayed in town. Up all night with the cattle and then have to ride straight back."

Whitmore made a small spitting sound. "We'll have plenty of time in town after this."

"Is that right?"

"Seen it for years. Once you ship the steers, the old man pays off all the extra hands, and that's it."

"Then we could have stayed over."

Whitmore laughed. "You'll be back soon enough. You'll see. He just wants us to bring the horses back, maybe oil the tack and put it away, and then he'll let us go." Whitmore hawked and spit. "Besides, he doesn't want me stoppin' in town while I'm on the payroll."

"Did he tell you that?"

"Not in so many words. But I can figger it out. Ask Russ."

Archer tipped his head. "He didn't come right out and say it to me either, but I think that's probably right."

"It don't hurt my feelings," said Whitmore. "The boss is no fool, and he needs to get his work done."

Archer left Whitmore and Beckett sitting by the stove when he went to make his report to the boss. Mercer answered the knock on the door and let Archer into the front room.

It was a plain room that looked the same every time. A straight-backed wooden armchair sat in the back corner on the left, and another just like it was pushed up to a dark rolltop desk along the right wall. The desk was closed as always. A hat tree stood on Archer's right, and an oval braided rug occupied the middle of the floor. The room was not large, maybe twelve by twelve, and with a doorway leading to the back of the house as well as one leading to the left into the kitchen, it did not look empty with its meager furnishings. Furthermore, it felt warm and comfortable, and embers glowed in the fireplace next to the desk.

Mercer stepped back in the direction of his desk. He waved his hand toward the chair in the corner. "Pull up a seat," he said. "I hope everything went well."

Archer took off his hat and stood in place. "Yes, it did. We didn't get any more rain, and we got to the shipping pens just at dark. We stayed there all night. We had the steers loaded in the boxcar by ten this morning, and we came straight back."

"Good. I'm glad to hear it."

Archer took the shipping papers from inside his jacket and handed them over.

"Thanks. Sit down."

Archer pulled the chair to the edge of the rug and took a seat. He hiked a leg up and set his hat on his knee. He could hear the ticking of the clock on the mantel.

Mercer turned his own chair around and settled into it. His dark brown eyes held on Archer for a second and relaxed. "Well," he said in his smooth voice, "we're getting to the end of the season here."

"That's what I figured, once you've got

your cattle shipped."

"You can feel it in the air, can't you?"

"Oh, yeah."

Mercer sat forward in the chair he had just settled into. He leaned over to his left, picked up three sticks of firewood, and laid them on the coals. Then he took up a fire poker that Archer had not noticed before. It was a rod between three and four feet long, with a smaller-gauge hook welded to the end.

Mercer held the poker so that the hook end lay at the base of the firewood, and he put his mouth on the other end of the rod. He did not appear to blow very hard, but the coals glowed, and small flames grew up around the bark of the firewood.

"It's hollow," said Archer. "I haven't seen one like that before."

"Oh, haven't you? It's pretty handy. You can blow air right into the coals without stirring up a cloud of ashes. Like a forge."

"I can see that."

Mercer blew again, and the little flames grew stronger. He withdrew the poker and let the tip rest on the hearth.

"That's nice," said Archer.

"Thanks. I made it myself." Mercer gave a faint smile.

For a moment, Archer was touched by

what seemed to be a genuine bit of pride. Then the man laid down the poker, turned in his chair, and spoke like the boss again.

"And how do you like your work at the Bar M?"

Archer sat up straight. "Just fine, sir."

"I rather thought you did." Mercer paused, then raised his eyebrows and said, "How would you like to stay on?"

Archer took a couple of seconds to absorb the question. From what he understood, a ranch that was a pure cattle operation, no hay and no crops, usually kept no more than the owner, the cook, and the foreman through the winter. "That sounds like a good opportunity," he said. "Did you have some particular work in mind?"

"Not another building or anything like that." Silence hung in the room for a minute until Mercer spoke again. "Russ, I'd like to make you an offer."

Archer kept his voice steady as he said, "All right."

"I'd like to make you my junior partner."

Archer felt dazed as the words washed over him, and he had to take a breath. "Well, that's, um, quite an honor. What would it consist of?" He imagined it meant no wages for the winter.

"We'd have to have papers drawn up. I'm

thinkin' of something like thirty-seventy, and maybe it could go up with time. You would get a draw each month, probably a little more than you're makin' right now."

"And what do I do through the winter?"

Mercer gave a casual shrug. "Why, you stay on here. Look after the horses, go out and check cattle when the weather allows it."

"A hired hand could do that."

"Oh, I know. But I want to build this ranch, and my idea is that if you've got an interest in it, you'll work for it."

"I'd say you're right about that. I don't want anything I haven't worked for."

"You've shown that, time and again." Mercer waited a couple of seconds and said, "I like the way you work with horses and cattle, and I like the way you take responsibility."

"Well, thank you, sir. It's good to know."

The boss's manner relaxed. "And there's another part to it. You know, I've never had a family of my own — no wife, no children — and a man ought to have someone to leave his property to. I don't mean to get sentimental, but —" He left the words hanging.

"I know, sir. Not having a family, you feel

like the rest of the world has something you don't."

"That's right. Of course, you're young, and you've got time. But when you do settle down, maybe you'll have somethin' to get started on." Mercer's face had softened, and his smile was like a grandfather's.

Archer felt a tightness in his throat. Even that much talk about family gave him a strange, mixed feeling. "Well, that's very . . . generous of you."

Mercer shifted in his chair and gave a more humorous smile. "Of course, we could both go broke in five years."

Archer laughed with the break in tension. "Yes, but you'd still have the land. You can always do something with it."

Mercer glanced at the small blaze of the fire. "That's true. Even if your cattle all die and your money runs out. You can't eat grass, but I guess the land is worth something."

Oscar and Whitmore had the pegboard out and were playing cribbage when Archer opened the door of the cook shack and stood in the doorway.

"Where's Boot?"

"He went to the bunkhouse," said Oscar.

"I'll find him there."

Archer straightened his jacket as he walked in the cool air across the ranch yard. Life seemed to have grown in importance, and he needed to keep things straight. He opened the door of the bunkhouse and walked in. Boot Beckett looked up from where he sat on his bunk, cleaning his revolver.

"What's new?"

"The boss asked me to stay for the winter."

Beckett's mouth went down as his eyebrows went up. "That's good for you."

"Well, I can't say I feel a hundred percent good about it."

"Why's that?"

Archer closed the door behind him and took a few seconds to frame his words. "He made me an offer. Said I could be his junior partner. Something like a thirty-seventy deal."

Beckett's face brightened. "Well, hell, that's great."

Archer shrugged.

"What's wrong with it?"

"I don't know. It's more than I could have expected, and on top of that, I feel like I'm . . . cuttin' you out."

Beckett set the gun aside. "By no means, old buddy. You've worked hard, and he appreciates it."

"So have you."

"Oh, hell. He's had his eye on you, so go ahead. Don't worry on my account. I can always find work, ridin' horses or somethin'. And like I said from the start, you were first in line here anyway."

"Still, here I am, all set up, and you're about to be sent off."

"No more and no less than I was expectin', for me at least. And as for you, that's your good luck."

"That's pretty decent of you, Boot. Some fellas would be jealous."

Boot gave a light laugh and shook his head. "I just never saw any profit in wishin' I had somethin' the next fella did."

"I try to be the same way." Archer shifted his feet. He had not taken off his hat. "I think I'm going to go out and stretch my legs," he said. "Let this sink in."

"Go ahead. I'll be here when you get back. And don't worry. Not about me, anyway." Beckett picked up the revolver and the oily rag and began rubbing the grooves on the cylinder.

Archer walked out into the cool afternoon, which was turning to evening now. The shadows were stretching out, and he decided to climb the ridge that looked like a dinosaur's back.

Up on top, some of the rocks had tiny pools of water in the hollowed spots. He found a slanted rock that was dry, and as it was not cold to the touch, he sat down. He was warm from the climb, so he opened his jacket and let out a slow breath. The ranch buildings below him were silent as the shadows crept over them, and he imagined the men sitting inside. To the east, the ridge of grey hills caught the slanting sunlight, and the grassland in the middle distance had a tawny shine. He turned in his seat on the rock and took in the vast country to the north where he and Beckett and Whitmore had gone all the way to the Cheyenne River for a few head of cattle. He recalled the place where they had camped, a hillside with rocks and cedars overlooking a waterhole. Maybe he could find a spot like that for himself. He had a hazy picture of a house with a woman and a child, something beyond what Lidge Mercer was offering him. It would mean adding on to the Bar M, or using his position at the Bar M to acquire something for himself, but he was ready to try. He could do it in a way he could be proud of. As the man named Tuesday had said, there was a lot of opportunity in this country.

CHAPTER SIX

Archer rested the smoke-colored horse when he came out on top of the pine ridge. He had hoped the air would be warmer once he left the shadows, but the sun was pale and a breeze blew out of the northwest. The grass here on top, greyish tan after a few frosts, bent with the wind, and Archer felt the tang of cold air on his cheek. He pulled off his glove, felt the horse's warm neck, and touched the cold leather of the saddle fork. This was the feel of November. He tensed his shoulders. The canvas coat with its blanket lining kept the wind out and the warmth in, and his wool pants were thicker than the trousers he had worn in the summer, but he knew the weather could get much colder. Frigid. Ponds would freeze a foot or more down, and the ground would turn hard as a brick. Pity the man who got stranded, and admire the power and heat of a horse.

Archer set off across the high rolling country toward town. Smoky puffed and snorted and kept up a fast walk. From overhead came a familiar whistling, wheezing sound. Archer looked up to see a V-formation of geese, not quite close enough for him to pick out the feet. Things were on the move. Earlier in the day he had seen a band of antelope that numbered a hundred or so, and now this, the wild geese of winter.

A couple of miles from town, another horse and rider appeared from the swells of the land. It was a tall, yellowish-brown horse, and the rider wore a sheepskin coat. The man waited as Archer rode ahead. The trail went down into a swale and back up again. The other rider came into Archer's view again. He waved. Archer rode another hundred yards until he recognized the hat and facial outline of Boot Beckett.

"Whoa," said Archer as he came to a stop. "I was wondering who'd be fool enough to be riding out on these windy hills on a day like this."

"I was wonderin' the same thing. I thought I knew that horse, though."

"How about that one? Did you trade for it?"

"Oh, no. I'm just ridin' him for a man. Got a little jumpy when the weather changed, and the fella didn't want to find himself on foot between here and Orin Junction."

"I thought maybe you traded your little sorrel for that big horse and the coat you're wearin'."

"Not that good of a trader. I've still got the sorrel. Good time to buy horses, though. People don't want to feed 'em through the winter."

"If I need some, I'll let you know. Shall we keep movin'?"

Beckett turned his horse onto the trail, and Archer rode alongside.

"So how are things at the Bar M?"

"Settling in. Not much real work. Lidge doesn't feed in the winter, you know, except the horses."

"You get to town when you want, then?"

"Pretty much, and stay over as I please. Like on this trip, I'll stay two nights. That's my plan, anyway. Other than fetching supplies, my hardest task is setting my watch by the train station clock."

"Must be nice, bein' a man of leisure."

"Well, that's winter for you. At the same time, there's the responsibility. If anything goes wrong, it's my loss to worry about."

"I suppose so. By the way, not wishin' to be too inquisitive, but did you get the thirty percent?"

"The papers are with the lawyer, but I'm supposed to. Meanwhile, I draw my forty a month."

"That's not bad. Who's the lawyer?"

"Fella named Cunningham."

"Why, hell, that's who I'm ridin' this horse for."

"Then don't let him break his neck."

In town, Beckett said, "I'm leaving this one at Lawrence's stable. I imagine you're goin' to Garvin's as usual."

"That's right. And I need to get myself a room."

"Let's meet at the Drover, then."

"All right."

When Archer arrived at the saloon, he found Beckett seated at a table not far from the stove.

"Weather's changing," said Archer as he pulled off his gloves. "When I came out of the hotel, it was starting to smell like snow on the way."

"Could be."

Both doors to the saloon were closed, and a man who did odd jobs was stacking an armload of firewood next to the stove. The pieces were nearly a yard long, and they looked like lengths that had been cut from old corral posts and planks. The stove itself was a large cast-iron affair, about four feet long and two feet wide, with a shiny one-inch foot rail running in a horseshoe around three sides. When the man had the wood stacked, he began building a fire.

The waiter brought two glasses of beer. "Gettin' cold out there, I guess."

Boot pushed back his hat. The reflection of the fire showed on his sandy hair and blue eyes as he said, "We might have to switch to whiskey."

The front door opened, and a cold draft of air blew in as a couple of men walked toward the bar.

"Close the door," the bartender called.

One of the men turned back, closed the door, and headed for the bar again. He had large feet and walked leaning forward. "Just tryin' to let the flies out," he said.

The bartender set up a bottle and two glasses. "Not many flies now."

The next man who came in had snow on his hat and coat, and it melted in beads that caught the lamplight. The two men after him had enough snow that some of it fell to the floor.

"Maybe you'll get snowed in," said Beckett.

Archer yawned. "Not a bad place for it."

The fire caught hold, and the smell of pine came from the burning planks. A man came in and stood with his back to the stove, and the melting snow formed tiny puddles on the floor. As the man shifted his feet, the water turned to smudges.

The man went to stand at the bar, and a few minutes later another man came in. He carried a gripsack and looked like a traveler in his hat and overcoat. He had quite a bit of snow on him, and catching sight of the stove, he headed for it. There he set his bag on the floor and pulled off his gloves.

"Ahhh," he said, holding his hands toward the stove. "I walked the whole length of this town."

He wore a large black hat with a tall, peaked crown and a floppy brim, curled on one side. As he took off the hat, shook it, and put it back on, Archer noticed a horse-hair hatband that would cost a day's wages. Next the man took off his overcoat, a caped garment of dark gabardine, and shook it. He draped the coat over a nearby chair and held his hands to the fire again.

"What would you like?" called the bartender.

The man raised his head and smiled. He had long, dark hair almost to his shoulders, a mustache and goatee of the same color, and flashing eyes. "I'm almost embarrassed to say it," he answered, "but if I'm going to drink anything, which I wouldn't mind, it would have to come through the goodwill of my fellow man."

"You mean you're broke."

"Only for the moment. I'm trying to get to the Black Hills. I've got people in Deadwood, connections —"

"Well," said the bartender, "don't —"

Archer spoke up. "I'll buy you a drink."

"Bless you, my lad," said the stranger, who couldn't be ten years older than Archer. "I'll have a brandy, if it's not asking too much."

"Not at all. What's your name, friend?"

"LaRue. Richard LaRue." He moved to the bar, picked up the drink that the bartender poured, and returned to the stove. Hoisting the small glass, he said, "My many thanks."

"You're welcome. I hope you make it to the Hills all right. The weather's not helping."

"Not at the present." LaRue's eyes sparkled as he took in both Archer and Beckett. "And you chaps, what do you do?"

"We're punchers," said Archer.

"Ah, yes. Quite a bit of that around here, isn't there?"

"Not much else, and not much of anything

in the winter."

"Pity that."

Beckett waved his hand. "Oh, we don't mind."

"What I meant was, I was hoping for a little more prosperity in the population."

The bartender spoke from behind the bar. "Does that mean you think you want to take up a collection?"

LaRue winced. "I would hope I didn't have to beg. In a manner of speaking, I can sing for my supper."

"We've got singing in here later on."

"Well, in that case, if I'm going to do anything at all, I had better do it soon."

"Do what?"

"Why, sing a song. I know hundreds."

"Why don't you keep it to one?"

LaRue arched his eyebrows. "Very well, I'll do one for my benefactor here. Let me see." He cast his eyes upward as if he were reading his hat brim. "Ah, yes. Here's one." He took another sip of brandy and set the glass on the table near the overcoat. Then he swept off his hat and struck a pose. "Gentlemen, I give you the ballad of Jack O'Malley." With a voice suitable for the theater, he sang.

He was once an honest puncher
Who plied the cowboy's trade.
He rode the plains and mountains
Until one day he strayed.

His name was Jack O'Malley,
And at an early age
He fell in with bad companions
And robbed the Cheyenne stage.

His partners Pogue and Henry
Laid out a simple plan —
They said they had fast horses
But needed one more man.

With Jack to hold the horses
Out in the scrub and sage,
At Cheyenne River crossing
They'd stop the southbound stage.

The Tuesday coach from Deadwood
Came rattling through the rocks
When Pogue and Henry stopped it
And cried, "Throw down the box!"

The stage, now running lighter,
Rolled south toward Robbers' Roost
While Pogue and Henry hustled
To divvy up the loot.

Then mounted on their horses,
They passed the bottle 'round.
But before they got to Deadwood,
Jack's partners shot him down.

Sprawled in the dust and dying,
He watched them ride away.
With failing words he whispered,
"For this I hope you pay."

His blood was spent, but justice
Prevailed in its own way.
Pogue died in a hail of bullets
Out Rapid City way.

While Henry rode to the Badlands,
And in the August heat
His horse gave out beneath him,
And left him for buzzard meat.

Now here's to all you punchers,
Keep pointed straight ahead;
Don't stray like Jack O'Malley,
Whose partners shot him dead.

To enjoy your life in the saddle
And live past middle age,
Don't be like Jack O'Malley
Who robbed the Cheyenne stage.

A ripple of applause sounded from the half-dozen patrons of the Drover as LaRue bowed and made a flourish with his hat. Then he put the hat on his head and stood with his hands together.

Archer rose from his chair and handed the man a silver dollar. "That was a lot of fun. It's the same tune as 'Cowboy Jack,' isn't it?"

"Oh, yes. And thanks." LaRue covered the silver dollar with his other hand. "I know that one, too, of course."

"They sing it in here all the time."

"Then it's a good thing I didn't do it first. This other one's original, at least as far as the words go." The air of the showman seemed to have subsided for a moment. "Thanks again. I'll remember you."

"Glad to be able to. I know what it's like." Archer paused and looked around for Boot Beckett, who was going down the bar with his hat upside down in his hand.

After a minute, Beckett came back with the hat and held it forward. "Here's a little more."

"And thanks to you." LaRue gathered the coins and put them in his pocket. "Well, I'd better be going before I wear out my welcome. I understand there's another place in town." He put on his coat and downed the rest of his brandy. "I hope they don't mind a troubadour. Maybe I'll do 'The Little Brown Church in the Vale.' " He picked up his valise, touched his brim, and left.

As Archer and Beckett sat down, Beckett took out his cigarette makings.

"You must be pretty well set. Bought him a drink and gave him a whole dollar."

"I've been broke before. He put on a good front, like it was all a merry joke, but you know it's not a good feeling to be treated like a vagrant."

Beckett nodded as he shook tobacco into the trough of paper. "A man's got his pride."

"That's right, and this fellow's got his. On top of that, he worked for what he made here."

Beckett and Archer went to a café to eat and returned to the Drover after dark. At least a dozen men were present, including a couple who had stayed on from the afternoon. One of the patrons was Whitmore, who raised his whiskey glass in salute.

Another was Tuesday, who sat at a corner table with Fenton. They had glasses of whiskey in front of them but did not seem in any hurry to drink. As before, Archer had the feeling that the storekeeper avoided looking at him and did not care to be seen by him in a saloon. After a while, Fenton left without finishing his drink. Tuesday carried his to the bar, waving to Archer and Beckett and taking a place down the way from them.

A couple of men came in the front door, shaking off snow. Archer did not recognize them, but they made him think of Peavey and Wyse. It had been a while since he had seen either of them. The men who had just come in went to the bar and stood between Tuesday and Beckett. Archer let his eyes drift around the place, not taking in anything in particular until he settled on a man standing by the stove.

He leaned toward Beckett and said, in a low voice, "Say, aren't those the spurs you got from Whitmore?"

Beckett gave a casual glance. "Oh, yeah."

"Sell or trade?"

"Sold 'em outright. They look pretty good, don't they? Never wore 'em myself."

"Yes, they do. I'd think he's getting his money's worth."

The music had not yet begun when Rosanna appeared. She must have come in through the back door. She walked along the bar, slowed as she passed Archer, and moved along when he did not look her way.

He felt his heartbeat subside. In the past,

whenever he wanted to know if a woman like that was his type, all he had to do was be near her. If something happened inside him, he had his answer. Rosanna hadn't changed in that respect since the time he had gone to the room with her, but he knew he had to resist the temptation. It was too easy to throw caution to the wind, and here was Tuesday, who could tell Fenton, and everything would go worse from there.

He watched as Rosanna stopped to talk to Tuesday. The man responded in his confident, smiling way as he touched her on the arm and then the hip.

Archer looked away. A minute later, Rosanna was nowhere to be seen. A minute after that, Tuesday's drink glass sat on the bar but he was gone as well.

The bell on the front door tinkled as Archer closed it behind him. Fenton stood waiting at the counter, his pale face lifted and his mouth open. Archer's boots sounded as he walked down the center aisle. He did not see any other customers in the store, nor did he see Kate.

"Good morning, Mr. Archer. Something for you today?" The storekeeper's white shirt, collar, bow tie, and apron were all in place, as was his slick hair. The man was full of courtesy now that it was known that Archer was junior partner at the Bar M, but his glinting spectacles and hard features made a thin veneer over his resentment, which was unmistakable.

"I have a short list, but I don't need it filled until tomorrow."

"Something small for today, then?" Fenton motioned toward an open jar of licorice sticks.

"I'd like to see Miss Blackwell for a second."

The storekeeper's face stiffened, and his thin bristly mustache twitched. "I don't really care to mix business and personal —"

"Excuse me, sir, but she lives in your house." Archer felt his own resentment rising, but he kept himself from saying any more about who mixed business and personal interests.

Fenton had both hands behind the counter. "And so?"

"And so, if I'm going to talk to her, I'm going to have to go to one place or another."

The storekeeper was taking audible breaths through his nose. "I don't know that you have to."

"I came in the front door. I don't hide anything." Archer picked his words, making an effort not to put things in terms of the storekeeper himself. "I believe she's of age, and she's not anybody's ward. In other places, girls go out the window at night."

"Meaning?" Fenton's beady eyes tensed.

"No need to treat this case like one of those. She doesn't need a keeper."

Fenton's mouth pursed, but he made a quick recovery. "Mr. Archer, I value your business, but it is not so indispensable that I have to let you tell me how to conduct my business or anything else."

"I didn't put it in those terms, sir. Regardless of whether I ever buy another sack of beans in here, I'd like to talk to Miss Blackwell unless she says otherwise. I don't know if you can make her do that."

"I don't make people do things against their will, and I don't appreciate the implication."

"It doesn't have to be one."

Fenton's eyes were hard behind his glinting spectacles. "There doesn't have to be a conversation at all. Why don't you leave things be?"

Archer made an effort to keep his anger in check. "Like I said, if I want to talk to her, it's either here or at the back door. Would you rather I spoke to your wife?"

The doorbell sounded along with the scuff of the door opening. Archer turned to see the man who did odd jobs in the Drover.

"Yes?" said Fenton.

"Ben wants a side of bacon and twenty pounds of spuds."

"Just a minute." Fenton turned toward the doorway in back of him and called, "Kate!" When she appeared, he gave her a full looking-over as if by habit, then nodded toward Archer and said, "Make it short." In a louder voice, over his shoulder, he said, "Twenty pounds."

Kate smoothed her apron and moved to the counter. "Good morning. Do you have an order today?"

Archer took a calming breath. "That's for tomorrow. For now, I was wondering if you'd like to visit awhile this evening."

She glanced in the direction of her employer. "Well, I suppose so. It's been a while since I saw you, and I don't get out much."

"Maybe we could go for a walk. It might get cold sitting in one place."

"Won't it be dark?"

"We'll go where it's light. Stay on the main street."

She hesitated as Fenton set the burlap bag on the counter, not two feet from her.

"I'll get the bacon in back," said the storekeeper, and went through the doorway.

Kate raised her eyes to meet Archer's.

"That should be all right. For a little while."

"What time would be best? Eight?"

"Make it half past seven."

Kate was wearing a wool bonnet and a long wool coat, both of a dark grey tone, when Archer called for her. She was also wearing a pair of dark cotton gloves. She took Archer's arm as he walked her from the back porch to the side street and up to the main street. Patches of snow lay wherever it had been packed or trampled in the alley and streets, but the sidewalk was clear, and when they stepped up onto it, she let go of his arm.

The two of them took slow steps as they passed by businesses closed for the day. The sky was clear, and in the light of a three-quarter moon, Archer could see Kate's face well enough. He waited for her to speak.

"You must have had an interesting talk with Mr. Fenton."

"It wasn't very long."

"He said you had the idea that he was over-protective but he was just looking out for me."

"I think we understood each other."

She laughed. "More than he let on to me, I'd guess. He *is* jealous."

"Quite a bit, it seems. I tried not to make

things worse, but I had to say something if I wanted to see you. I said you were of age and not anybody's ward. I hope that wasn't out of line."

"I don't think so."

"He was still being difficult, so I had to ask him whether he wanted me to talk to him or to his wife."

"Oh."

"What's the matter?"

"That might have been a bit strong."

"Well, he seems to think he owns you, but he doesn't. You work for him and for his wife, and I thought he could use a reminder."

"Oh, he knows that. He and Mrs. Fenton treat me like an indentured servant, but they know I came here of my own free will."

Archer thought she was still giving it too light a treatment, so he said, "I don't like him trying to control who you talk to. He doesn't own you."

Kate gave a wave of her hand. "He knows that I came here on my own, and I can leave that way. When I do what I came for — though I haven't told them that."

Archer felt his hopes sinking. "Oh, then you don't plan to be here for long?"

"I don't know."

"I hadn't thought of that."

She turned her face to him and smiled. "I didn't give you reason to. For all you knew, I was a clerk and domestic servant who spent her spare time reading sentimental poetry. Which I do, but it's not the whole story."

Archer was quiet for a moment. Trying a cheerful tone, he said, "Have you made progress with *Evangeline*?"

Her breath was visible on the air as she spoke. "Oh, it's so lovely and so sad, but it's so long. I've got the opening part, as I told you. Now I'm working on the last part, sort of an epilogue, where we go back to the forest primeval and the lovers are sleeping in the graveyard." She clapped her gloved hands together. "Oh, it's wonderful, but I'm afraid I've gotten us off track."

"Actually, I think I did. You were saying that being a working girl and reading poetry wasn't the whole story about you."

"Oh, yes. That's right."

"You said something about doing what you came for, and I gather it's something you're not quick to talk about."

"Well, yes."

"But you mentioned it to me."

She stopped on the sidewalk in front of a dark shop and showed him her face in the moonlight. "And I've mentioned it to no one else. But if I don't ask anyone, I'll get nowhere."

Archer felt his optimism coming back. "Feel free to ask me, or tell me. I don't have any reason to repeat it."

"I didn't think you would." She resumed walking at the same slow pace. "I didn't come out here just to make a living, but once I was here, I had to find work to get by. And it gave me something to be doing — as far as people saw me, you know."

"I think I follow you."

"Perhaps I can be clearer. You see, Mr. Archer, I don't have people to go back to. My mother was all I had, and she passed away."

"I'm sorry to hear that. But please do call me Russ."

"Very well." She walked on for a couple of more steps. "I thought I was starting at the beginning, but actually it goes back further, to when I was born."

"That's fine. I'm following it."

"When I was a very little girl —" She broke off and laughed. "As you can see, I'm apprehensive about telling this story. But let me start again." She took a deep breath as she raised her head and lowered it. "I was born here, somewhere in this part of the country. When I was a little girl, my father took my mother and me to Indiana. After a short while he left us there and, I think, came back out here."

"And his name is Blackwell?"

Kate shook her head. "No. My mother married again, and please don't ask me the details of either marriage, because I don't know. But at any rate I had a stepfather, and I went by his name, largely because my mother did."

"And he's gone as well."

"Yes. A few years before my mother."

"And so, having no one there, you came out here."

"That's right," she said, looking straight ahead. "I came to look for my father."

"I see." Archer gave it a quick thought and suppressed an image. "Do you think he's a man of property?"

"I have no idea. For all I know, he's dead. But I just wanted to know. That's all. I don't care about anyone else's money or property. I just want to know about this part of my life."

"I can understand that."

She raised her eyes to meet his. "I've been very cautious and deliberate about it. You're the only person I've so much as mentioned it to."

149

"Well, like I said, it'll go no further than me."

She stopped and turned to him again. Her voice was lower as she said, "Do you know many people here?"

He stopped as well. "Not many, but you can try me. Do you know your real father's name?" He felt an edge of worry.

She looked both ways and brought her dark eyes back to meet him. With her voice almost in a whisper, she said, "I understand his name is Jack Doolin."

Archer's tension vanished. "Haven't heard that name, but I can keep my ears open. I won't mention it unless you want me to do some asking."

"Thank you," she said. She brought her gloved hands together in front of her. "For right now, let's leave it as something to listen for. I haven't gotten anywhere that way, but maybe you will."

"Good enough."

They walked to the end of the block, where the town ran out of sidewalks. As they turned around, Kate looked up at the moonlit sky.

"Sometimes it's incredible. There's so much to see out there."

"That's for sure. There have been nights when I've lain in my bedroll and been plumb amazed."

"Like a sailor at sea. I've heard that people say the prairie is like an ocean. They even call their wagons schooners."

He stole a look at her pretty lips and blushing cheeks. She was like a girl in a storybook. "And the highwaymen are like pirates," he said.

She glanced his way. "Have you known any of them? Highwaymen, not pirates."

"Oh, no. It's just that I heard a song about an honest puncher who fell into bad company and robbed the stage."

"Like the Scottish ballads, about young men who turn pirate. And get hanged, I'm sorry to say. Hanged in Glasgow or London town. But it's fitting, I suppose." She seemed uplifted by the idea.

"The gallows and the graveyard," he added.

She gave a light laugh. "Oh, yes. The paths of glory." After a few seconds she said, "But tell me about yourself. I've told you my story, so you can tell me yours."

Archer took a couple of seconds to answer. "Well, there's not much to it. I haven't been a pirate or sailed the high seas. I was raised without parents of my own, first in an orphanage and then in a kind of work farm."

"You never got adopted?"

"No, it was what they called a foster home. I learned to do farm work."

"Did you go to school?"

"Not much, once I left the orphanage. But I was twelve by then, so I had learned to read and write and do arithmetic. We had books to read at the foster home, and not much else for entertainment when the weather was bad, so I'm not so bad off. I know about Longfellow, for example, and Dickens."

"He writes about orphans. Or did."

"That's true. Anyway, once I got old enough, I went out on my own. When you do that, you don't feel as much like an orphan, or you don't see yourself as one. At least I didn't."

"So you've worked your way up."

"I don't know how far up. As you may have heard, Lidge Mercer has taken me in as a junior partner. I wouldn't have gotten that far if I hadn't worked, and I don't want to be satisfied with just that much. Not that I'm ambitious about property, but I'd like to earn something more on my own."

"It's good to have ambitions, as long as you're not ambitious, as Brutus would say." When Archer did not answer right away, she said, "Julius Caesar, you know."

"Oh, yes. He got his."

"Yes, he did." She seemed cheered as before, when she spoke of young pirates being hanged. She walked on for a couple of steps and said, "Anyway, back to you. And your ambitions are . . . ?"

"I'd like to have land of my own. I don't covet anyone else's. I've seen quite a bit of country since I've been here, and I have an idea of what kind of a place I'd like for my own."

"I can tell you've thought about it."

"All the time I was growing up. When you're poor, when you don't have anything, you build your dreams. At least I did, though I didn't talk about it very much. I didn't want anyone to laugh."

She turned her head and gave him a questioning look. "Who would laugh?"

"The other kids. They'd say things like once you're poor, you stay that way. The rich get richer and the poor get poorer, and that's how you die."

She frowned. "That seems so pessimistic."

"Maybe they had good reason. But I didn't. I held onto my idea. I thought the land was the most lasting thing you could get. It doesn't die on you like a horse, and it doesn't wear out like clothes or a carriage. If you've got land, you've always got something to go back to."

"And that's your mission."

"I suppose you could call it that. To have land that I earned for myself."

She heaved a sigh. "And mine is to find my father."

He felt the spark of optimism again. "I can help you on that, like I already said."

"I'd offer to help you on yours, but you seem determined to do it by yourself." She made what looked like a little pout, with her lips full.

"Mine's going to take longer, so we'll see. Meanwhile, I'll do what I can to help you on yours."

He took her gloved hand in his, and they stopped and faced each other. Her eyes were shining until he moved nearer. Her eyes closed, and his did, as their lips met. He felt lost in the kiss, but at the same time he had a sense of his presence on a board sidewalk, with snow around, and a vast sky above as he held a lovely girl in the moonlight.

CHAPTER SEVEN

Archer held the .25-caliber rifle at his hip and worked the lever action. He squeezed the trigger. The rifle jumped in his grip, and the bottle sat unscathed on top of the sawhorse. Archer worked the lever again and tried to get a feeling for what the left hand should be doing. Part of the problem was that the rifle was too light. Even though it was a small caliber, it had a good powder charge and kicked more than a heavier gun would. He braced his left elbow against his ribs and with his left hand applied forward pressure on the forearm where he held the rifle. Holding the stock against his hip with his right hand, he fired again. The bottle burst into glittering fragments, and the explosion gave Archer an immediate satisfaction.

He carried the rifle and leftover cartridges to the cook shack, where Oscar was cutting up a chunk of shoulder meat.

"How did it go?"

"Not too bad." Archer set the rifle in the corner by Oscar's bunk. "It took me a little while to get the aim, and then I had to work on keeping the gun steady at that level."

"Well, it helps pass the time."

"That it does. It also gives you a better feel for guns. If it came down to anything serious, though, I'd go ahead and fire it the regular way."

"Serious — like a coyote?"

"Even a prairie dog. Any kind of a live target." Archer took off his hat and coat.

"Hah. It should be a good varmint gun. I'll get somethin' with it yet, like a skunk."

"How long have you had it?"

"Me? Oh, it came with the place. I found it on top of an old mattress, underneath a pile of rags."

"Your good luck."

"I figger it belongs to the ranch, but I keep it here. If you want to use it as a saddle gun, go ahead. I think you could get a deer with it."

"We'll see. Is there any coffee?"

"There's some left in the pot there. Should be warm."

Archer poured himself a cup and sat at the table while Oscar continued cutting up the meat.

"This is when deer meat gets good," said the cook. "Antelope, too, for that matter. Lot better than when they're runnin' in hot weather. They've put on fat to go into winter. There's not much fat on an antelope, as far as that goes. Meat cooks up good in bacon grease."

Oscar went on to tell a story of how one winter he and the boss and two ranch hands went through nine antelope. They ran out of bacon and grease, so he melted beef suet and cooked the antelope meat in it. He didn't care to boil it in a stew. It kept too much of a gamy taste. That boss was stingy. As long as there was something else to eat, he wouldn't kill one of his own beef, and all the cattlemen kept an eye on one another, so it wasn't easy to kill someone else's.

Archer listened to the story and thought about other things at the same time. He was picturing the process of laying out a corral when he heard the thump of hooves in the ranch yard. He went to the door and opened it.

A wagon pulled by two bay horses had come to a stop. The driver was bundled up in a brown wool coat and a lap robe, but his battered hat and lean features gave him away. Whitmore raised a gloved hand in greeting.

Beside him on the seat, also bundled and wearing a winter cap, sat a man with dark hair and a drooping mustache.

Archer called out. "What have you got?"

"Coal," said Whitmore.

"I'll be right out." Archer closed the door and went for his hat and coat. "I didn't know we had any coal coming."

Oscar said, "Lidge ordered it for the forge. Do you know how to work iron?"

"Not yet. What kind of forge work is there to do?"

"A little of everything, I guess. You know, Lidge does his tinkering, but there's the regular work as well. Winter's the time to get caught up on those things."

"Well, I'd better go out and make sure they unload it in the right place, though I imagine Whitmore knows where to put it."

"Oh, is that him?"

"Him and another fella."

"Tell 'em to come in when they're done. I'll get some more coffee going."

Whitmore's swamper was a man named Henkelman. He looked well suited for the work, as he was a stocky fellow of average height, round-featured and round-muscled. When he took off his mittens to handle the shovel, his thick hands were impressive. Whitmore let him do at least two-thirds of the work.

When they had pulled the wagon around to the cook shack, Lidge Mercer came out and took the bill. He talked to Whitmore for a couple of minutes as Henkelman put blankets on the two horses. Then Mercer went back into the ranch house, and Whitmore led Henkelman into the cook shack.

Archer was left to his own thoughts as he followed them in. The scene with Mercer was curious in a small way. He had barely glanced at Archer, which would not have been unusual if Archer were still a ranch hand. Archer had the sense that Mercer was withdrawing. Maybe the man felt he had gone too far in allowing familiarity or equality and wanted to make sure he was still in command. It might be a simpler matter. Mercer might feel uneasy at having ordered the coal and not told his partner, and so he was keeping his distance now. Whatever the case, he did not waste time in getting back into the ranch house.

Oscar was loud and jovial as he welcomed the two visitors. Whitmore introduced Henkelman, who shook hands and stepped back. When Oscar told them to sit down and have a cup of coffee, Whitmore opened his thick wool coat and took out a quart bottle of whiskey.

Archer was glad to know that Mercer had gone into his own quarters.

"We'll lace it with this," said Whitmore.

"Whuh-ho. I'll say we will." Oscar put four mugs on the table.

"Just straight coffee for me," said Henkelman.

Archer said, "Me, too."

Whitmore paused with the bottle in his hand. "Oh, you're a boss now. I forgot."

"Don't worry about me. I just don't care for a drink yet."

"We'll just have a little nip," said Oscar. "Weather like this."

Henkelman said, "It's really not that cold."

"Nah," said Whitmore. "Not if you're movin' around. But it's a long way out here, just sittin' on your ass."

Oscar poured coffee into the cups. "What news in town?"

"Nothing. No interesting obituaries, no bankruptcies, embezzlements —"

"Why don't you get to work, then?"

Whitmore had his head raised as he watched the movement of the coffee pot. "Oh, I'm not important enough to kill someone or steal a satchel full of money."

Oscar finished pouring. "You would be if you did."

"Don't know if I could rise to the occasion." Whitmore twisted the cork, and it came out with a squeak. "Here's this."

"Sit down, all of you," said Oscar. "If I'd known someone was comin', I'd have baked something."

Whitmore poured whiskey into his cup and Oscar's. "Maybe I'll send a messenger next time."

"Send the bottle with him, heh-heh." Oscar seemed to light up even at the prospect of a drink. He lifted his cup and drank. "Oh, this is good. Mighty fine of you to remember old Oscar."

Whitmore glanced at Archer. "Takin' a chance. Maybe Lidge won't want to hire me next season."

"You do your work when you're here," said Archer. "That counts for plenty."

Oscar gave a wide smile. "Tell him it was Christmas. We're pretty close. Less than a month."

Whitmore set down his cup. "Ah, that makes a man feel good." He leaned back to reach into his pocket, and he dragged out a white tobacco sack with yellow strings. With a less guarded sidelong glance at Archer, he said, "See your pal Boot Beckett once in a while."

"He's riding horses, is he?"

"That, and other things. Said he went out

to Tuesday's place and pulled the shoes off half a dozen head there."

"He gets by."

"Oh, yeah. See him with his little gal, too."

"That's good."

Whitmore began to roll a cigarette, and Henkelman took out a pipe and tobacco pouch. Archer took off his hat and coat and sat back in his chair.

Oscar launched into a detailed story about two hunters who got caught in a sudden storm at this time of year. One was the owner of a ranch, and the other was a foreman on a neighboring ranch, and they both knew the country like the back of their hand. But they both got caught, one down in a creek bottom and the other up in some breaks. They must have lost their bearings, the way everyone figured it out later. The neighbors got up a big search party, and it worked out of the ranch where Oscar was. He cooked day and night, and on the third day after the storm they found the two men, each one of 'em dead as a post. It was a big funeral, and everyone brought food. Hell of a blow. The man who was a foreman had a wife and kids. The fellow who had his own ranch was an old bachelor, but he had men dependin' on him, just like a family. The ranch ended up getting sold. The other one got a new foreman, but the owner let the widow and kids live on at the ranch until they had a place to go. It was a big thing to happen in that country.

Whitmore got up, took off his coat, and poured more coffee. He filled Henkelman's cup and Archer's, but he poured only half in Oscar's cup and his own. Before he sat down, he poured two generous slugs of whiskey.

Oscar was in a mood for telling stories. He told one about two men who were trapping coyotes for the winter. One of them got sick with what was later thought to be appendicitis, and the other got bucked off and broke a hip when he went for help. The first man died, and the other man was crippled after that, but he married the dead man's wife and helped her raise the two kids.

His next story was about a parade he saw in Bismarck. A team of horses spooked and ran over a handful of people in a marching band. They were playing so loud they didn't hear the wagon coming. Oscar said he could still hear that music.

Da-dum-da-dum-da-dum-da,
Da-dum-da-dum-da-dum
Da-dum-da-dum-da-dum-da,
Da-dum-da-dum-da-dum.

He waved his arms as he chanted the rhythm.

"I know that song," said Whitmore. "It's the 'British Grenadiers.' It goes like this.

> Some talk of Alexander,
> And some of Hercules
> Of Hector and Lysander,
> And such great names as these.
> But of all the world's great heroes,
> There's none that can compare
> With a tow, row, row, row, row, row,
> To the British Grenadier."

He sang three more stanzas, and then he lifted his cup and raised his voice for the next one.

> "Then let us fill a bumper,
> And drink a health to those
> Who carry caps and pouches,
> And wear the loupèd clothes.
> May they and their commanders
> Live happy all their years
> With a tow, row, row, row, row, row,
> For the British Grenadiers."

Oscar clapped his hands together twice. "That's it, all right. I can hear it clear as day." He and Whitmore downed their drinks. Then Oscar took the bottle and poured two more without the coffee.

A loud knock came at the door, and Oscar flinched. He set the bottle on the table away from him.

The knock sounded again. Oscar's eyes, a little bleary by now, were fixed on the door.

"That's not Lidge," said Whitmore. "He'd come right in." He put on his coat and tucked the bottle under it.

The knock came again, five loud raps.

"Come on in," Oscar shouted, putting on a tone of impatience. "The door's open."

The doorknob turned, and the door swung inward. A man stepped inside and closed the door behind him. He was a tall man in a dull black hat and a grey wool overcoat. He had hair the color of steel dust, a rough complexion, red-rimmed eyes, and a straight, prominent nose. Even more than before, Peavey reminded Archer of a large rat.

Peavey cleared his throat, but his voice still sounded coarse as he said, "I'm lookin' to talk to Lidge Mercer."

Oscar motioned with his head. "He ought to be over in the big house."

The ranch house wasn't all that big, but Archer was used to Oscar's habit of calling it that, just as he was used to Whitmore referring to Mercer as the old man.

Peavey showed little reaction. He gave a straight nod in the direction of Whitmore and Archer. Back to Oscar, he said, "I heard a bunch of noise, so I thought I'd try here first."

"Just singin' a couple of hymns. Practicin' for a funeral."

Peavey scowled.

"Hah-hah," said Oscar. "Just a joke. We like to have a good time."

"I can see."

"Would you like a cup of coffee?"

"No, thanks. I'd rather talk to your boss." Peavey made a hawking sound in the bottom of his throat.

"Well, I think you can find him over there, like I said."

"I'll try it."

When Peavey was gone, Oscar said, "Not much humor in that fella. You'd think he'd sit down and sing a verse or two with us."

"Not very likely," said Archer. "He's not a big lover of music."

Oscar picked up his cup, sniffed at it, and drank.

Whitmore spoke. "We'd probably best be goin'. I'll finish this up, and we'll leave."

Henkelman, who had kept to himself the whole time, nodded in agreement.

Whitmore raised his cup to his lips and

tipped back his head, all in one movement. As he set the cup down, he smacked his lips and said, "Ahhh." Then he reached into his coat, pulled out the bottle, and handed it toward Oscar. "You'd better keep this."

"Oh, no. You take it."

"There's plenty where I'm goin'. You'll regret it tomorrow if you don't. Here, just take it and put it away." He set the bottle on the table.

Oscar eyed the bottle and lifted a brow toward Archer.

"It's a small thing to me," said Archer. "It's halfway gone anyway. Just don't let it cause any trouble."

"Like what?"

"Like joking with Peavey about funerals."

"Is he dangerous?"

"I don't know, but it's better not to antagonize him. Like you said, he's humorless. I've seen him in the saloon, and even then, he doesn't seem to have much patience with people who're havin' a good time."

"Well, I've seen him before, too, but this is the first time I've talked to him. You can bet I'll remember him."

Archer stood at the window of the bunkhouse and watched the grey shape of Peavey ride away on the brown horse. The man had visited with Mercer for about an hour, and Archer could not imagine him having come on any business that was good for the Bar M. Not this time or the time before. Archer shivered. It was cold in the bunkhouse, as he had not lit a fire all day. He was wearing his hat, coat, and gloves, and he could see his breath in the air. Across the yard, sunlight on the barn told him that the sun had not yet slipped behind the ridge. When it did, the afternoon would get colder. Whitmore and his swamper would be glad for all the bundling they had. They were traveling light going back to town, so they should make good time. Unless Peavey was headed somewhere else, he should pass them before they made it to the pine ridge.

Movement to the left caught Archer's eye. Lidge Mercer had come out of the ranch house and stood on the porch. Archer walked out of the bunkhouse and headed toward the cook shack so that Mercer could call to him if he wanted. Archer waved, and after he had taken a couple of more steps, Mercer called his name.

Archer turned and paused, and Mercer beckoned to him to come over. As Archer approached the steps, Mercer spoke.

"If you have a little while, you could come in. I've got something I'd like to talk about."

Archer followed him into the dusky front room. The door to the kitchen was open, and light fell through the doorway onto the oval rug. Mercer led the way into the kitchen, where two chairs sat opposite one another at a small table. Mercer took the chair near the stove, a sheet-iron box with the door cracked open. Fire glowed inside. Archer sat in the other chair and took off his hat.

Mercer took off his and set it on the table. He let out a long breath and gazed off to one side, past his hat. He had a tired, heavy look about him, as if the extra weight on his hips and around his waist had caught up to him and was pulling down his spirit. His dark brown eyes were clear, but his face sagged below them, and his greying beard, though trimmed close, had an old, jowly cast to it.

"I guess you know this fellow Peavey," he began in his smooth voice.

"Somewhat. Only in passing."

"Well, he's been the source of a lot of trouble for me."

"That's not a surprise, knowing him, but I didn't have an idea of how much you two were acquainted."

"Oh, we go way back. We're cousins."

Archer widened his eyes. "Really?"

"Yes. We grew up in the same town in Missouri."

Archer was able to place the smooth voice now. He said nothing, just nodded for Mercer to go ahead.

"He came out to the ranch earlier. During the summer."

"I saw him as he was leaving."

Mercer went on. "It was the first time I'd seen him in a few years. I had a hunch he might have followed me here, but I didn't know."

Archer felt it was his turn to speak. "When I first met him a few months back, not long before he came out here, he said he was working for a man named Scott."

"He didn't say anything about that, not then and not now."

"I usually see him in the company of a fella named Wyse."

Mercer shook his head. "Don't know him."

"Not the best company, either of 'em."

"I wish he would stay away, leave me alone, but I'm afraid he never will." Mercer let out a weary breath. "This does me no credit at all, but I'm going to have to tell it to you. Because of our arrangement."

Archer nodded.

Mercer had his hands together on the

table in front of him, and he stared at them for a long moment. His brows drew into a frown, then released. He took in a breath through his nose, raised his eyes, and said, "A little over twenty years ago, somewhere around the time you were born, I guess, Phillip and I were young men in our twenties, not going anywhere at all. My father had a clothing store and I worked there, but no more than I had to. Phillip's father, my uncle on my mother's side, was a grain broker and did pretty well. Phillip pretended to work for him, but he did less than I did. Within a year's time, both of our fathers died — mine from diabetes, and his from a stroke. The money was all tied up, and I was working for a clerk's wages. Phillip had no job at all. Quite a change from the leisure we'd been accustomed to."

"I can imagine."

"What we did have was a grandmother, and she had settled her estate largely on Phillip and myself, so that we could get ahead on our own. Rather nice of her. I think she thought we were more enterprising than we were. Or more responsible." Mercer paused. "I can imagine how this strikes you, growing up as you did."

Archer shrugged. "Not many of us choose how we start out."

"No doubt about that. Anyway, here we were, two worthless young men, waiting for our grandmother to die. The trouble was, she was taking too long. She went on for months, in and out of a haze. Half the time, she didn't know who we were. She'd think we were her brothers, or that Phillip was his father — her name was Peavey, too. Finally, we got impatient. I think Phillip was worse than I was, but I can't blame it all on him." Mercer's eyes met Archer and moved away. "I think you can see where this is going, but —"

"It's not troubling me. Go ahead."

"Not yet, maybe. At any rate, we could see that the old lady was done for, but it might drag on for quite a while longer. We convinced ourselves that all we were doing was bringing about the inevitable. Just saving time. I didn't have the nerve to do the deed myself, but Phillip said he did. And he proved it. He smothered her with a pillow while I kept a lookout."

"Whew."

Mercer stared at his hands. His eyes had the defeated look of a man who had nothing left to lie about. "Like I said, it doesn't do me any credit. Anyway, once it was done, there was no turning back, no turning aside. Even if I had had the courage to admit what

172

we'd done, and Lord knows that I wished many times that I did, I would have had Phillip to deal with. He was a physically powerful man back then. He still is. So I saw it through, took my inheritance, and hoped to separate myself from him for good."

A piece of firewood made a soft clunk against the inside wall of the fire box. Mercer's eyes rested on Archer for a second and slid away. He opened the door and poked at the burning wood with his poker.

"Easier said than done," he went on. He closed the door of the stove. "I went to the northern part of Missouri and bought a farm. Within a couple of years he had squandered his money, and he came to leech off of me. I gave him some money and asked him to stay away. He did for a while, and then he came back. I was trying to make an honest life for myself, and he knew it. I'll tell you, I wasn't a very good farmer, but I had good men working for me, and I was making a little. He would come around and hover like a vulture, laugh in my face, threaten to ruin me and my reputation. And I deserved it. That was what I told myself. I had done this hideous thing, or had taken part in it, and this was my punishment."

Archer studied the tired face. He pitied

the man for his weakness, for having come under the power of such a vermin. He imagined Peavey, half rat and half bird, enfolding Mercer with his wings like a vampire in a Gothic tale.

"I don't know if it was in me to marry anyway, but his coming around made it a certainty that I couldn't. When I wasn't plagued by guilt, I was paralyzed by fear. I knew I could never have a wife, never have a family. I was always on my guard, keeping up a good face. I didn't drink or go to the races or go to the whorehouses or anything that comfortable bachelors do. Yet I knew he would come around again, and he always did. Finally when I gave him a pretty good sum and thought I was rid of him for a while, I sold all of my property and cleared out of Missouri."

"And came here."

"Not right away. I traveled around, looking at opportunities and trying to cover my trail. Then I bought this rundown ranch in the middle of nowhere. Before long, I had the feeling of being watched. It wasn't the same as before. Normally he would come knocking on my door, brazen as could be. But he waited. He came that first time, a few months ago, and then again today."

"No shyness at that."

"I should say not."

"Are you sure he's the one who's been watching you?"

"Well, no. First, I can't say beyond a doubt that I've been watched."

"I thought I saw someone out there, one time, when I first came here."

Mercer shrugged. "You probably did. But even if there has been someone, I don't know it's him, even if he's been around."

"There was that fellow I had a tangle with one day. Jenks. Said you were off your range. You remember him."

"Of course I do. The first day in months that I'd ventured out very far at all."

"At the time, I thought Jenks was the spy. But I haven't seen him since that day, or his friend Crowell either. And I haven't come across anyone else who says he knows 'em. I wonder if they're connected to Peavey in some way."

Mercer's face drooped as he shook his head. "I don't know. The whole thing has worried me sick. Yet it's no less than I deserve." He paused. "I'm sorry to have to drag you into it. I feel ashamed to even talk about it. But since I've taken you in as a partner, I thought it was only fair to let you know." He took a slow breath. "I haven't felt right about keeping it from you, but I guess it's just natural for a fella to hope he can get away without having to tell someone. At least now, you're forewarned."

And forearmed, Archer thought. So much for being taken in as a partner and heir. As much as anything else, he was filling the role of a watchdog — or bodyguard.

"It's all right," he said. "As long as everything else is aboveboard between us."

Mercer's spirits seemed to pick up at the prospect. "It is. And if you've got any questions, I'll be glad to answer them."

Archer cast his mind back. "Maybe one."

"What is it?"

"You've never lived out in this country before?"

"No."

"Or had kids."

"No, none at all. I'm sure of that. Why?"

"Just trying to keep some stories straight. I guess that was two questions, not one."

"I'll answer any I can."

Archer moved among the horses, patting them and looking them over for nicks and cuts as they ate from the grain boxes. Dusk had fallen, but he could see the animals well enough as he came close to each one. By habit he counted them, the six horses they kept in for the winter. All the rest, including the sorrel that had bucked him off, were running shoeless on winter range. Archer was the only one who rode these horses now, and he couldn't ride them all with any frequency, so he enjoyed this daily contact with them. When he was done, he stood back and counted them again. Five of the six belonged to the Bar M, and it gave him an uncertain feeling to look at them and not know his relation to them. By agreement, he had an interest in the Bar M, so these horses should be partly his — either thirty percent of each one or thirty percent of five head. The same went for the stable, the bunkhouse, and the rest.

Even the thirty percent seemed nebulous. For as much as he felt the temptation, or the right, to salvage something for himself, his better angel told him that all he stood to acquire was tainted. Not that the horses themselves had any such blemish — just the possession of them did. No wonder Lidge Mercer seemed so much like a duck out of water. He was not only a late arrival to ranch country, but he knew deep down that none of this should be his. Maybe that was part of the reason he could be generous with it.

A thin dust hung in the air of the stable, raised by a stamping foot here and a swishing tail there. Daylight was fading, and the farthest horses were but shadows. None of this was going to change today. He would be friends with these horses again tomorrow, and the next day, until he decided where he stood. He didn't think it would be right to just walk away, but an inner voice told him that sooner or later he was going to have to renounce what little he had gained through his association with Lidge Mercer. Maybe it would be for the best and leave him free to pursue his larger purposes. In a very short time, what had seemed a path to his dream had become a barrier, and he needed to get past it. For the time being, though, he needed to stay levelheaded and find the best way of easing out. The man who had offered to be his benefactor deserved at least that much.

CHAPTER EIGHT

Archer tossed a leg bone in the direction of a clump of sagebrush and watched the bone disappear in the snow.

"More chicken?" Sadie asked.

"No, thanks."

"There's one piece left. Boot, you eat it."

"What part is it?"

"Here." She held the plate toward him. "It's a thigh piece. And there are two biscuits left."

Archer took a biscuit, and Sadie set the tin plate on the canvas next to Boot.

Archer exchanged glances with Kate, and they both smiled. Sadie was a go-ahead kind of girl. If she was going to kill and cut up the chicken herself, as she said she did, she was going to make sure none of it went to waste. And she wasn't squeamish about saying "thigh" or "breast," as some women were.

She stood up on the spread-out tarpaulin

and went to the sleigh. She had a straight walk without much motion. Archer looked away as she bent into the sleigh to bring out the cake. As she came back with the pasteboard box in both hands, he smiled her way. She was neither tall nor short, wide nor slender, but her brown wool coat and knitted cap made her look bigger, and when she carried the box with her elbows out like an equestrian's she looked like she meant business. She was the perfect girl for Boot, who ate what came his way and did not worry much about tomorrow.

She set the box in the middle of the canvas.

Kate asked, "Did you make it yourself, Sadie?"

"Oh, yes." She raised her head in what looked like a small gesture of pride as she lifted the top from the box. "Mrs. Montgomery lets me use the kitchen for anything I want. She frets a little over the amount of firewood we use, but then Boot brings us some once in a while. Don't you, Boot?"

"When I can't sell it anywhere else."

"See how he is? He doesn't want to admit to doing anything that isn't rough and tough. Why, you should see him gathering eggs."

"I just did that once."

Archer said, "I believe he's embarrassed. I don't know if I've ever seen him blush before."

Kate spoke. "Is it very hard to raise chickens?"

Sadie shook her head. "Not very. It's mostly a matter of whether you want to look after them all the time. Some people don't."

"The Fentons don't have room, but Mrs. Fenton says her mother always kept chickens. I know people had them in town in Terre Haute, but I always thought of them as something people had in the country."

"It's easier to let them run loose there, and shut them up in the evening."

"Did you grow up in the country, Sadie?"

"On Snake Crick. My folks still live there. My pa works for a man. When I got old enough to work away from home, I came here."

"That's over in Nebraska, isn't it? In what they call the sandhills?"

"Close. The real sandhills are a little farther over."

"Do you have younger brothers or sisters to help out your mother?"

"I have a younger sister, and a brother after that."

Kate turned. "Have you met them, Boot?"

"Not yet. Sadie doesn't want me to meet

her sister."

"Oh, I do, too." Then in a matter-of-fact tone, Sadie said, "It's just that she's prettier than I am."

Kate's voice was soft. "Don't say that, Sadie."

"Well, she is. But I'm not homely. Am I, Boot? Watch what he says."

"If you were, I wouldn't have had to rub out so much of the competition."

Sadie beamed. "You see? Boot's no fool. He just acts like one so he can get the best of people in a trade."

"One of these days, I'm going to get you somethin' real nice in a trade."

"He keeps telling me he's going to get me a pair of skunk-skin slippers."

"I know a fella who's got a pair. Says his wife wore 'em before she died."

"This is how he shows affection, in public."

Boot tossed away the bone, and it, too, disappeared in the snow. "Last thing I traded for was an iron bar, good for diggin' postholes. Not much call for them this time of year, so the price was pretty good."

Archer spoke up. "I could use one of those, come spring."

"I thought you might. I'll make you a real good deal on it."

"Next time I'm in town with the wagon, I'll take a look at it. I've got to get some grain before long, and I'll pick up some kerosene at the same time. I also want to get a length of chain."

"It'll go along just fine, then."

Sadie was holding the cake knife upright, as if she was waiting for the boys to get through their talk. "Let's have the cake," she said.

"No coffee?" said Boot.

"We'll have that when we get back to town."

Kate spoke. "And you made the frosting as well, Sadie?"

"Yes, I did. It's not very good. All I had was lard to hold it together, so I didn't spread it on very thick. If anyone wants to scrape it off, don't be afraid of hurting my feelings."

"A little bit of lard don't hurt no one," Boot said.

"Doesn't hurt anyone." Sadie cut out the first piece and put it on the tin plate that had held the biscuits. "See? It's not very thick at all."

The evening shadows lay long and dark across the snow as Archer and Kate walked along the board sidewalk from the café to the cross street.

"Coffee warms you up," she said.

"It does. And food keeps the fires burning to begin with. Sadie made a real nice picnic for us."

"She did." After a second, Kate added, "I think a great deal of her. She's straightforward, and there's not a bit of pretense about her."

"Competent and proud of it. No nonsense, but not too serious, either. This whole excursion is like a breath of fresh air after being at the ranch. Everything's been so glum out there of late."

Kate turned with a look of concern. "Oh, really? Are there problems? Or maybe I shouldn't ask."

"I should probably wait to say any more. Sorry I said as much as I did."

"That's all right. Back to Sadie. She seems so solid and dependable."

"You can tell she's had a good upbringing. Working class, but who isn't? And certainly of the better kind. Clean and well-mannered."

"I like the way she spoke of her family."

"You mean her sister being prettier?"

"Oh, that. No, I meant that whenever she mentioned her folks, she had a tone of respect. Even in little things, like when she talked about her mother teaching them how to make jam from the wild plums. It must be a very basic existence on Snake Crick." Kate pronounced the last two words with deliberation.

"I'm sure it is. That kind of work doesn't pay much for a man with a wife and family, so they've all got to pull together. If spuds are all they've got to eat, no one complains."

"Doesn't hurt anyone." Again, Kate pronounced each word separately.

The two walked on without speaking until they came to the cross street. She took his arm as they placed their steps in the trampled snow.

"You remember," said Kate, not very loud, "when I told you there was something I came here to look for?"

"Of course."

"You haven't picked up anything, have you?"

Archer looked each way as they reached the middle of the street. "Oh, no. If I had, I would have told you."

"I was sure you would. Anyway, I think I've gone on long enough, and it's time to take the initiative. I'm still apprehensive, because I don't know what I'll find or who else might turn up. But if there was a quiet way to do it, maybe you could ask about it."

She kept her gaze fixed ahead as she spoke.

"I can give it a try."

"You still remember the name, don't you?"

"Oh, yes. I remember it perfectly. And I'll be on the lookout for a quiet way to ask."

"Thank you, Russ." They turned the corner, and the back porch of the Fenton household was right ahead. "And thank you for such a delightful day. All of it."

"All I did was hire the sleigh. Sadie did the biggest part. And Boot took care of the coffee."

"We've already thanked them. But I wanted to make sure I thanked you — for everything."

"You make it sound as if we're done."

She smiled as she shook her head. "Far from it. I'm also thanking you for what you've agreed to do."

"Like this?" He put his arms around the waist of her coat, and he felt the grasp of her hands on his upper arms as she held him.

She turned her face to him and said, "This, too."

The length of chain clunked and rattled as Archer dropped it into the rear of the wagon box. The sacks of grain were stacked in the front part, and the five cans of kerosene were lined up behind them. In the rear of the bed, cushioned in three inches of straw and wrapped in canvas, were the food supplies for the month.

Boot Beckett stood by with the digging bar, holding it with the flared tip upright. In his fur cap he looked like a trapper, while the bar itself reminded Archer of a spear he might have seen in a painting of noble tribesmen.

Boot raised the bar and handed it to Archer, who hefted it before he rotated it a quarter-turn and lowered it into the box.

"Fifteen pounds or a little more," he said. "I'm glad I didn't try to take it home on horseback. I might have had to leave it some place."

"It'll ride fine this way. If you see a badger you can brain him with it."

"If I see a badger, I'll stay in the wagon."

"Pelt's worth something."

"I'll treat him like a brother. Share the bacon with him. Actually, I've got Oscar's rifle if I have to shoot something."

"That's good."

Archer paused. "Sure I can't give you something for it?"

"Plumb certain. Consider it my Christmas present, just a little bit late. You can buy me a drink sometime."

"Well, be that way. But it's worth something."

"So was the horse and sleigh. I didn't feel that I held my own that day, and when this diggin' bar came up in the conversation, I figured that was how I'd get even."

"That's good. I was afraid you meant it about the Christmas present. But I still come out ahead."

"Maybe I did mean it about buyin' me a drink."

"Good enough, Boot. You're hard to bargain with." Archer climbed onto the wagon seat and unwrapped the reins.

"So long. Have a safe trip."

"See you later, and give my best to Sadie."

Archer drove the team northward. As he passed an empty lot near the edge of town, he saw a man chopping wood. The workman stood up straight and waved. Archer recognized the lean frame and battered hat. A thought ran through his head, and he stopped the wagon.

Whitmore came ambling over as Archer climbed down by the wheel.

"What d'you have to say, Russ?"

"Not much. And yourself?"

"Probably less. How's everything out at the ranch?"

"Well enough."

"Just you and Lidge and Oscar still?"

"That's right. In three different houses. Don't get on each other's nerves as much that way."

"Just as well. Come a big freeze, and you can all bundle up, like the Rooshians."

"Do they do that?"

"Ones I knew did. They lived in a dugout. Man and his wife and his cousin. Come spring, they found the man like a block of ice under a pile of hay in the stable, and the cousin and the wife were long gone. Law caught up with 'em in Chicago."

"Whose fault was it?"

Whitmore gave a short toss of the head. "Oh, the husband's. He should never have shared his blankets, and once he did, he should never have gone to sleep."

"They couldn't say he just froze to death."

"Not with a gash in his head like that."

Archer winced. "That would be a good story for Oscar."

"I've told it to him. You'll probably hear it someday. See if he dresses it up. Then again, maybe he won't tell it around Lidge. I guess him and that fella Peavey are cousins."

"Oh, is that getting around?"

"Somewhat. Peavey says Lidge beat him out of some inheritance money quite a while back, and he's tryin' to get it." Whitmore raised his eyebrows. "You think there's anything to that?"

Archer shook his head. "I can't say. Lidge told me a little about it, but it's his story. It sounds like Peavey has got his as well."

"Oh, yeah. I didn't mean to be puttin' you on the spot to answer for him. Just curious."

"No harm in that." Archer paused. "As far as curiosity goes, there's something I was interested in."

"What's that?"

"You've been here quite a while, know quite a few people and some of the old stories."

"Well, some." Whitmore gave a clever smile. "There's some stories, of course, that nobody knows the straight of."

"Sure. But this is more about a man than a story. At least to begin with."

"Who is it?"

Archer lowered his voice. "Did you ever know a man by the name of Jack Doolin?"

"A lot of people did, or still do, as far as I know." Whitmore gave a close look. "He's not caught up in this Mercer-and-Peavey business, is he?"

"Oh, no. This is a whole different line. I happen to know someone who'd like to know how to find this Jack Doolin. And it's not about money or old grudges or any of that."

"He shouldn't be hard to find. He lives over in Glenrose, the last I heard. Used to run a card game."

"Is he dangerous?"

Whitmore shrugged a shoulder. "I don't think so. Maybe to himself. Drank like a fish when I knew him."

Archer reflected for a few seconds. "That should be enough to go on if he's not hard to find. Thanks for telling me."

"No trouble."

Archer took out a four-bit piece and tried to put it in Whitmore's hand.

"What's that for?"

"You can get yourself a drink."

"I don't need it. Not the money, that is. I might want a drink later, but I've got money to buy it." He motioned toward the wood-pile where he had left his ax. "I get paid for this."

"I can't give money away today."

Whitmore had a droll expression as he said, "Not every day will be like that. We get deeper into the winter, I might take you up on it. But not today, and not for tellin' you somethin' that any fool on the street knows. At least in Glenrose."

■ ■ ■ ■

Archer let the bay horse run, and it stepped out at a trot, pulling the buggy at an even pace. Small chunks of snow with mud on the underside flew up from the roadway. The morning was clear and sunny, and the temperature was in the ten-degree range. Archer did not feel cold. He was wearing layers consisting of an undershirt, a wool shirt, and the lined canvas coat. His leather gloves had cotton lining, and his wool pants had a layer of long underwear beneath them. Adding to his comfort was the lap robe he shared with Kate. She was bundled up as well in her wool cap, wool overcoat, and an unknown number of layers of garments. She didn't look chubby, though, and her cheeks had a pretty blush.

Glenrose lay a little more than ten miles west of Ashton. If things went well, they could make the trip in one day. Archer turned to Kate and gave her a wink.

"Don't worry. It'll be all right."

"I just don't know what to expect."

"Try not to expect anything. That way you won't be disappointed."

She put on a brave smile.

Glenrose was a noisy town for being

smaller than Ashton. It had a steam-driven rock crusher, a blacksmith shop, and a train station. A locomotive idled and hissed, and men shouted above the noise. Archer gathered that the train had left off a full coal car at the siding and was about to move on.

In the center of town, Archer helped Kate down from the buggy and up onto the sidewalk in front of a café. Inside, the smell of baking bread carried on the warm air. Archer and Kate took a small table by the window where the sunlight slanted in. After a few minutes, Archer warmed up enough to take off his coat and gloves. The waitress brought coffee and said that lunch would not be ready for another hour. The bread had just come out of the oven, though, and she recommended it with butter and strawberry jam.

The waitress looked stout enough to help unload the coal car or to work in the blacksmith shop, and she was not too delicate to talk and joke with a couple of teamsters. One of them spit tobacco juice on the floor, and the other kept teasing her with promises of gifts he was going to buy her — a pair of fat grey geese, a milk cow, a white mule that would kneel down for her to get on. She laughed and batted the air as if she were swishing flies.

When she came by to see if Kate and Archer needed anything more, Archer asked her what her name was.

"June."

"Do you know most of the people in this town?"

"Some of 'em."

Archer lowered his voice. "Do you know a man named Jack Doolin?"

She twitched the left side of her nose and said, "Not very well. But I know who he is."

"Do you know where we might find him?"

"This early in the day, you can probably find him where he lives. He rents a room."

"In a boarding house?"

"Something like that. A lady rents out rooms in her house."

"Is it far from here?"

The waitress raised her arm and pointed. "You go out on the street and go two blocks north. You come to High Street. Turn right there. Second block on the right, in the middle of the block, there's a two-story house painted grey. What they call battleship grey."

"Has the place got a name?"

"Not that I know of. The lady who runs it is Mrs. Pitts."

"It should be easy to find."

"Oh, yeah. I've never been to the shipyards, but you'll know that grey when you see it."

When the leaden-hued two-story house came into view, Archer had no doubt that he had found Mrs. Pitts's place. He left Kate in the buggy and walked through pocked, frozen snow to the slanting porch. The steps and floorboards gave under his weight, and the grey door casing was loose when he knocked on it.

Footsteps sounded inside, and the door opened. A thin woman with short, straight grey hair gave Archer a looking-over.

"Can I help you with something?"

"I'm looking for a Mr. Jack Doolin. I was told he lives here."

"He does."

"I'd like to talk to him if he's in."

"And who should I say is here?"

"My name's Russ Archer, though I doubt that he has any reason to know who I am."

"I'll tell him." The woman shut the door.

Archer tossed a smile and nod in Kate's direction. When the door opened again, the grey-haired woman told him to come in. As he stepped into the front room and took off his hat, she pointed to her right.

"Over there," she said.

The front room was a plain area with no family pictures or personal knickknacks. On

195

the near side it had two chairs covered with a worn corduroy fabric, on the left end stood a wooden chair with no arms or cushions, and across the room sat a divan that looked as if it was upholstered with old drapes. At the end of the divan, with his back to a door leading into another room, stood a man with dark circles under his eyes. He raised a lit cigarette to his lips as Archer approached.

"Are you Jack Doolin?"

"I am."

"My name's Russ Archer. I'm here on behalf of someone else."

Doolin nodded as a cloud of smoke drifted upward in front of his face. He did not offer to shake hands but rather had the defensive air of someone who was used to keeping creditors at a distance.

When the smoke cleared, Archer got a better look at him. The man had dry, straight hair the color of winter grass, rising on top of his head where he had it combed back. He had a long face with soft flesh hanging on his jaws and under his chin.

Archer said, "This person asked me to go first, to see if you'd be willing to have a meeting."

"Depends on who it is and what he wants." Doolin's elbow went up as he took another pull on his cigarette.

"It's your daughter."

Doolin's brown eyes showed no expression as he blew out smoke and said, "She doesn't need any go-between. She wants to talk to me, she can just come up to me and talk. That's the way I do things."

"Well, since it's been so many years, and she was such a little girl when she saw you last, she didn't know how open you would be."

Doolin raised his cigarette again and took a slow drag. His eyes skimmed over Archer. "So what are you to her?"

"Nothing formal. We've gotten to know each other a bit in the last few months."

Doolin sniffed.

Archer said, "Well, all right. I'll be more direct. I'm the young man who courts your daughter, Kate. But that's not why I came."

"Kate. I called her Katie." Doolin now leveled his gaze on Archer as if he was trying to size him up. "So why did you come?"

"To do this asking for her. To see if you wanted to meet her. She's waiting outside."

Doolin frowned. "Oh, well, bring her in. It's cold out there."

Archer went out to the carriage and escorted Kate into the house. Doolin was still standing by the divan and no longer held a cigarette. He gave Kate a wary look as she approached.

She stopped about six feet away. Her face was flushed and her lip was trembling as she took off her gloves. "Papa," she said, "I'm Kate."

He drew his brows together. "Little Katie. I wouldn't have known you."

"I wouldn't have known you, either. But here I am." She put on a bright smile.

"And your mother?"

The smile disappeared. "She passed away. About a year ago."

"I'm sorry to hear that. I never had any ill will towards her. I heard she married again."

"She did. To a man named Blackwell. He passed away a couple of years before she did."

Doolin's eyes, brown but not very dark, moved from Kate to Archer and back to Kate. "So you came out here with this fellow?"

"No, I came on my own. I met him after I got here. I've been staying in Ashton."

Doolin seemed to be studying his own left hand as he said, "I don't have anything to offer you. I had a card game for quite a while, but I never made so much that I could put any money back. I rent a room here, and I barely get by. A few people owe me money, and I pick up a little playing cards. I'd offer to help you out, but —"

"Oh, I didn't come to ask for help. I just wanted to meet you, to know who you were and what you were like."

Doolin did not speak. His eyes had little expression as they roved over her.

Kate's voice was quick, with a nervous edge to it. "I realize I caught you off guard, took you by surprise, so I won't stay long. But I'll be in Ashton, and if you'd like, I'll come see you again."

Doolin gave a nod. "That would be all right."

"And if you wanted to get in touch with me, you can find me at Fenton's general store. I work there and help his wife in the house."

Doolin seemed to be still absorbed in the process of recognizing her. "So you're little Katie. All grown up now, and living in the next town."

"That's right. I go by Kate. Kate Blackwell."

He took in a breath through his nose. "Girls change their name anyway."

Kate glanced at Archer and back at her father. "Well, I guess we'll go now. We can get back before dark."

Doolin shifted his attention to Archer.

"How did you get here today?"

"In a buggy. We wouldn't have been able to come and go all in one day if we'd taken the train."

"You live in Ashton too?"

"North of there. I have an interest in a ranch."

"Oh. Well, I guess that's all right. Get a little time off this time of year."

"I'm doing all right with it."

"You run cattle, then."

"A few. Trying to build up."

"Sure. Takes time and a lot of work. And a head for business. Lotta men go broke that way. It's not for me. And besides, I never liked horses — not workin' with 'em, that is."

"I get along at it." It occurred to Archer that Doolin was making small talk with him because it was easier than facing his daughter. Archer turned to Kate and said, "Are you ready to go?"

"I think so." She took a quick breath. "Goodbye, Papa. I'll come to see you again. If you come to Ashton, don't be too shy."

"Sure. I'll see you again." Doolin had both hands in his pockets. His head was lowered, and the dark circles under his eyes were noticeable.

Archer said, "So long," and offered his

arm to Kate. She was keeping up a smile as she took his arm and walked away.

As they rolled down the street in the buggy, she sounded worn out when she said, "I thought it might have amounted to a little more."

Archer patted the robe that covered her lap. "I think you were right when you said you took him by surprise."

Halfway from town to the ranch, Archer smelled snow on the way. A storm was blowing in from the northwest. He turned up the collar of his coat and pulled down the brim of his hat. The saddle horse picked up his pace when Archer touched him with the stirrup. Snow began to gather on the buckskin's black mane and forelock as well as on the sleeves of Archer's canvas coat. By the time Archer turned off the trail toward the ranch, an inch of snow had gathered on the ground.

At the ranch, he put the horse away and walked through a couple of inches of snow on his way to the cook shack. Smoke was coming out of the stove pipe, and he figured he was in time for noon dinner.

Oscar was sitting by the stove drinking a cup of coffee. "Back, huh? I was wonderin' who-all I'd have for dinner."

Archer brushed the snow off his sleeves, drew close to the stove, and held out his hands to the warmth. "What's Lidge up to? Anything in particular?"

"Don't know. Haven't seen him yet today."

"Is he in the house?" Archer took off his hat and coat and held them as he waited for an answer.

"I assume he is, unless he froze to death in the outhouse. I didn't go call him for breakfast because he's been in a poor mood lately. Keeps to himself. You've seen it."

"Maybe I should go check on him. Have him come over here to eat with us. Get him out of his own company."

Oscar stood up. "Go ahead. I'll get some grub started."

Archer put on his hat and coat again and went outside. Snow swirled in the grey daylight. He crossed the yard and went up the steps to the ranch house. No sound came from inside as he knocked on the door. The wind made an irregular whooshing as it came around the corner of the house. Archer knocked again and waited. Still nothing. He hoped Mercer wasn't sick. It would be a long trip to the doctor in this weather.

After the third knock, Archer brushed the snow off the door handle, turned the knob, and pushed the door open. He stepped in.

The house was cold and quiet. Archer closed the door behind him and stood for a moment as his eyes adjusted to the dim, shadowy atmosphere. The ashes were dead in the fireplace, and the poker was standing idle against the wall. The clock on the mantel had quit ticking. Archer was about to call out when his glance was drawn downward. A body lay on its back on the oval rug. Archer could not see the face from where he stood, but he was pretty sure who it was. The man's large midsection was prominent, and the grey shirt and dark vest were just like Mercer's.

Archer spoke in the cold, still room. "Lidge?"

No answer.

Archer stepped closer and nudged a foot with his boot. The leg was rigid. Archer took a couple of more steps and looked down on the haggard face and greying beard. Archer spoke again but did not expect an answer.

"Lidge?"

He noticed more details — a hole in the chest of the grey shirt, a dark stain that had spread and soaked into the braided oval rug. Questions came crowding in about who had done this, when, and why. But one thing

was certain. Lidge Mercer had come to the
end of his trail.

CHAPTER NINE

Archer knocked on the door of the sheriff's office and pushed it open. He felt the warm air and saw the lit interior.

"Come on in," said the sheriff. "Close it good behind you."

After he made sure the door was snugged, Archer faced the sheriff, who was standing with his back to a small potbellied stove. "Good morning, Sheriff," he said.

"The same to you." Sheriff Morris was cleaning his fingernails with a small penknife. An overhead lamp cast a glow on him. He was a short, thin, bald man with a drooping grey mustache. The blade of his knife was thin and pointed, and veins were prominent on the backs of his hands. He clicked the knife shut and put it away. "Have you got anything new?" he asked.

"I came to see if you did."

"The trail's been cold on this from the very start. Literally."

"I know." An image arose in Archer's mind, a scene of all white with the blanket of snow that fell after Lidge Mercer was killed. Any tracks that might have been left would be hard if not impossible to see when the snow finally melted. Archer shook his head. "I still think Peavey had something to do with it, even if he wasn't there."

"Maybe he did, but you sure can't place him there. Everyone saw him right here in town for three days, from the day before the killing to the day after. Him and his pal Wyse, both of 'em."

"Took the trouble to establish an alibi."

"Maybe they did, but they weren't at the ranch when Mercer got killed."

Archer felt his blood rise. "But I know Peavey was antagonizing Lidge."

"You know what you were told. And I know there's usually two sides to every story. Peavey's got his."

Archer's brows tightened. "I haven't heard it."

"I think you can pick it up in various places around town, but the short of it is that Mercer beat him out of his inheritance and ran with the money."

"I heard some of that before. It's an even easier thing to say now. But I told you what Lidge told me."

"Sure. Like I said, two sides." The sheriff turned and held his hands out toward the stove. "You hear it from Peavey, and the old lady was about to change her will, cut Mercer out, and then she up and died. Even after that, Mercer took more than his share."

"I don't believe it." Archer moved to the other side of the stove to face the sheriff.

"You don't have to. Neither do I. But if any of this is true, even Mercer's version, you didn't exactly have a gem for a business partner."

"He may have had his failings, but he was honest with me."

"As far as you know."

Archer paused in taking off his gloves and gave the sheriff a close look. "Is there something I should be told about?"

"Figure for yourself. But you never signed any partnership papers, did you?"

Archer stuffed his gloves in his coat pocket. "No, but he was going to let me know when they were ready."

"Well, I've looked into it. They were ready for two months, but he never signed them, and neither did you. My guess is that he wasn't sure he wanted to go through with it."

"But there should be something in his will. He told me that."

The sheriff opened his hands wide above the heat of the stove. "Oh, yes, he had the lawyer draw up the will, but he never signed it, either. Just put it off."

"But his intentions were clear, in both parts, if he had the lawyer draw up the papers."

"I'm not a lawyer, and I'm not a judge, so I can't tell you what his intentions were, how firm they might have been, or how the case will stand up. But when the judge comes around on his circuit, the case will be put before him."

"When will that be?"

"He usually comes around in April or so."

Archer reflected. "Then everything is just hanging in the air until then, as far as the business aspect goes."

"Could be. Most probably will be. My only interest in it is how it sheds light on a murder case I have on my hands."

"And how much does it do that?" Archer took off his coat and hung it on a peg.

"Not much at all."

"Then what are you going to do?"

"It's what I'm doing. I'm trying to find out if there were other people who might have had reasons to want Mercer dead."

"And what would those be?"

The sheriff gave a light shrug. "I don't

know. But like I said before, whatever part of this story is true, your boss, Lidge Mercer, was a shady character who pretty much hid out on his ranch. That kind of person can give reasons to different people."

"I don't know if I would call him shady."

"You don't have to. And the point I was making was that various parties might have had something against him."

Archer huffed a breath. "So you don't think Peavey had anything to do with it."

The sheriff's eyebrows went up. "Oh, I didn't say that at all. I just said I couldn't put him there at the time of the killing."

"You seem sympathetic to him, or to his version that Lidge beat him out of money."

The sheriff waved his right hand. "I was just telling you what he said. As for getting his own share back, or what he says is his share, that's up to him."

"How so?"

"He's already filed a petition to contest the unsigned will and the unsigned partnership papers."

"How can he contest something that was never signed or filed?"

"What you said. Intentions. Anyone who wants to make a case for what Mercer's intentions were had better be prepared for an opposition. You may not end up with anything, son."

Archer felt a sting. "Who said I wanted anything?"

The sheriff looked at the stove. "Who could say you didn't? Why else would you be hounding this case?"

Archer took a full breath to keep himself from saying anything too hasty. "Lidge Mercer was not a saint. We both know that. He told me himself that he got his start in a corrupt way. And there may well have been other things about him that he kept hidden. Still, he did right by me. He was fair with me when he was my boss, and he offered me something he didn't have to. From my point, at least, he deserved more than just a bullet through the chest."

The sheriff tipped his head to one side. "Oh, I'll go along with that."

"Call it loyalty, or just basic decency, I think it's only fair to try to do right by him in return. Whoever killed him should be brought to account."

"And that's your whole stake in this?"

"As far as coming to hound you, as you say."

The sheriff gave him a sidelong glance. "You'd like to hang it on Peavey, wouldn't you?"

"I'd like to hang it on whoever did it and

whoever was in on it."

"So would I."

"And I wouldn't be surprised if that included Peavey."

The sheriff shook his head. "You can't go into something like this with your mind already made up and then try to prove it."

Archer tried to keep the impatience out of his voice. "What other ideas have you got, then? You said there could be other people who had reasons to get him."

The sheriff pushed out his upper lip and let it fall. "That's just an assumption, what we call a premise. But the actual reasons, I'm yet to figure out. On the face of it, the two most obvious suspects would be the two that you said came by last summer and started a fight."

"Jenks and Crowell."

"Those are the names I wrote down. Problem is, hardly anyone knew 'em to begin with, and no one has seen or heard of 'em since the fall season was over. Most likely went somewhere else for the winter."

Archer was about to ask a question when the sheriff answered it.

"Funny thing is, no one seems to know which outfit they were workin' for."

"I'd bet they were working for someone. If they were just living off the fat of the land, to put it in nice words, they would have laid low and wouldn't have come around to start trouble like they did."

"You saw 'em. I didn't." The sheriff smoothed his mustache. "Can you think of any other strangers that came around the place?"

"The only one I can think of is a man named Henkelman. He came out with Whitmore to deliver a load of coal."

"Coal? All the way out there?"

"Blacksmith coal. For the forge."

"What kinds of things do you turn out on a ranch?"

"I don't know how to do that kind of work myself, but I understand that Lidge did."

The sheriff laughed. "A forger." Then, catching Archer's glance, he said, "Sorry."

"From what Oscar told me, Lidge knew how to repair wagons and farm equipment, along with any hardware around the place, like hinges and gate bolts and the like. I saw a fireplace poker he made."

"All that's common enough."

"Oscar said he thought Lidge was planning to build a bar for inside the door of the ranch house — actually, one for the front door and one for the back. But he didn't want to go out and work at the forge when the weather was so cold."

The sheriff moved his open hands above the stove. "That's warm work, but I guess you'd have to go out to the barn and get the fire going first."

Archer shrugged. "Anyway, this fellow Henkelman rode along on the coal delivery. But he kept to himself. I wouldn't suspect him of anything."

"Neither would I. From what I've seen, he knows his place and keeps to it. Anyone else?"

"Oh, there was Middleton the carpenter, but he was out there quite a while back. And he's no stranger."

"Nah, he wouldn't get mixed up in something like this." After a pause the sheriff said, "Just have to keep on lookin'."

"For possible suspects, or for reasons?"

"Either one." The sheriff opened the door of the stove and threw in a couple of sticks, each about an inch thick. "You get an idea, you let me know."

"I'll do that." Archer took his coat from the peg where he had hung it. The sheriff did not move from his position by the stove, and Archer wondered how much the man was going to put himself out to try to follow a cold trail.

Archer went to the door and opened it. As he stepped out onto the sidewalk, he almost bumped into Peavey. During the interview with the sheriff, Archer had caught a glimpse of someone lingering at the edge of the window, and now Peavey stood on the sidewalk not three feet from the recessed doorway.

He looked as much like a rat as ever with his steel-dust hair, red-rimmed eyes, straight nose, and stubbled face. He moved his grey overcoat aside and pulled a watch from his trousers pocket. Ignoring Archer, he flicked it open, as if he had been waiting for an appointment and Archer had delayed it.

"Excuse me," said Archer, nodding his head at the narrow space on his right.

"By all means." Peavey stepped aside with the watch held open at waist level.

Archer walked away, and in the corner of his vision he saw Peavey move toward the door. Something about the watch lingered in Archer's mind until he placed it as the one that Whitmore had gotten in trade from Boot Beckett. Like anyone else, Whitmore needed to get through the winter.

The last rays of the afternoon sun lent a feeble warmth to the surface of the building in back of the bench where Archer sat with Kate. The shop behind them was closed, and Archer could see anyone who might come close enough to overhear.

Kate said, "So it doesn't seem as if much progress is being made."

"Not much, and it's been two weeks. I think that if it happened to someone more important, or with a better reputation, the sheriff might be pushed into doing more. As it is, though, things don't seem to be going anywhere very fast. I sure wish someone could solve this before the judge comes in April."

"Someone? Who else would have a reason to?"

"That's just it. No one else has an interest in it. And the way the sheriff's poking along, I feel as if I ought to be doing something."

"Like what?"

"I don't know. But I think I can try to find out what I can."

Kate laid her hand on his arm but did not state the obvious.

"I know," he said. "I'm careful already, and I'll be even more so. But I can't let someone get away with doing him in like that, and I can't let someone walk all over him and take his property. I feel I owe it to him — or to some sense of fairness. Like I told the sheriff, Lidge did right by me. Sure, he may have wanted me for protection as much as anything, but I do believe that he did want someone to pass things on to. And even though I don't want his property, since I know where it came from, I think I should look out for it until it gets settled in a proper way."

"Isn't that strange? I hadn't quite thought of it before."

"What's that?"

"You just lost a kind of a father, something you never had, and I just found one. Thanks to your help, of course."

Archer realized Kate had taken a side-track. As he considered what she had said, he found himself comparing Mercer and Doolin. He stifled the impulse to make a judgment. "I suppose so," he said. "But regardless of how someone might define what he was to me, he was something, and I need to do right by him."

Kate got back on track with him. "Realistically, though, what do you think you can do?"

"Well, for one thing, I'll stay on at the ranch and make sure no one moves in ahead of time. The lawyer has it set up to pay wages and regular expenses. Oscar said he'd stay on, which I appreciate, but he was pretty rattled by what happened, and he doesn't like being by himself. I think I might hire this fellow Whitmore to come back ahead of the season. He and Oscar get along, and I don't think anyone's going to harm them, especially if there's two of them."

"And how about the other part?"

Archer lowered his voice. "You mean finding out who did it?"

"Yes."

"That's not going to be as easy. Once we go through the most obvious possibilities of the two men who were seen in town the whole time, the trail thins out. The fellow I tangled with back in June is like a phantom. No one knows who he worked for or where he went." An idea hit him. "Say, I wonder if he ever came into the store that you would remember."

Kate's eyes widened. "I don't know. What did he look like?"

"Oh, pretty common, I'd say, but not in the sense that he looked like everyone else. He was a tall fellow, a little sloppy in his build with weight hanging over his belt. He had a tight face with small eyes, a pug nose, and a chin that was pushed up." Archer laid the back of his hand under his own chin and lifted. "His face looked as if it had been squeezed."

Kate shook her head. "I don't remember anyone by that description — not in the store." She drew her brows together. "But I think I saw a man who looked something like that the day we went to Glenrose."

"Really?"

"Yes, he rode by when you went in at the beginning to talk to my father. I thought he looked me over, but I tried to ignore it as I usually do when men look that way. Then later, as we were leaving town, I thought I saw him behind the window of one of the businesses. I didn't think much about it, but you know how it is. You go to a strange town, and if you see the same person more than once, it's notable."

"It could be the same fellow. Keeping an eye on me."

"I hope he's not keeping an eye on me as well. I really didn't care for his looks."

Archer gave it a quick thought. "I think if he was, he would have come into the store at some point. It's much more likely that he's watching me, if anyone. If I go back to Glenrose, I'll keep my eyes open."

"Are you planning to go there before long?"

"It was only half an idea until now. But if that fellow Jenks is hanging around there, it might be worth my while to see what I can find out." Archer noted the tinge on Kate's cheek. "You got pretty cold when we went there last time. Did you want to go?"

She frowned. "I don't think so, not right away. He didn't seem very excited about meeting his long-lost daughter. I can wait until the weather's better, though I didn't mind it so much anyway."

Archer tipped his head as a way of inviting her to say more.

"If this man Jenks, as you call him, is connected with Mr. Mercer's death, and if he's lurking around, I might be an inconvenience to you."

"That's putting it nicely. Of the three reasons you gave, the weather seems to be the least important."

She rubbed her bundled shoulder against his. "I don't mind the cold, though it did take me a while to thaw out last time." Her eyes met his, and she smiled. "When do you think you'll go?"

"Not right away. I owe Boot Beckett a visit. The last time I saw him, which was right after Lidge met his end, he told me he got a little place out northeast of here, near Hat Creek."

"Did he file on some land?"

"He bought a relinquishment from someone who didn't want to try it anymore. Boot says it's got a shack and a well and some pens, and he'll be out there working on it."

"That sounds good, or I hope it is. He might have a great deal of work to do all by himself."

Archer smiled. "Some people can work themselves into the ground, but I wouldn't worry about him."

"And Sadie?"

"I suppose she's still in the picture. He didn't mention her, but if he's getting a place of his own, I would expect she's in on the idea."

Kate's eyes twinkled. "Or behind it."

Archer returned her nudge from before. "Might be. I'm planning on going out there tomorrow, so I might get a hint then."

Archer tipped his head back to appreciate the rock formations above him. They rose out of the pine ridge as he crossed the eastern edge of the Hat Creek Breaks. Below, the land spread out in a valley of rumpled dry land with watercourses marked by pallid cottonwood trees, leafless now in winter. The valley, or bowl, was bordered by a line of hills some eight or ten miles to the northeast. Straight east at the same distance, the grassland rolled into Nebraska.

Archer followed the road as Beckett had told him. It was the old Cheyenne-to-Deadwood stage route. Riding down from the ridge, he crossed two large dry washes and a wide sandy draw. At the bottom, he turned in the saddle to look at the towering sandstone formation he had ridden past. Confident that he still had his bearings, he veered off the main trail to the northeast. A mile later as he came out on higher ground, he saw a sod shanty sitting in the middle of a flat. Past the house sat a couple of nondescript pens made of poles and wire.

Archer rode into the yard and called out a greeting. He wondered if he had come to the right place, as a half-dozen chickens, some red and some brown, were scratching around in the yard. As he stopped the horse, the door of the shanty opened. Framed in the doorway, wearing her wool cap and coat, stood Sadie.

"Well, hello," said Archer. "Look who's here." He swung down from the horse and walked forward.

Sadie had an uncertain look on her face. "Boot's out back," she said. "I'm sure he'll be glad to see you."

"Thanks. I'll go look for him. We'll see you in a little while."

Archer led his horse around to the pens, where he found Boot Beckett tying up a corral pole with a length of old telegraph wire. Inside the corral stood a grey roan, a bay, and a dun.

"Is this your trading stock?" he asked.

Beckett straightened up from his work. "I've been ridin' the bay, and the roan is Sadie's, but any of 'em's up for sale or trade. What kinda horse are you lookin' for, mister?"

Archer laughed. "None right now." He glanced around. "Looks like you're gettin' settled in. Did Sadie come out to help?"

" 'Magine." Beckett pulled off his gloves and picked at his left hand. "Damn splinters go right through these leather gloves."

"Chickens," said Archer.

"Those are Sadie's."

"I thought they might be." Archer motioned with his head toward the other pen. "And the milk cow?"

"She brought that, too."

An idea began to dawn in Archer's mind. "So she's not just leavin' these critters for you to take care of."

"Oh, no." Boot gazed off in the distance.

"Well, I guess I'll be goin', then." Archer pulled his reins out to separate them.

"What for?"

"You seem to have a lot on your mind, not in much of a mood to talk."

Beckett turned his head downward, kicked at the ground, and looked up. "Oh, all right, damn it. I got hitched."

Archer could not suppress his smile. "Hitched? Did you think I was going to read about it in the newspaper?"

Beckett shrugged. "It came up on me pretty sudden." He shook his finger. "But not for any of those reasons." He paused. "We went over to Nebraska so I could meet her folks, and they asked us what kind of plans we had, and it sort of got out that we were thinkin' of somethin', and her folks said, well, why don't you tie the knot while you're here, and you can take some stuff back with you."

"The cow and the chickens. Something like a wedding present."

"Somethin' like that."

"So how long ago was that?"

"We been back three, four days."

"Oh, so you *are* just gettin' settled in." Archer smiled again. "Didn't mean to put you on the spot like that."

Beckett gave a simple expression as he tipped his head side to side. "Not used to talkin' about it yet."

"Well, I hope you're happy with it."

"Oh, yeah." Beckett slapped Archer on the shoulder. "Tie up your horse for a while. We'll go in and have a cup of coffee."

The inside of the shanty was dim but very

223

neat and clean. Sadie built up a fire in the cookstove, and in a few minutes the warmth spread through the front room. Along the partition wall, which was made of lumber, Sadie had her enamel kettle and cast-iron skillets hanging. As the room warmed up, she took off her cap and coat and hung them on a hook to the left of the cookware.

Boot and Archer did likewise with their hats and coats. To the left of the last hook, Archer noticed a broom hanging with its head up. Something curious caught his attention. The handle of the broom was poked down through an iron ring that was fixed to the wall with a bent-over nail.

"Is that the extra cinch ring you had?"

"Yep. I gave it to Sadie right after I met her, and she said she could find some use for it."

Sadie spoke over her shoulder as she measured flour. "Boot didn't want anyone to be able to say he didn't give me a ring."

Boot wrinkled his nose. "We'll get a nicer one, a little later on." He pulled a chair out from the table. "Sit down, Russ."

Archer took a seat. "These places are all right. They hold the heat in, don't they?"

"If you don't mind a little dirt trickling down from the ceiling. No matter how they do these dirt roofs, you're goin' to get some of that." Beckett took out the makings for a cigarette.

Sadie lifted her measuring cup and poured water into the mixing bowl.

Archer smiled at her industry. "What are you making, Sadie?"

She spoke over her shoulder again. "Biscuits. And you're going to stay long enough to eat some."

"I won't argue."

"You're our first visitor." She turned and gave a half-smile. "Lord knows how long it would have taken Boot to tell you on his own. It's a good thing you came out."

Archer smiled back. "Everything's ducky, it looks like. By the way, how did you get the chickens over here?"

"In burlap sacks."

"On horseback?"

Boot paused as he was about to lick the seam of his cigarette. "We went in a wagon I hired. We took a couple of things over there and expected to bring somethin' back. Just ended up more than we thought."

"So you tied the cow to the back of the wagon?"

"It's that easy." Boot finished building his cigarette and lit it. With the cigarette still in his mouth as he shook out the match, he said, "Has anyone found out who put the bullet through Lidge?"

Archer absorbed the bluntness of the question. "Not that I know of. I talked to Sheriff Morris yesterday, and things don't seem to be moving very fast. You haven't ever seen that fellow Jenks again, have you?"

"That one? No, not at all. His pal, neither."

"They were supposed to have been working for someone out here, but no one seems to know who."

Beckett shrugged. "I sure don't."

Sadie rolled out the dough and cut round biscuits with an empty tomato can. By now the Dutch oven was hot, and she laid in the first half-dozen pieces of dough.

As the biscuits baked, Sadie put a crockery jar on the table. "Chokecherry jelly," she said. "We don't have butter yet."

When she went back to work the remaining dough, Beckett tipped his ash in a sardine can. "Are you plannin' to ride across country to get back to the ranch?"

"I was thinkin' of it earlier, but now I'll probably go back to town."

Sadie's voice came up. "Oh, are you going to tell Kate? About us?"

"I probably will, if you don't mind."

"I hope you do, and I hope you'll bring her out to visit."

"Let her see the real thing," said Boot. "Dirt and chickens. Keep her from gettin' big ideas too soon."

"Don't listen to him, Russ. Bring her out."

Archer sat on the back porch with Kate that evening. After he told her about Boot and Sadie and described their homestead, their talk moved on to other topics. When the conversation hit a lull, Archer asked how her poetry recitation was going.

She said that with the lines of *Evangeline* being longer and not rhyming, her progress was slower. However, she lit up at his request to recite some, and she delivered the opening and closing passages about the forest primeval, women's devotion, and the lovers in the graveyard.

When she was done, her face was radiant. She said, "It's always beautiful, every time I go through it."

"You're beautiful." He held her face with both hands and kissed her.

"Well," she said, catching her breath, "there was quite a bit to that one. What are you thinking about, Sadie's chickens?"

He raised his eyebrows. "Not all the time. I hope you're not in a hurry."

"Oh, no. I don't even know where I stand with my father. By the way, when do you think you'll go to Glenrose again?"

"Now that I'm back in town here, I could go tomorrow. If you'd like to go, you're welcome."

"No, thanks. For one thing, I have to work, and — well — we talked about it yesterday."

"Yes, we did. Maybe I'll wait a couple of weeks, then, and go by myself. Probably easier that way."

"Be careful on your way home tomorrow, then."

"Of course. I've got plenty to come back to."

"That's a good way to think, Mr. Archer."

CHAPTER TEN

Archer rode the buckskin horse down the main street of Glenrose as the racket of the rock crusher filled the air. The horse made small splashes as it picked up its hooves and set them down in the yellow-brown slush of the street. Archer could smell the moisture of the melted snow as well as the smoke from the steam engine. People on the sidewalks did not pay him much attention, and he didn't see anyone who looked like Jenks. He turned right off the main street, rode past the café, and came to High Street. Everything was in place, including the grey rooming house of Mrs. Pitts.

In the month since Lidge Mercer died, the days had gotten longer. The sun still set in the southwest, but it was higher in the sky and the rays felt stronger. At the same time, the north side of buildings like Mrs. Pitts's house stayed in shade, and the piles of snow did not melt fast. Archer tied the buckskin to a hitching post and picked his way along the walkway, careful to avoid the trampled snow that had iced over.

He had barely finished knocking when the door opened, and there stood the landlady with her short grey hair and pale blue sweater just as before.

Recognition registered in her face as she said, "Yes?"

"I'd like to speak with Jack Doolin if I could."

"Just a minute." She closed the door, and footsteps faded away. They came back, and the door opened. "Come on in," she said.

Archer walked inside and took off his hat. On the other side of the front room, Jack Doolin stood in his doorway.

"How do you do?" he said.

"Not too bad, and yourself?"

"Gettin' through the winter." Doolin's eyes wavered. "Did you come by yourself?"

"I did."

The light-brown eyes settled. "Anything in particular?"

"I had a question or two to ask. Nothing very personal. Do you have time?"

"Sure. We can go into my room and talk." Doolin gave a toss of the head.

He led the way into a dim room where the smell of stale tobacco smoke hung in the air. The room had a bed, a dresser, a wash stand, and two chairs. Doolin sat in one chair and pulled the other around for his visitor.

Archer sat down, hiked up a leg, and set his hat on his knee.

As Doolin began to roll a cigarette, he glanced up. His pale hair looked as if it hadn't been washed in a while, and his brown eyes with the dark circles below them looked tired. "What's on your mind?" he said.

"To begin with, I'm curious as to whether you know a man named Jenks."

Doolin shook tobacco into the paper. "Not that I recall."

"Tall fellow with a tight face. Has a pal named Crowell, a fellow with blond hair and a crooked mouth. By the way, if Jenks takes off his hat, he's bald."

Doolin shook his head.

"I had a little set-to with him last summer, and I haven't seen him since. But the last time I was here, with your daughter, she thought she noticed a man who answered to that description. She said she couldn't be sure, but it looked like he was keeping an eye on us."

"Wouldn't know." Doolin pulled the drawstring with his teeth.

"I didn't mean to suggest that you had anything to do with him."

Doolin pushed out his lower lip and gave a small shake of the head. "Not at all. I didn't think you did."

"How about a man named Peavey, then?"

Doolin stuck the rolled cigarette in his mouth and brought up a match. He struck it on the rough iron bar of the bed frame and lit his smoke. With the cigarette in the corner of his mouth, he squinted and said, "Now him I do know." Doolin shook out the match and tossed it in a can by his chair.

"Through the card game?"

"That's right. I don't recall that he ever played, but he hung around and got acquainted. Asked questions, didn't like to answer 'em."

"Did you ever hear him mention a man named Lidge Mercer?"

Doolin blew out a cloud of smoke. "He asked questions about him. Seemed to me he came through this way to look for Mercer, and when he found out what he could here, he moved on to Ashton."

Archer let his eyes meet Doolin's. "You know, Lidge Mercer was killed a little while back."

Doolin flicked his brows in a matter-of-fact expression. "I think I heard something like that. Out at his ranch."

"That's right. It's the ranch where I live. I had, or still have, an interest in it. I found him dead when I got back from my last visit here."

Doolin's eyes went upward, as if he was reading his forehead. "That's about right, as far as time goes."

"He and Peavey were cousins."

"I didn't know that."

"According to what Mercer told me, Peavey followed him out here from Missouri. That goes along with what you said."

"That's the impression I got."

"Did he have a partner named Wyse who went around with him?"

"Oh, him. The talker." Doolin took a drag. "You could tell they were in cahoots. Peavey showed up first, and then Wyse came along a little later. They acted like they just met, but Wyse isn't a good actor. Plus his tongue gets loose when he's had a little fire water."

Archer hesitated, not sure how much to tell Doolin, but he figured he was going to have to give out information if he was hoping to get some. "From what Mercer said, and from what I've heard since he died, it seems that Peavey's got designs on Mercer's property."

Doolin held his cigarette in front of him

and stared at it. He turned down the corners of his mouth and tipped his head side to side. "That goes along with what I heard, though I picked it up in pieces, here and there. You sit in a card game every night, plus you sit around listenin' to the talk when you're waitin' for a game to start, and you pick up lots of scraps. Most of it never amounts to anything, but it's all worth knowin'."

Archer picked his words. "If there's anything you know about Peavey and Wyse as it pertains to Lidge Mercer, it might help me."

"Knowin' somethin' is one thing. Repeatin' it is another."

"I imagine. You don't have any reason to tell me, and you never know when someone else might want to get even."

Doolin sniffed, took a pull on his cigarette, and blew out two streams of smoke through his nostrils. "I don't let tinhorns determine what I do and don't say."

"Even so, I wouldn't want to put you in a spot."

"I don't have any secrets with them. And I know things they don't."

"Well, I'll assure you of one thing. This won't go any farther than you and me."

"Hah. It's nice of you to say it, but I'm not goin' to stake much on someone else holdin' a confidence. You know, there's an old sayin' about secrets."

"Oh, I think I've heard it. A secret is something you tell just one person at a time."

"Nah, that's a joke. The true sayin' is that the only way two men can keep a secret is if one of 'em is dead. So if it's a real secret, you don't tell anyone at all."

Archer waved his hand and sat back. "That's fine. But if there's something you can tell me, I'd appreciate it. And even though it's not a secret, I know how to keep my mouth shut."

Doolin took one last drag, a long one, and pinched out the butt of his cigarette as smoke drifted up in a cloud. He tossed the snipe in the can by his foot. "Well, it goes like this, as I put it together. Peavey wanted money. He didn't want a ranch, with all the work you have to do and the low return you get from it. But someone else wanted Mercer's ranch. So the plan was that Peavey would take the ranch from Mercer and sell it to this other man."

"I see. And what was this fellow's name?"

"That's where you got me," said Doolin. "I guessed it was the man they worked for, but I never heard a name."

"Peavey told me, or me and my friend,

that he and Wyse were working for a man named Scott. That was back in the summer."

Doolin shook his head. "Don't know."

"Last I heard around town, they weren't working for anybody, but that's not uncommon this time of year."

"Huh." Doolin ran his fingers through his hair and rubbed the back of his neck.

Archer pushed ahead. "Whoever it is, he must want Mercer's place pretty bad. There's other land to be had, and easier. Maybe Peavey's a good salesman."

Doolin raised his eyebrows and peeled another cigarette paper out of the pack. "Maybe he thinks he is."

"I think I'm missing something."

The brown eyes settled on Archer. "I go along with you. It's got to be a hell of a nice ranch to kill someone over it. If Peavey did it, he don't care about the place itself. He just wants the money. But if somebody wants the land, then it's like you say. A lot of trouble for a common grass ranch."

"So how does that fit with Peavey thinking he's a good salesman?"

Doolin stuck his tongue out the corner of his mouth as he shook tobacco into the trough of paper. "Peavey might be sellin' somethin' of greater value than he realizes."

"You mean, there's more to it than the land."

Doolin looked down at his work. "Could be. Dependin' on who knows what."

"Well, I sure doubt there's any gold or silver mines there."

"So do I. But there might be somethin'."

Doolin seemed to be enjoying his position as the man who knew something that someone else wanted to know, so Archer humored him.

Archer waited until Doolin had the cigarette rolled and lit. Then he said, "Whatever it is, it's probably underground, because on that whole ranch there's not much more than rocks, grass, and an occasional tree."

Doolin took the cigarette away from his mouth. "Now you're gettin' closer."

As Archer followed Doolin's motion, he noticed that the man's fingers were yellow with tobacco stains. He wondered if Doolin ever went outside. "Is there something buried there?" he asked.

Doolin sniffed. "There might be, but I've never heard anyone around here mention it. No one."

Archer gave him a skeptical look. "Then how do you know about it?"

"I heard about it somewhere else."

"Oh." Archer thought he might have been

too direct, but Doolin seemed inclined to say more, so Archer let him go ahead.

Doolin rose from his chair and pulled up his shirt. His pale abdomen bulged out, and a purple scar ran from his navel to the tip of his sternum. "A fella did this to me, tried to gut me like a fish. It was the last thing he ever did. He went to the undertaker, and when I got sewed up I went to jail. From there I went to the pen in Laramie."

"How long ago was that?"

"Sixteen years. I was in there for two years, and I got out. Not everybody did." Doolin tucked in his shirt, sat down, and tipped his ash.

"I imagine."

"But while I was in there, I met a man named McGraw. His name won't mean anything to you. It didn't to me. But accordin' to his story, he was the only one left out of a gang that robbed the stage up on the Cheyenne River, at a place near Robbers' Roost."

"I know where that is. An old hand named Whitmore pointed it out to me when we were up in that country gatherin' cattle."

"Sure. I know that country, too, so I know what I'm talkin' about." Doolin raised his head and squinted as he took a drag.

"How long ago did this robbery happen?"

"About twenty years ago. Just a little more. I remember it. I was workin' up that way at the time. I was cook's helper for a big outfit there on the Cheyenne River. Jake Bishop was foreman. Some of the punchers wanted to join a posse and go after the reward, but Jake wouldn't let 'em."

"How much did they take?"

"A hell of a lot. More than twenty thousand in gold dust and bullion."

Archer gave a low whistle. "That *is* a lot."

"Comin' out of the Black Hills, of course."

"That was the regular route then, wasn't it?"

"Yeah. A little while after that, just about everything went guarded. Outriders, someone ridin' shotgun, riders trailin' behind. I think there might have been someone ridin' shotgun on this one, but it was a job where the robbers got away."

"And you met one of them."

Doolin gave a curt nod. "That's right. He wasn't anyone to like, but that don't matter much when you're behind bars. I listened to his talk. He said there was four of 'em. One of 'em got shot in the holdup and died later. They buried him somewhere up in that country, north of Old Woman Creek. They left the main trail, of course, and somewhere out there north and west of Hat Creek Station, they buried the gold. It was too heavy and was slowin' 'em down."

"That's big country out there," said Archer, "but that's the area where the Bar M is. That's the ranch that was Mercer's and I'm still taking care of."

"That's where I had it placed. But as to where exactly they buried the gold, McGraw wouldn't ever tell me." Doolin took another puff. "Anyway, they buried it, and they took off across country, plannin' to catch the train in Orin Junction. But a group of fellas hopin' for a reward caught up with 'em, and they had a big shoot-out. McGraw's two partners got killed, and he got shot up pretty bad. Not bad enough to keep him from goin' to trial, though. He got life because someone got killed in the holdup and a couple of the fellas in the posse were killed as well. Both of 'em named George, same as him, but that's just a coincidence."

"So he got locked up, and he kept the secret to himself."

Doolin spit a fleck of tobacco from his lip. "Yeah, and we already know about secrets. He'd tell the story, but he wouldn't ever tell anyone where they buried the loot. Not while I was in there, anyway. I did hear, though, that he told someone."

"I see. If you don't mind my askin', who

did you hear it from?"

"From a fella I knew when I was in there. He had more time to do than I did, but when he got out, he drifted through this way. He sat in on my card game, and of course we recognized each other. When there was just the two of us, he filled me in on things that had gone on after I left."

"Is he still around here?"

"No. Not above ground. He fell off a freight car up by Douglas."

"That's too bad."

Doolin made half a shrug. "He didn't know that much. But he did tell me that before McGraw died, he told someone. I don't know who, and this other fella didn't know either, but the story was that McGraw told someone who was going to be gettin' out. That man was supposed to help McGraw's kin, but you can imagine how far that's likely to go."

"So whoever it was, there's a good chance he's out now, and there's another good chance that he's the only person left who knows where the gold is buried."

"Or supposed to be buried."

"Well, that's something. I've heard stories like that before."

"Oh, so have I. But if there's anything to it, there's a shit-pot full of money out there somewhere, and even if there isn't, there's someone who thinks there is."

"Hmm. I'm not much of a treasure-hunter myself. But I'd sure like to know who might be interested in it."

Doolin twisted his mouth, as if he was about to say something and thought better of it.

Archer leveled his gaze at the man and said, "So you don't know his name, then."

"No. But if he really knows where it is, and someone seems to be makin' a move to take Mercer's property, that gold might be right under your nose."

"The Bar M has got thirty-two hundred acres. That's five sections. A lot of area to go over, one foot at a time. It would be hard to know where to start."

Doolin looked down his nose at his cigarette as he drew on it and burned it down to his fingertips. He blew away his smoke and said, "When the weather gets warmer, I wouldn't mind goin' out and pokin' around."

"At the rate things are going, I'll probably still be there. Feel free to come out."

Doolin put on a nonchalant air as he manipulated the stub of his cigarette between his thumb and forefinger. "I'll keep it in mind."

No wonder, thought Archer. No wonder Doolin was willing to tell as much as he did. It was the same idea Archer had about himself earlier — a fellow had to be willing to give in order to get something in return. As he had heard a gin rummy player put it, "I give you cards, I get cards back." For all Archer knew, Doolin had the exact location of the cache. But it didn't seem likely. Doolin was hanging back like a buzzard — or maybe like a coyote, waiting for the buzzards or crows to tell him where the treasure was.

"It's not a bad place to visit," Archer said. "Especially in good weather. There's company. We've got a cook named Oscar, and this old hand named Whitmore that I mentioned earlier has come back out to stay on with us."

Doolin nodded. His cigarette was pinched out, so he dropped the butt in the can. His face looked shadowy in the dim room, and he had the air of a man who felt he had talked enough.

"Well," said Archer. "Maybe I should be thinkin' about headin' back."

"To Ashton."

"I'll probably go that way."

"You've kept up your acquaintance with Katie?"

"Oh, yeah."

Doolin showed little emotion as he said, "That's good."

Archer hesitated. He felt as if something still hung in the air. "Was there anything else?"

"Ah, no. It's not that important. Maybe next time."

"That's fine." Archer stood up, put out his hand, and obliged Doolin to shake with him. "If you're ever over that way, such as to see your daughter, let me know. I'll take you out to the ranch."

"Sure." The brown eyes rested on Archer as Doolin, still seated, retrieved his hand. "It would be something to do."

Archer left the dim, smoky room and passed through the front room of the house without noticing much. Once outside, he took a breath of the cold air. It was a clear day, and the buckskin horse stood dozing in the pale sunlight.

The day remained cloudless and the road became drier as Archer rode east out of Glenrose. Though the sun was not very strong, he enjoyed its warmth on his back. The horse generated warmth as it picked up a fast walk. Archer took off his leather glove and patted the buckskin on the neck, felt the animal vitality beneath the matted winter coat.

Archer's thoughts drifted back to the dusky room and the confidence he had been taken into when Doolin showed him the scar. In those narrow confines, the gesture had seemed almost normal. Even now, as Archer reviewed it in the clear light of day, it did not seem unreal. For all his distance and noncommittal expression, the old card player had shown Archer his hand. At first it had seemed that he was trying to get something in return. Now, with the clear blue sky reaching out all around, other possibilities presented themselves. Maybe Doolin wanted to share something he knew; maybe he felt he could trust the young man who had an interest in his daughter.

Archer sorted through it a little more. It was a confidence, not a secret. In Doolin's book, a secret was something a man didn't tell anyone at all. The only way two men could keep a secret was if one of them was dead — like McGraw. Maybe Doolin had other confidences, such as the thing he seemed to be on the verge of saying and then deferred until next time. If he had any real secrets, he wouldn't be sharing those until he thought he was ready to cash in his chips.

A speck brought Archer back to the present moment. A speck, a spot, a figure — something off in the hills to his left, nearly a mile away. It might have been the upper part of a man's body. That was how things appeared and disappeared in this country — a man on horseback rising partway out of the folds in the land and then settling back in. Archer studied the grey hills, but the figure did not show again.

The buckskin kept up its brisk pace, snorting now and again. Archer tried to review everything he had seen and heard on the way out of Glenrose. Nothing distinct came up. There had been the pounding of the rock crusher, horses and wagons in the muddy street, people on the sidewalk. Nobody in particular.

That was it. After hearing Doolin's stories about Peavey, the scar, and the lost treasure, Archer had been absorbed. He had forgotten about Jenks and the need to be on the lookout. The ride out of Glenrose had been a series of bland, superficial impressions.

Archer kept his wits about him for the rest of the way to Ashton, but he felt jumpy. He turned left on the main street and stopped at the café. The dinner hour had passed, so he ate bread and cold beef as he sat by the window. Nothing conspicuous passed by outside. Archer fidgeted as he watched the street. He made himself think about calm, everyday details. Kate was at work. He could stop long enough to pick up a few provisions, but he had a long ride to the ranch if he was going to get there before dark. The buckskin had plenty of steam left in him, but it wouldn't hurt to give him a bait of oats.

Archer counted the horses in the stable. There were six, as usual. Evening was closing in, and dust hung in the air to blend with the warmth and smell of the horses. Archer moved among them, patting each one with his gloved hand. Except for the sounds of the animals breathing and eating, the ranch was quiet.

With the chores done, Archer headed back to the cook shack, where he had left the supplies earlier. Weak light from the window fell on a pile of snow, and the smell of woodsmoke carried on the cold air. Archer opened the door and stepped inside. He was met by the comfort of warmth and lantern light. Whitmore and Oscar did not look up from their cribbage game. Archer took off his gloves and put them in his coat pocket, then hung his hat and coat on the row of pegs.

"I'll get busy on supper in a minute," said

Oscar. "We just chunked up the fire."

Archer pulled a chair around and sat about four feet away from the stove. "Long day," he said. "Didn't realize I was tired until I sat down."

Oscar snapped his cards on the table. "We'll finish this later," he said as he got up.

Whitmore turned in his chair to face Archer. "Learn anything new this time?"

"Not as much as I'd like. You remember the story about Jenks, don't you?"

"The one you had a fight with?"

"Yeah, that one. Did you ever meet anyone in town who went by that name?"

Whitmore shook his head.

"No one seems to know much about him or his partner — who they worked for, where they hung out, where they went."

Whitmore shrugged.

"You know Peavey, of course."

"Oh, yeah." Whitmore bobbed his head.

"I wonder if they've got any connection."

"The only one I've seen Peavey with is that fella Wyse, and I think he's gone now. I didn't see him for the last couple of weeks I was in town, and I heard that someone from the law from somewhere else was lookin' for him."

"Huh," said Archer. "You wouldn't think

it would be so hard to turn up a little bit of information. I did talk to Jack Doolin again, though."

"Oh, what's he say?"

"He's never heard of Jenks. He knows who Peavey is and how he's had designs on Lidge's property."

"Oh, yeah, Doolin picks up as much gossip as a barber does."

"He talked about a few things. One was about some old stagecoach loot that's supposed to be buried somewhere out in this country."

Whitmore fished out his makings and hiked one leg over the other. "Yeah, there's a hunnerd stories like that. Truth is, most of those robberies were tracked down."

"This one where they got away with the money was supposed to have taken place up by Robbers' Roost."

"Oh, yeah. I've heard of that one, and another down by Hat Creek Station. In both of 'em, the gold was never found, not that anyone knew about. In that one down by Hat Creek, a few years later there was a couple of fellas who said they were meat hunters, and the rumor was that they had shovels and dug a lot of holes. But I didn't hear that they ever found anything."

"And the other one, farther up this way?"

"Bah, it's the same. I've worked with fellas that every time they dig a posthole, they think they're gonna hit a treasure chest or a saddlebag full of gold coins. But all they ever get is dirt if they're lucky and rocks if they're not." Whitmore paused as he shook the yellow grains of tobacco onto the paper. "You're not gettin' the fever, are you?"

"Oh, no. Not me. I'm just trying to figure out if someone else is."

"Someone else?"

Archer shrugged. "Trouble is, I don't know who it might be."

CHAPTER ELEVEN

Archer stabbed a chunk of fried beef with his fork and dragged it from the platter onto his plate. Whitmore speared a smaller piece with his knife and held it with his fork as he cut off a bite. Oscar was taking his time eating as he told a story about a preacher in Miles City who had become obsessed with a saloon girl.

"He wanted to cleanse her soul and help her live a righteous life. She wanted to keep makin' money with her heels in the air. But he'd set his mind on it — what mind he had left for straight thinkin'. You know, they say that stuff backs up when there's no petcock to let the steam off. Some say it's liquid, some say it's fumes or vapors, but it backs up and rises on up into your head. He should have just laid down a couple of dollars every week. Done 'em both some good."

A knock sounded at the door.

Oscar hollered, "Come in!"

The knock came again in three clear raps.

"Come in! The door's open!" Oscar laid down his knife and waited. When the door did not move, he got up, marched across the room, and pulled the door inward with a rush of cold air.

A round-featured man with a winter cap, dark hair, and a dark mustache stood in the doorway. Archer recognized him as Henkelman, the man who had helped Whitmore deliver coal a couple of months earlier.

"Why didn't you come in?" said Oscar.

"I wasn't sure." Henkelman stepped inside and closed the door behind him.

"Wasn't sure of what? You've been here before."

Henkelman shrugged in his overcoat.

"Well, sit down. There's hot grub, unless you're not sure of that either."

"Thanks." Henkelman took off his cap and sat in the empty chair. As soon as he sat down, he rose again to take off his coat. In the process, his thick hand came forward with a paper object folded and sealed, though not very neatly, in the form of a letter. "This is for you."

Archer saw his own name written in pencil. The handwriting was uneven, like that of a man who did not write very often.

Archer said, "Thanks," and put the letter in his vest pocket.

Whitmore took a drink of coffee. "Did you come all the way out here for that?" he asked.

"Just partly." Henkelman's eyes widened as Oscar set down a plate of fried meat and potatoes. "I was going up to Jim Tuesday's, so I came across this way."

Whitmore set down his cup. "Deliverin' mail all over the country?"

"Not exactly." Henkelman picked up his knife and fork. "I went to see Mr. Tuesday about some work."

Oscar cut in. "What kind of work would he have? Where is his place, anyway?"

"His ranch is north and west of Hat Creek."

"South and east of here, then," said Archer. "You came over that big line of hills, did you?"

"That's right."

"I haven't gone that way. How is it?"

"About like you'd expect. Quite a bit of snow in some places, where the sun and wind don't get at it."

"I see," said Archer. "Well, go ahead and eat."

"Thanks."

Oscar spoke again. "What kind of work?"

"I'm going to be hauling rock out of the Hat Creek Breaks."

"Russ is good at that," Whitmore said. "He could help you."

Oscar asked, "Why do you have to haul it that far? Doesn't he have rock closer by?"

"I'm sure he does, but he wants a few loads of flat rock, and there's places in the breaks where you can pick up a lot of that kind of sandstone."

"What's he want that for?"

Henkelman cut off a bite-sized piece of meat. "He says he's going to build an icehouse. He wants the flat stone for the floor."

"Lot of work," said Oscar, "but it's his business. Go ahead and eat."

All four men settled into the meal, and before long the food was gone. Oscar poured the last of the coffee, a little in each cup, until sludge ran out the spout.

Henkelman finished at the same time as the rest of them. He set down his coffee cup and wiped his mustache with the cuff of his shirt.

"Get enough?" said Oscar.

"Just fine."

"Sorry I don't have any pie or cake. You came on the wrong day."

"That's all right. I need to be going

254

anyway, to get back to town before dark."

Archer sat back in his chair. "Well, thanks for stopping by. Appreciate it."

"No trouble at all. And thanks for the meal." Henkelman took in Oscar as well with his nod and smile, then rose from his chair and put on his cap.

Archer stood up, went to the door, and waited as Henkelman put on his coat and dug out his gloves.

As Henkelman paused at the door, Archer handed him a silver dollar.

"Oh, that's too much, Mr. Archer."

"It's all the change I've got, and you came quite a bit out of your way."

Henkelman tipped his head to the side. "Well, thanks." With his gloves in his left hand, he slipped the coin into his right coat pocket. Then he put out his thick hand to shake. With that courtesy taken care of, he went out.

Archer stood at the doorway until the man untied the horse he had left at the rail and mounted up. Archer shut the door and went back to his seat.

There he took out the letter and broke the candle-wax seal. As he unfolded the paper, he saw more of the same handwriting as on the outside, pressed in pencil with letters slanting each way. The message was simple.

Mr. Archer. Am staying in the Royal Hotel. Would like to go out and visit like you offered. J.D.

Oscar's voice piped up. "For as much as you paid, you'd think you'd have gotten a long love letter."

Archer opened the door of the stove and tossed the letter in. It curled, turned black, and disappeared in flame. "It would be nice," he said, "but if I remind myself that I paid for the delivery and not the letter, I won't feel so disappointed."

Archer saddled the smoke-colored horse and rode out of the ranch yard in the chill of morning. The sun had cleared the hills in the southeast, and as he glanced in that direction, he formed a general idea of where Tuesday's ranch was. He imagined a straight line from the Bar M to Hat Creek Station. After the crow flew over the rough hills, it would cross some portion of Tuesday's spread.

Having formed that picture, Archer constructed a new one, approaching the layout the way Henkelman had gone. It was the road north out of Ashton to the Black Hills, the old Cheyenne-to-Deadwood stage route. When it crossed the Hat Creek Breaks, Boot and Sadie's place lay on the right. As the road curved northeast and then ran straight north, Tuesday's place would lie on a broad, grassy plain that sloped upward to the north and west. Henkelman would have picked his way through the hills on the western edge of Tuesday's place and would have come out a couple of miles south of where Jenks and Crowell had appeared that day.

Archer was satisfied with being able to put Henkelman on the map, but his uncertainty about Jenks nagged at him. The man had shown up east of the Bar M headquarters, then may have been in Glenrose, well to the south and west of here. He may have been lurking in the hills between Glenrose and Ashton, or he may have left the country and had nothing to do with Lidge Mercer's death or the lost gold. Archer half-expected to see the man with the scrunched-up face materialize before him now on the trail, but the only thing that came anywhere close was a brindle cow, lean in the flanks, that kicked up its heels and ran back into the draw it had come out of.

Archer found the Royal Hotel a few doors down from the Drake, where he usually stayed. Inside the Royal, a clerk with a thin neck and sparse mustache had his feet on the desk and was reading a newspaper. He swung around and stood up, and with the newspaper still in his hands, he asked Archer how he might help him.

"I'm looking for a man named Jack Doolin. I understand he's staying here."

The clerk folded his newspaper as he spoke. "Yes, he is, and I think he's in his room. I haven't seen him come out yet today."

"My name's Russ Archer. I think he's expecting me."

The clerk's eyebrows wavered upward. "You can knock on his door yourself. It's room eleven, down the hall on your left." The clerk pointed at a hallway that led straight back into the building.

"Thanks."

"Not at all." The clerk sat down, opened his newspaper, and shook it. He raised his chin and gave his attention to the paper.

As Archer turned and walked down the unlit hallway, his eyes adjusted to the faint light. The first number he saw on his left was a three. Four was on the right, five was on his left, and so on until he came to eleven, the second-to-last door before a person would step out the back door and into the alley.

Archer knocked on the door. He expected

to hear footsteps or bed springs, but no sound came from inside. He knocked again, and still no answer. After his third knock, he tried the handle. The knob turned, and the door gave inward.

"Jack," he said, in a normal tone of voice. After another few seconds with no response, he pushed the door open.

The room was dark, with no window and no lamp light. Archer opened the door to ninety degrees to let in what little light came from the dim hallway.

The bed on his right was empty, but apparently someone had been lying on it at some point, as the covers were rumpled. On the nightstand close at hand, a clear bottle had about three fingers of whiskey in the bottom. The room smelled of tobacco smoke but nothing recent.

After a minute, Archer could see better. He stepped into the room. It was narrow, with the bed on his right and the wall on his left almost close enough to touch. On the far side of the room, past the foot of the bed, stood a dresser with a swivel frame but no mirror.

"Jack," he said again. He walked toward the foot of the bed and paused to listen. No sound came from the rooms on either side or above.

He looked down to be sure he wasn't going to stumble on anything, and a stockinged foot came into view. Two feet. He took a wide step around and peered at the floor between the dresser and the foot of the bed. He made out the shape of a man's body, a man fully clothed except for his shoes.

Archer leaned on the iron bed railing to confirm what he was already sure of. Jack Doolin lay chin-up in the murky light. His eyes were closed, and the darkness of his lower eyelids was visible. A bruise appeared between Doolin's forehead and left ear, and the hair that had looked like winter grass had a dark, sticky smudge on it.

Archer straightened up and stood back. He took a deep breath to calm himself. A sense from within told him not to touch anything. What was done was done, and it was someone else's business to look into it.

Archer took another breath and tried to collect his thoughts. He hadn't seen any bullet holes, and whoever had done this would know not to touch off any shots in here. The person had come with a purpose. Whether it was to keep Doolin from talking any more or to keep him from finding the loot didn't matter now. If Doolin knew the precise location after all, he had taken that knowledge with him. It may or may not have been the thing he said he might tell Archer next time.

Archer shook his head to try to clear it. It was too bad Doolin came to his end this way, but there was nothing Archer could do to change it. And he was going to have enough to do in order to look out for himself and Doolin's daughter.

Kate's hands did not stop shaking, and her voice was a dry whisper. "And no one knows anything?"

From their corner in the café, Archer could keep an eye on the rest of the place. Even though no one was within twenty feet, he spoke in a low voice as well. "They know what they can see, and that is that he was bludgeoned. But as for why, all they know is what I told them, and — I shouldn't even be saying 'they.' It's just the sheriff. Anyway, he doesn't put much stock in the story about the hidden treasure. He thinks Doolin and Mercer might have been part of some mysterious ring where everyone had something on someone else."

"Oh, my word, what could that be?"

"I don't know. It's just an idea of his."

Kate lowered her voice even more. "I don't think my being his daughter is such a deep, dark secret that someone could blackmail him about it."

"No, and I don't think the sheriff even knows it. I didn't tell him. When he asked me how I came to know Doolin, I said I looked him up so I could ask him some questions about Jenks and Peavey. Which I did, the second time."

"Speaking of this man named Peavey, he seems to have had the ear of Mr. Fenton in the last little while."

Archer drew his brows together. "I wonder what that would be about."

"From Mr. Fenton's comments, at least some of it has been about you."

"Me? What does he have to say about me?"

"I don't know details."

"Well, I'm sure your boss is willing to listen to anything about me, but if Peavey's trying to make me out to be a scoundrel, he's going to have to make up quite a bit." As Archer ran a quick review of the handful of times he'd crossed paths with Peavey, he recalled the first occasion. It was the night he went to the room with Rosanna, and Wyse had made some suggestive comments afterwards.

"What's the matter?" asked Kate.

"Oh, nothing. Just remembering a couple of times when I bumped into him."

Kate was still fidgeting with the napkin in her hands. "So they don't know we're related?"

"Huh? Oh, no. At least I haven't told anyone. And if you haven't, the only person who could have said anything was him. So I don't think you have very much to worry about. I don't blame you for being afraid, though."

The door of the café opened, and Boot Beckett walked in. He tossed a look of recognition and made his way to Archer and Kate's table.

"How-de-do?" he said, tipping his hat to Kate.

She blinked her eyes and said, "We're fine. How's Sadie?"

"Oh, she's doin' swell. You should go out and see her."

"One of these days I will."

Archer said, "What's new with you, Boot?"

"Not much. Just runnin' some errands. Saw your horse and thought I'd drop in."

"Glad you did. I suppose you're keeping busy."

"Oh, yeah. Actually, there is something new. I'm supposed to go to work for Jim Tuesday in about a week. You remember him."

"Sure. Are you going to build his icehouse

263

for him?"

"Whoa. You know everything, don't you?"

"Not quite. I just heard it from Henkel-man. He said he was going to haul rock for it."

"That's what I understood. As soon as the ground's soft enough to dig, we'll do the foundation."

"I think there's some places where you can dig already, but it's your job."

"We'll see what the boss says. I don't care much for the diggin' part anyway, you know. For me it starts to get interestin' when we run the walls."

Archer appreciated the self-assured tone, as if Boot had built a dozen houses. "I hope it all goes well," he said.

"Me, too." Boot smiled and touched the brim of his hat. "Well, I'd best be goin'. Good seein' you both."

"You bet," said Archer. "Give our best to Sadie."

When Boot was gone, Kate said, "He seems to be in good spirits. Married life must agree with him."

"Looks like it. And his clothes are always a little cleaner now."

Kate did not speak right away. She took a long breath and said, "It's just as well you didn't say anything about this other business."

Archer gave a toss of the head. "He's busy and has got things to do. I'll bring him up to date the next time I see him. In the meanwhile, it's nothing for him to worry about."

"Not like it is for us." She paused. "Will there be a funeral?"

"There'll be something, but don't fret about it. Look out for yourself. I'll go to it, and I can go with you to pay your respects later on."

Tears started in Kate's eyes. "It's such a sad way to go," she said. "No one to mourn for you."

"Well, he's got someone. You just can't be very outward with it for the time being. And as far as that goes, he'd be the first one to tell you to look out for yourself first. I think you'll agree that he wasn't very sentimental."

Kate's features brightened as she wiped away the tears. "You're right about that. It helps to think of it that way."

Archer stood at the rail and watched the crowd in the Drover. About a dozen men had come in and taken places along the bar, and the women were beginning to show up.

Archer knew some of the men by sight, and he recognized the woman who sang, but a couple of the girls were new to him. He thought he might see someone more familiar, such as Peavey, Fenton, or Tuesday, but none of them appeared. Archer took his time drinking one glass of beer and then another. He didn't mind being left to himself, although he had come in with the idea that he might hear something about Jack Doolin.

The man who did odd jobs around the saloon had just come in from carrying an armload of empty bottles out back. As he walked past, Archer spoke.

"Say, Wally, what do you know?"

The swamper was a slight man whose head hung forward. He wore a narrow-brimmed hat and had four or five days' worth of stubble on his face. He shook his head and said, "Not a damn thing."

"Buy you a drink?"

"Bad manners to turn it down."

Archer signaled to the bartender, who brought two glasses of beer. Wally took one of them and lifted it in salute.

"Thanks," he said.

"My pleasure." Archer looked out at the crowd, took a sip, and came back to Wally. "Nobody knows anything."

"It's always that way."

"I thought you had the inside track on things, seein' as how so much knowledge flows through this place."

"Like so much beer through a man's body." Wally took a second drink, and his dull face brightened a bit. "Was there somethin' you were wonderin' about?"

Archer shrugged. "Maybe one little thing." He took another look around. "Have you heard anything about that fella who was found dead in the hotel?"

"The gambler?"

"Yeah. The old card player."

Wally hunched his shoulders. "Not much. Just that they found him there. Chances are that he owed someone money and they caught up with him. He didn't live here, you know."

"I knew that. Actually, I knew him."

"Oh, if he was a friend of yours, I didn't mean to say anything —"

"I don't know if he was a friend. I was just wonderin' why someone would have it in for him."

"Don't know. Not any more than I already said, and that was just repeatin' what I heard."

"That's all right. Just makes a fella curious, is all." Archer took a sip of beer. "Looks like they got a couple of new girls in here."

"Oh, yeah. They come and go." Wally turned his upper body as he looked around. "Is there one you like?"

"No, not really. There was one I met quite a while back. I don't see her this evening."

Wally's face went long. "Which one was that?"

"Brown-haired girl. Name of Rose-Ann or something like that."

"Rosanna."

"That's her. Nice girl."

"Yeah, she's not in here tonight. Didn't show up last night, either. You know, sometimes they disappear for a day or two, at about the time some fella with a roll of money comes to town."

"Everyone has to work. I wasn't lookin' for anything like that this evening anyway."

"There's always later." Wally leaned his head forward and took a drink.

"You're right there. By the way, I'm going to need someone to shoe a half-dozen head of horses before long. I'd want someone to come out to the ranch. I've got coal and all that. I just need someone who's handy at the shoein'."

"I don't know anyone right off hand."

"Well, if you think of someone, maybe you can let me know."

"Sure. I'll do that." Wally tossed off the rest of his beer. "Thanks again for the drink."

"Don't mention it." Archer handed him a half-dollar. "Buy yourself another one later on."

The man's eyes were bleary, but he held them steady as he said, "I'll do that."

Archer hefted the digging bar as the water dripped off the flared end. The ice in the horse trough was only a quarter-inch thick, and the days were getting longer. Each day, the sun came up a couple of minutes earlier and went down a couple of minutes later. Before long, he would be able to dig postholes two to three feet deep.

He carried the bar upright like a heavy spear. The flared tip pointed upward, and the tamping end pointed down. As he opened the door to the barn, daylight fell on the straw and debris scattered on the floor. He stepped inside as usual and then heard motion behind him. A strong hand grabbed his left upper arm, and a small, cold object pressed against the base of his skull just above his collar.

"Don't move, or this thing'll go off."

Archer held still. He smelled the stale odor of sweat. The hand on his left arm relaxed, then patted his hip and his coat pocket. As the man shifted his feet and went to transfer the pistol to his left hand, Archer rammed the flared end of the digging bar onto the toe of the man's boot.

An inarticulate cry of "Agghh!" rose out of the man's throat. Archer whirled, ducked aside, and crouched as the gun bobbled and fell with a *thump* on the floor. The man was drawn up to his full height, and his face was distorted with the pain. His eyes were wide open, and his yellow teeth were bared. The man's lower face was covered with a winter beard, but even at that, there was no mistaking the pug nose and pushed-up chin of Jenks.

He and Archer both dove for the gun. Jenks got his hand on it first, but he fumbled and the gun went off with a roar. Archer pinned the hand and the gun onto the dirt floor and tried to twist the gun away. Jenks gave it a yank and stumbled back, then brought it up and around. The cylinder clicked, but the hammer did not fall. The gun was jammed.

Archer dropped back and laid his hand on the iron bar where he had let it fall. Jenks had both hands on the pistol and was jerking it as he pulled on the trigger. His small eyes were concentrating on the gun itself, and his face was drawn tight.

Archer pushed up with his legs and swung the bar around with both hands. Jenks's eyes were still focusing their hatred on the gun that had failed him, until the bar rose into his field of vision. The eyes opened, and he tried to pull his head back, but it was too late. The bar caught him with a thud on the left side of the head, knocking his hat off. His bald head showed in the dull light as he spilled to the floor, bounced half an inch, and settled.

Voices were calling as footsteps came pounding across the ranch yard. Whitmore burst into the barn with the .25-caliber Stevens held ready at waist level. Oscar stood behind him, pushed up against the door frame. Both men were bare-headed.

"What the hell happened?" asked Whitmore.

"This fella pulled a gun on me." Archer realized he was pulling in deep breaths. "Then his gun jammed. I had to give him one with this bar."

Whitmore's eyebrows went up. With the rifle still ready, he stepped in front of the body. He pushed with his boot at Jenks's arm, then leaned over and laid his finger on the man's neck. After a few seconds he straightened up and said, "I think he's done for. Any idea who he is?"

"It's Jenks. The one I told you about."

Whitmore frowned as he took another look at the body. "I don't recognize him, but it seems like your hunch was right. That is, you had a hunch about him, didn't you?"

"I thought he might still be around, but I didn't think he'd be this close."

"Do you think he's the one that did in Lidge? Or Doolin?"

Archer gazed at the lifeless head, bald and bearded. "He could have done either one, or both."

"He could have done the same to you. Good thing you fetched him a wallop like you did."

Archer continued to stare at Jenks but could get no sense out of what he saw. After a few seconds he said, "Yeah, I was lucky. But he reminds me of the last dead man I saw. He took a lot of information with him."

CHAPTER TWELVE

Archer took the gravy tureen as Kate handed it to him, and he set it next to his own plate. From his seat at their corner table, he could keep an eye on anyone who came near enough to listen in. The waitress was keeping her distance, so he felt free to speak in a normal tone.

"Sometimes it amazes me to see how little can come out of something that you think is a big event. Someone tries to waylay you in your own barn, you react, and you have what you think is a huge outcome. Not only do I do this thing with my own hands, but I think it's a breakthrough in the Doolin case at least, and probably in the Mercer case as well. Then the sheriff treats it like a bushel of turnips. It's all opinion on my part, he says. He needs proof. Same with what happened to Doolin. He's got facts, but not enough to connect them. It's clear that Jenks had the ability and could easily have found the opportunity — and this is in the sheriff's words — but there's no way to prove that he did it or that he even had a motive. I tell you, finding Doolin was no small thing for me, either, but the sheriff treats it like a routine occurrence. And it doesn't seem to have made much of a dent anywhere else."

"I haven't heard mention of it," said Kate. "Not that I would expect Mr. and Mrs. Fenton to discuss it at supper, but I haven't heard a word from anyone, much less anything about any relations between Jack and, we'll say, someone else. Do serve yourself some gravy."

"Oh. Right." Archer reached for the curved handle of the ladle.

Kate had a wistful expression on her face as she said, "It's sad to think that a person amounts to so little. It's like Marc Antony says in the play —

But yesterday the word of Caesar might
Have stood against the world. Now lies he
  there,
And none so poor to do him reverence.

As for Jack, he was no Caesar to begin with, but you'd think he would deserve someone to care about him."

274

"You do. And I do, in a different way."

"That's right. At least there are two of us who are that poor." Kate dabbed at her eyes with her napkin. "It's as if there's some virtue in being an orphan. I hope you don't mind my using that word."

"No, not at all. You used it before, when you mentioned Dickens."

"I use it now because that's what we both are. I know it's not the same with both of us, but I was struck with the parallel. Here I was, finding a father I never really had, and he wasn't much of a father after I found him, and then I no sooner had him than I lost him. As I thought about it, it occurred to me that you had gone through something similar. I understand that Mr. Mercer wasn't your actual father, but in a way he was that kind of a figure."

"I suppose."

"And so, in that way, we're in a similar place in life's path. Don't you think?"

"I see what you mean. I can't say that I feel the same way, though. I'm not so concerned about what kind of a figure Lidge was to me as I'm caught up in what he left behind. Whether it turns out that I do or do not have any legal interest in the ranch, I really don't want any. The whole thing feels tainted, and I want to earn my own way.

Right now, though, I'm tied to it. I think it would be terrible, no justice at all, if Peavey ended up with it. Lidge's lawyer, Cunningham, has written to Missouri to see if there's anyone there who might be in line for the inheritance, but who knows how long that will take. Meanwhile, I've got to look out for the place until I see how Peavey's lawsuit turns out."

She reached across and patted his hand. "It won't be very long."

"Oh, I know. It's just frustrating to be stalled like that. On the other hand, at least it gives me something to do. I like the work. And on the practical side, I've been able to draw wages every month, just like Oscar and Whitmore. The lawyer's seen to that."

"That's good. But it'll all pay off in other ways as well. When you get your own place, you'll know exactly how to go about every bit of work."

He laughed. "Maybe the daily chores. But there's so much you learn just by doing it, and there are lots of jobs in settling your own place that I haven't done yet. So I expect to muddle my way through and have to do lots of things over again."

Her dark eyes softened. "Do you think you'll get a place close to here, like Boot did?"

"I don't know. Boot was lucky to find that place and get a hold of it before someone else did. Except for places like that one that come up every once in a while, a fella has to go where the land is being opened up for new claims. From what I've heard, the government is supposed to open up a tract of land north of the Cheyenne River. When that happens, I hope I'm all done with things around here."

Her face had a sad expression as she said, "I suppose you have to move on to other things that are more important."

"Oh, no. I didn't mean it that way. I just meant that I hoped I was done looking out for the Bar M. Plus I hope someone gets to the bottom of the Mercer and Doolin business. I wouldn't like to leave things unfinished, but I don't want them to stand between me and what I want to do next."

"But you've already said, or at least suggested, that there's not much you can do to nudge the sheriff."

"That's true, but I might be able to do something on my own. I know, I tried that when I went to see Doolin by myself, and if anything it made things worse. But he did give me more to go on, and I think I need to take the initiative instead of waiting for things to come my way. Actually, that's already happened with this fellow Jenks. I tell you, it's pretty unsettling to find out that someone has come right into your own quarters and wants to do you in. I can almost imagine how Lidge and Doolin felt, though it didn't go up to the last minute with me."

"What kind of initiative do you think you'll take?"

"I've got a couple of things in mind." He lowered his voice. "For one, I'll see what I can find out about the man Peavey was supposed to be working for. Name of Scott. For another, I want to find out if this fellow named Tuesday has anything to do with it. Jenks may have been working for him at one time, and for all I know, Peavey's in with him as well." Catching her uncertain look, he said, "Tuesday's the fellow Boot Beckett said he was going to work for. He may have started by now. I can drop by there to see Boot, and I might be able to pick up an impression or two."

"And what if neither of those two works out?"

He shrugged. "I guess I'll have to think up something else."

"Please eat," she said. "Your food's getting cold."

"I feel funny eating by myself, in front of you."

"Oh, please. It's just the way things are right now."

As he ate, she raised her reticule from the floor, set it on her lap, and opened the drawstring. She took out a very thin packet tied with string. As she unwrapped it, he saw that it consisted of two pieces of pasteboard about five by seven inches, with a sheet of drawing paper and a cover leaf of tissue lying protected between the two stiffer pieces. She lifted the tissue and let him see the drawing. It was of a cow horse, saddled, with a coiled rope tied on.

"That's a nice picture. Did you do it?"

"Yes, I did."

He raised his eyes to meet hers. "I didn't know you could draw."

She gave a soft smile. "I haven't talked about it."

"Is it something you've always done?"

"Yes, since I was very small. You know, we didn't have a great deal when I was growing up, and we moved around. But even if I didn't have much to call my own, this was something I could do. All I needed was paper and a pencil. People used to ask if they could keep my pictures. And it wasn't just a portrait of their baby. It might be a

279

drawing of a chair, or a cart, or a horse. I liked drawing horses, and I still do."

Archer let his eye wander over the drawing again. "This looks good." A thought crossed his mind. "Do you do people at all?"

"Sometimes I try my hand."

"Do you think you could do one of Jack?"

Her face fell. "I've thought of it, but I don't have enough to go on. I saw him just that once, and not for very long. The image I have in my mind just isn't filled in enough. Maybe I should try, though."

"Only if you want to."

"I might."

Archer rode the buckskin horse south toward an area called Silver Springs. According to the directions he had gotten in town, he was to follow the trail for eight miles until he came to a deserted homestead with a fallen-in root cellar. There he was to turn west and ride four miles into the Scott ranch. As he rode, he saw that the country was coming out of winter. Newborn calves lay curled on the sloped ground where they could catch the rays of the morning sun. The first green of the year was pushing up beneath the tufts of dead grass, and the stock pond he saw had only shore ice around the edges.

He found the abandoned homestead site with no trouble and headed west. Except for scattered cattle and an occasional band of antelope, the land was empty. It was rolling country with buttes in the distance. Trees were scarce, and he saw no buildings or fences or windmills.

It seemed as if he had ridden more than four miles when he came to a hill like all the others and rode to the crest. At the bottom of the hill was a fence with a wire gate. Right inside stood a tall grey horse.

The horse stayed put, watching him, as he rode up to the gate and dismounted. He opened the wire gate, led his horse through, and closed the gate behind him. Fifty yards beyond the horse lay the bleached skeleton of a cow. Archer rode over the next hill and into the ranch yard.

A mottled brown dog came out of the barn, barking. A moment later, a man emerged. He was a normal-looking individual in work clothes and a short-brimmed hat. He squinted in the sun as he walked toward the center of the yard.

"Help you?"

"Looking for the Scott place."

"This is it." The man had a toothpick in his mouth and moved it from one side to another. "I'm Bill Scott."

Archer dismounted and faced the man. "My name's Russ Archer. I come from the Bar M, up north. Maybe you know of it. I worked for Lidge Mercer and became a junior partner a while before he died."

Scott's eyes traveled over Archer, to the horse, and back to Archer. "I think I heard some of that. Don't know the place itself. It's a ways from here. Of course, you know that."

"You're right. And I didn't come all this way looking for stock or anything like that." Archer paused for a couple of seconds. "I came to ask about someone who said he was working for you a while back."

Scott's eyes narrowed. "And who would that be?"

"Fella named Peavey. He and a pal of his named Wyse said they were working for you."

Scott frowned. "That was quite a while ago. They worked for me for less than a month."

"Is that all?"

"Yeah. The tall one didn't care for any of the jobs I gave 'em. Didn't like buildin' fence, checkin' pastures, workin' cattle — nothin'. The other one didn't complain as much, but he went along with whatever his pal wanted."

"Sounds like them. Do you know where they went to work after they left here?"

Scott shook his head. "They didn't say anything, and they haven't come back to pay me a visit."

"I guess Wyse isn't around anymore."

"I wouldn't know." Scott tipped his hat against the sun. "Are you lookin' for 'em?"

"Not really. I've seen Peavey around, but I don't know what he's doing. That is, I don't know where he keeps himself. I do know, or I've been told, that he's trying to get possession of the ranch that Mercer left."

Scott shook his head as he turned down his mouth. "Well, I'm sorry I can't help you any more, but I don't know anything."

"That's all right. You've been plenty of help. Whatever he's up to, he's not doing it from here."

"I'd say not. I do wonder about him trying to run a ranch, though."

"Oh, I don't think he wants to run it. I think he's just interested in its value."

"Grass isn't worth much."

"No, and there's hardly enough cattle to call a herd."

"No tellin'," said Scott.

Archer gave it one more try. "I don't suppose he ever mentioned the name of any friend from around here."

Scott moved the toothpick and shook his head slower than before. "If he's got any friends, he keeps 'em to himself."

"Well, thanks." Archer set his reins, put his toe in the stirrup, and mounted up.

The grey horse was standing in the same place as before. He looked even taller from up close. Archer figured he might go seventeen hands. He didn't have any saddle tracks on him, and he had his full winter coat. Archer wondered what it was like to be way out in the far-flung country and not have anything to do. He wasn't going to find out today, though. When he had the gate snugged behind him, he mounted up again and headed for the Hat Creek Breaks.

Archer rode past the sandstone formation on the crest of the pine ridge. The sun in early afternoon brightened the surface, and Archer enjoyed the soft warmth that reflected. A cottontail rabbit darted into a shelter of small rocks at the base. Straight out from the ridge, a half-mile away, a hawk with a pale underside turned and tilted as it drifted over the valley below.

Archer left the main road and followed the trail as before until he arrived at Boot Beckett's homestead. The grass was cropped short for quite a ways out in every direction, and a half-dozen chickens scratched at the meager ground near the house. In the pen in back, a couple of horses looked toward the visitor.

Fifty feet from the house, Archer called out a greeting. When the door did not open, he called again. Motion from the area in back caught his eye, and a few seconds later, Sadie came from behind the pens and into the open. She waved a gloved hand and walked forward. She was wearing her wool cap, a heavy wool overshirt, and a pair of corduroy trousers. As usual, she walked straight without much motion.

Archer dismounted and waited for her to come within speaking distance. "Afternoon, Sadie. Enjoying the weather?"

"I'd better." She brushed away a wisp of her blond hair. "Lookin' for Boot?"

"Thought I might talk to him if he was around."

She motioned with her light blue eyes as she gave a toss of her head toward the northwest. "He's at work. He took a job with Jim Tuesday."

"I was wondering if he'd started yet. Does he stay there?"

"Sometimes. He comes and goes."

Archer lifted a light smile. "You get along all right on your own."

"It would be pretty poor if I didn't. Most dangerous thing so far has been a coon that wanted to eat my hens."

"Did you get him?"

Her small nose and mouth went up and down as she nodded her head. "Just a little too late in the year for his pelt to be worth much, though."

Archer glanced away to the northwest. "How far is it to where Boot's working?"

"About seven miles. It's not hard to find. Are you goin' there?"

"I could. Just seven miles?"

"Well, maybe a little more. You get back out on the main road, you go four miles north until you come to a place where the road runs next to a creek. It's dry now, but you'll see a big cottonwood all by itself. You pick up a trail there, and you go west and a little north for about three miles. Tuesday's place is just before you come to a line of hills that runs north and south."

"I know those hills, at least from the other side."

"That's what Boot said. Your place ends just a few miles from Tuesday's."

"I'll probably go home that way, just to get to know the country."

Sadie looked up at the sun. "You ought to have plenty of time."

"I think so." Archer evened out his reins. "Well, thanks for the directions, Sadie. We'll see you again before long."

"Bring Kate out to see me."

"I will." Archer put his foot in the stirrup and swung aboard. He touched his hatbrim and said, "So long."

He found the cottonwood without any difficulty, as it was the only one of its kind within a couple of miles. He picked up the trail as Sadie told him, and in about half an hour from the main road he came upon the small headquarters of a ranch.

The house was like many others in the country — square with a pyramid-shaped roof. It faced east, and right next to it, facing the same way, sat a bunkhouse with a single-slant roof. A barn, situated perpendicular to the bunkhouse, faced south. Archer's glance moved around as he took in the details, and as the trail approached the headquarters at an angle instead of straight on, he did not see the building in progress right away. When the gap between the ranch house and the bunkhouse came into view, the gleam of new lumber showed from behind.

The sound of a hammer, five raps and then a sixth, carried on the air. A minute later, the same pattern sounded again.

Archer rode into the yard, dismounted, and tied his horse at the rail. The hammering started again, so he did not bother to call out. He walked between the two buildings and paused at the icehouse-to-be.

The stone floor was already laid, and the foundation rose above it about a foot all the way around. A skeletal framework rose up on the front and left sides, while the walls on the right and back sides had been boarded all the way up on the outside and halfway up on the inside. A stack of lumber sat on the right or north side of the building, and within a few seconds Boot Beckett appeared with three ten-foot boards on his shoulder. He tipped his head up and waved with his free hand.

"Caught you at work," said Archer.

"Good thing. You can give me a hand." Beckett lowered the three one-by-eights to the ground in front of the structure.

"Did you do the floor and foundation yourself?"

"Actually, he did the floor ahead of time, and I did the foundation when I got here."

"Wasn't it harder that way?"

"He said he wanted to get a jump on the weather."

"Huh." Archer glanced around the building. "What is this, about twelve by twenty?"

"That's it. And six-inch walls. Gonna fill 'em with sawdust. That'll have to be hauled in, too, of course. A few wagonloads."

The afternoon sun was at its warmest, and the pleasant smell of fresh lumber hung on the air. Archer noticed the walls again. "Are you keepin' it all square and plumb?"

Beckett smiled. "Just as best as I can. They say a good carpenter can hide his mistakes, but I'm not that far along yet."

"Well, I didn't come to inspect."

"Good. Why don't you help me put up these three boards, and then I can take a few minutes."

Archer held each board in place as Beckett pounded the nails. The lumber was rough, and while it might have been straight when it was milled, it now had curves on the flat side as well as on the narrow edge. Beckett tried to straighten out each board as he nailed it, and Archer had to apply full pressure to keep the board in place as Beckett whaled away with the hammer.

"That's pretty good for right now," he said when he had driven the last nail. "I don't suppose you came by just to be a carpenter's helper."

"Good guess." Archer shot a glance at the bunkhouse. "Are you the only one here?"

"For right now."

"I'll try to keep it short anyway."

"Let's sit down." Beckett walked across the stone floor and sat on the foundation where the wall had not been closed in yet.

Archer did the same. When he was seated, he said, "You might have heard about a fella who was found dead in the Royal Hotel a little while back."

"I heard somethin'. Gambler, wasn't he?"

"Of sorts. He ran a card game for quite a while, and more recently I think he just sat in on a game when it looked good."

"Did he get killed because he owed someone some money?"

"I think that's what most people would think of first, but I don't. I happened to know the man."

Beckett looked straight at Archer and opened his eyes. "Did you?"

"Yes, I did. In fact, I was the one who found him."

Beckett gave a quizzical expression. "You haven't taken to gamblin', have you?"

"No, I was talking to him about other things. Trying to see if I could find out why someone might have wanted to do in Lidge."

Boot flicked his eyebrows. "He may have been the right kind of fella to ask."

"Seemed like." Archer paused. "I asked

him if he knew anything about that fellow named Jenks."

"Oh, that one. What did you find out?"

"Nothing, from him." Archer looked around. Seeing nothing, he went on. "But Jenks showed up on his own, out at the ranch."

"The hell. I would have thought he was long gone."

"Well, he wasn't. He came up behind me in the barn and stuck a pistol in back of my head."

"Not very neighborly. I suppose he told you why."

"We didn't get that far. We had a little scuffle, and I laid him out with that digging bar you gave me."

"Huh." Beckett creased the corners of his mouth. "You got him good, then."

"Oh, yeah. Trouble was, no one could get any information out of him once he was done for. I had a hunch that he killed Lidge and Doolin both, but there's been no way to connect him."

"Doolin bein' the gambler."

"Right."

Beckett reached into his vest pocket and took out his tobacco sack. "Well, it's too bad you couldn't get anything out of him, but at least he's not gonna pull any more stunts."

"And you never heard any of this?"

Beckett shook his head. "Nope."

"And you don't know if Jenks ever worked here?"

Beckett shrugged. "Could be, but I've never heard him mentioned."

"And I doubt that you've heard Tuesday say anything about the Bar M."

"Not that I remember. Why?"

"Oh, I think he might have had a reason to want to own it."

"Hmm. From what I've seen, he's no great shakes at runnin' what he's got. Spends half his time in town. But you never know." Beckett moved his head back and forth in slow motion as he shook tobacco into the trough of his cigarette paper.

Movement beyond the frame of the front wall caught Archer's eye, and he felt a lurch in the pit of his stomach. It was like reacting to a snake before a person identified it. But this was no snake. A tall man in grey, with coarse hair the color of steel dust, stood between the ranch house and the bunkhouse. He had his head tipped up as he surveyed the two young men. Even at the distance, the man's red-rimmed eyes and pointed nose reminded Archer of a rat.

"I'm back," said Peavey.

Beckett raised his eyes. "Good enough,"

he said, and he resumed smoothing out the little mound of tobacco.

Peavey turned and walked away in the direction he had come from.

When he was gone, Archer spoke in a low voice. "Is he working here?"

"For as much as he works." Beckett stuck his tongue out between his lips as he rolled the cigarette and made ready to lick it.

"What about his pal Wyse? I heard he was gone."

"I believe he had to hat up."

"Well, I had some questions about them, but I guess they'll have to wait."

Beckett seemed as nonchalant as ever. He licked the seam edge and patted it down, then stuck the quirly in his mouth. "Sure. We can talk about it later." He took out a match, popped it, and lit the cigarette.

That's what Doolin said, Archer thought. But out loud he said, "How much longer do you think you'll be working on this thing?"

"Maybe two more days to get it boarded up. Whenever the sawdust gets here we'll fill the walls, and then we'll build the roof after that."

"You think you'll work here the whole time?"

"No tellin'. If I have a couple of days off,

I can work on my own place. I suppose you came by that way."

"I did. Sadie gave me good directions. She's been out this way, I'd guess."

"She came with me one time, so she'd know where to find me if she needed me."

"You're not getting close to — but she probably wouldn't be ridin' then anyway."

"Oh, no. None of that. But if someone was interested in a horse, she could tell me, and I could go home that evenin'."

"I see." Archer sat without speaking as Beckett smoked his cigarette. After a couple of minutes, Archer stood up. "I think I'll move along, try to get home before dark. You don't know the way through these hills, do you?"

"Not yet, but I think you can find it all right."

"I'm sure I can. Meanwhile, if you pick up something you think I ought to know, don't forget to tell me the next time I see you."

"Hah. You're the one with all the news. Leave it to me, and I wouldn't even know about Garfield."

"I wouldn't mind being off the main trails myself, but news seems to find me." Archer motioned with his head toward the bunkhouse. "So do people I don't care for."

Beckett shrugged in his light way. "Nothin' special there. He doesn't like anyone."

Archer made his way back to the Bar M as the sun began to fall in the west. He took his time going through the hills, and he imagined Jenks having come this same way. Archer studied the landmarks and turned every few minutes to look at the layout in back of him. It was a good habit in any country a man hadn't traveled in, so he could see what the land would look like if he came from the other direction. It was even a better practice when he knew some-one like Peavey was at his back.

CHAPTER THIRTEEN

Archer closed one eye to line up the post with the others. Hacked as it was from its natural state, the cedar post had twists and bends in it, so it did not line up straight on either side. Archer held the post where he thought the center of it was in line, and with his foot he dragged dirt so that it fell into the hole around the base of the post. The smell of the damp earth mixed with the aroma of cut cedar, and the sun was warm enough that Archer had taken off his jacket before he began to dig the hole. He felt the energy of the sun and of the blood coursing through his body. It was simple, clean work. Dig the hole wide and deep enough, get the post as straight up as he could, and tamp it in solid.

He walked back five paces to get a view, then walked around ninety degrees to get another sighting. Back at the post, he adjusted it and pushed in a little more dirt.

After a look around, he picked up the bar and started tamping.

When he had packed the first layer and was shoveling in dirt for the next one, Whitmore came through the corral and stood a couple of yards away.

"I've got everything in the wagon and the horses hitched."

"Good enough. I should be done here in a few minutes. Have yourself a smoke."

"I think I will." Whitmore sat down on the old post that they had dug up and tossed aside. "Found a centipede," he said. " 'Bout as big around as a pencil and damn near as long. But he twisted and curled up when I stomped on him."

"That's good." Archer thumped at the dirt around the post.

"Another month and the snakes'll be comin' out."

"That'll be time to brand. See how many calves we've got."

Whitmore did not look up from rolling his cigarette. "You say you're not plannin' to stay on. Does it ever seem odd to be workin' for a dead man?"

"Oh, yeah. But if there's work to do, it gives you something better to think about."

Whitmore glanced toward the hole. "You

think about that dirt you're packin' in there?"

"A little bit. But for me at least, this kind of work frees your mind to think about things you'd like to do in the future."

"Things like what? Or should I ask?" Whitmore lit his cigarette and blew the smoke away.

"Dig more postholes. Build new corrals instead of fixing old ones."

"Don't you dream of havin' a few slobberin' cows of your own as well?"

"That, too." Archer thought of asking Whitmore if he hadn't ever wanted a place of his own, but he decided not to.

"I'll tell you one thing," said Whitmore.

"What's that?"

"These cedar posts'll last a hell of a lot longer than those cottonwood and pine that the last fella put in. That one you're settin' is liable to still be there when you're gone. Damn sure outlast me, though I don't always like to think about that."

Archer moved a quarter of the way around the post and kept tamping. "When I was digging this hole, I remembered what you said about men who always hope they're going to dig up treasure."

"Ha-ha. Were you disappointed?"

"Not much. Even if I was, there's always

more holes to dig."

"Isn't that the truth? No matter how old you get. 'Course, if you've never dug any to begin with, you're not likely to later. Take Lidge for example. It was too late in life for him to take to some of this work."

An image of Doolin passed through Archer's mind. "Maybe some people could take to the digging if they thought they were going to find something."

"Good luck to 'em," said Whitmore. "But if you don't want to be disappointed, you best be satisfied with your wages."

"And with doing the work." Archer gave a pull on the post, and it did not move.

Archer handled the reins as the wagon rolled out of the ranch yard. Not far to the east, the land began to slope upward. Archer recognized some of the gullies and outcroppings from the time when he and Boot came out this way to gather rock. He also recalled the spot where they had the run-in with Jenks and Crowell, but he did not mention it to Whitmore. He drove on toward the hills on top.

"There should be two good cedar trees up here," he said. "Both of 'em dead. I came through that gap the other day, and they were up on top to my right, about a hundred yards apart." He clucked to the horses and gave the reins a shake.

The horses leaned into the steeper climb, and the going got rougher. Archer had a hard time trying to keep the wagon on level ground, and it tipped to one side and the other. At one point when the wagon rose up on the left front end and then fell, Whitmore gave out a groan and slumped off the seat and into the wagon box. The crash of a rifle shot came right after.

The horses bolted, and the wagon moved in hard, jarring bounces. Archer pulled on the reins, but the horses kept surging ahead. When the ground rose up steeper, they cut to the left. The wagon teetered and slammed back down onto all four wheels. The .25-caliber rifle, which Archer had wrapped in a piece of canvas, slid back in the box with the axes and the crosscut saw. The wagon banged again, and the horses dragged it down across a gully and up on the other side. A whistling sound split the air, and the boom of the rifle followed. Archer whipped the horses down into the next gully and yanked them to a stop.

Whitmore was writhing on the floor of the wagon box and clutching his right shoulder. A splotch of blood had appeared on his jacket and had picked up dirt from the floorboards.

"What the hell's goin' on?" he asked.

"Someone's shooting at us. I think we're out of his line of fire." Archer crawled to the back of the box and unwrapped the rifle. "Just stay put," he said. "I'm going to see if I can find where he is. I've got an idea of where the shots came from." He slipped out of the wagon, and in a crouch he went twenty yards up the gully. Taking off his hat, he crawled to the rim.

Searching the rocks to the southeast was harder than he would have imagined. His vision was blurred, and the ridge was hazy in the warming sun. The rocks seemed to move. He closed his eyes for a moment, rubbed, and opened them. He could see a little better, but his heart was still pounding and his breath was heavy. As he settled the rifle into place, he could not keep the sights lined up steady. He relaxed and tried to take regular breaths. He rubbed his hands on his pants.

Now he saw movement, a spot that was a different color from the rocks. He levered in a shell, lined up the sights for a second, and squeezed the trigger. A small wisp of dust lifted, and the *spang* of the bullet hitting rock came back to him.

He waited for several long minutes, sweating now, but he saw no more movement. Whoever it was had either holed up tight or gone back.

Archer scurried down the gully to check on Whitmore. The hired man was lying on his back in the box of the wagon. "Are you all right?" Archer asked.

Whitmore heaved a breath. "I'm still alive, but it hurts like hell. You didn't do any good, did you?"

"I don't think I hit anyone, but I let him know we had something that would shoot farther than a pistol."

"How long are we gonna have to stay here?"

"Not too long, I don't think. We can follow this gully down a ways. Once we get onto easier ground we'll be out of his range, and I don't think he'll come out into the open."

"We're goin' back to the ranch, then?"

"That's my idea."

Whitmore raised his head about an inch off the floorboard. He winced and said, "Don't get yourself shot, too."

"I think we'll be all right. This gully broadens out as it goes down, so we should be able to get out of it. Just before we do, I'll get down and take a peek. But I think he's done trying for today."

"You say 'he.' You didn't see him, did you?"

"No, but I've got a pretty good idea of who it was."

Archer pulled up at the door of the cook shack and hollered for Oscar. The door opened, and the cook stood in the doorway. His bald head, light skin, and white apron made him look fragile.

"What's going on?" he said. His forced tone of authority was gone. "Where's Whitmore?"

"He's lying on the floor here. Someone took some shots at us, and they hit him."

"Holy smokes! Is he hurt bad?"

"Enough that I think we'd better take him to town."

"You want me to go?"

"I think it would help. You don't want to stay here by yourself after this, anyway, do you?"

Oscar's eyes seemed to stare at nothing. Then he looked at Archer and said, "Probably not. What do we need?"

"I'd say some blankets, some water, and some grub if you've got some." Archer looked over his shoulder and said to Whitmore, "Hang on, pal. We'll get you there."

Oscar went to the big house for blankets

and a stoneware jug wrapped in burlap. Archer filled the jug as the cook threw together some cold biscuits and meat. A couple of minutes later, Oscar was ready to go in a flat-crowned hat and a wool coat. As he took his seat in the wagon, he said, "I could sure use a drink."

Archer opened the door of the hotel room and found Oscar and Whitmore in good spirits. The cook was sitting on a spindle-back chair, and the ranch hand was propped up in bed. A bottle of whiskey sat on the stand next to the water pitcher, and each man had a glass in his hand.

"How do you feel?" said Archer.

"Better than I deserve," Whitmore answered.

Archer nodded at the glass. "You lost quite a bit of blood."

"I know. I'm goin' easy. Oscar's the one that needs the medicine. Shot his nerves all to hell."

The cook grimaced with one side of his mouth. "I'm not that bad off, but I will admit that the first drink went down pretty fast." He looked straight at Archer as he asked, "What did you find out?"

"Nothing good. The sheriff asked around, and he found people who could say that

Tuesday and Peavey came into town last night, took a room in this same hotel, and checked out at noon today. No one can vouch for where Peavey was at the time of the shooting, and I think he could have ridden out there and come back, with an alibi set up and waiting. But just like always, we've got no proof."

"Too bad you didn't put a bullet through him," said Oscar. He pointed at the rifle standing in the corner. "Someone comes in here, he'll get a belly full."

"Speakin' of which, I think you two should eat something. I'll go down and send up some grub. I'll eat while I'm down there, so don't expect me back right away. I might ask a question or two if I see someone I know."

"You be careful," said Oscar. "I don't like the way things have been going."

"Neither do I. But I've got to do something other than try to hide."

Archer sipped on his glass of beer as he took in the crowd in the Drover saloon. As he had expected, he did not see Peavey or Tuesday. The women had not shown up yet, neither the woman who sang nor the women of the night. Archer kept an eye out for Wally, the man who did odd jobs.

When Archer was on his second beer, Wally came shuffling into the saloon. He stopped to exchange words with one man and another. When he came to the place where Archer stood, he put on a broad smile and said, "How're you doin' this evenin', governor?"

"About like always. And yourself?" Archer signaled to the bartender.

"Same as you." With his head hung forward in its unusual posture, Wally smiled again, and the corners of his eyes creased. He gave a small, quick turn as the bartender set his glass of beer on the bar. He reached for the glass, lifted it in salute, and said, "Thanks."

"Glad to." Archer let the man take a drink, and then he said, "What's new?"

"Not much to speak of."

Archer looked out at the crowd. "That's normal."

Wally took another sip. "Maybe one thing."

"Uh-huh." Archer nodded without turning to look at the man.

"You might remember a person you mentioned to me last time we spoke."

Now Archer turned. "I do."

"Name of R.O. and so forth."

"Right."

"Well, she went missing."

Archer made a small frown. "I think you said something like that before."

Wally's voice took on a low, confidential tone. "Maybe I should say she's still missing."

"I see. Any speculations?"

Wally moved closer and spoke even lower. "Everyone acts as if it's bad luck to talk about it, but the talk's gone on among them. It turns out she was the daughter of that gambler that got killed."

It took Archer a couple of seconds to absorb the information. "Doolin? Are you sure?"

The yellowed eyes held steady. "It's what I heard. I've been keepin' an eye out for you, because I thought you'd want to know."

"I sure do. But how certain is it?"

Wally took a drink of beer and licked his lips, as if he needed the priming. "I picked up as much as I could, and it goes like this. Her last name is Clare. She was his daughter by a woman with that name. The woman's husband was a no-account, and he left her. Doolin took up with her, but they didn't stay together."

Archer could hear Doolin's words. *Maybe next time.* "And she knew it? That is, the girl did?"

"Oh, yeah. She knew him. When he was doin' better, he gave her a little money once in a while." Wally took another drink.

"Did he see her when he came to town the last time?"

"I don't know. I haven't heard."

Archer recalled a picture of Tuesday, smiling in his confident way as he touched Rosanna on the arm and then the hip. "I don't suppose it would be that hard for a fella to get her off somewhere alone if he had a reason to."

"Probably not, but I don't know why someone would want to."

"I would guess it would be to keep her from saying anything she might have heard from her father."

"That part's obvious." Then, as if he had caught himself over-stepping his bounds, Wally said, "But it doesn't answer the question of why someone would have it in for him."

"When I said that to you, you said he probably owed someone some money."

"Well, that's what a person would've thought, but it's got to be more than that if they took it further. That is, with the girl."

"That's what I think," Archer said.

Wally looked each way and tossed off the rest of his beer. He did not seem to be inclined to linger. His voice had a detached tone as he said, "No tellin'."

Archer reached his hand forward, palm down at waist level, and let a half-dollar fall into Wally's hand. "Thanks for remembering me," he said.

"Thank you, sir."

"Don't mention it."

"I won't."

Archer walked along the main street with Kate at his side. They stepped down from the end of the board sidewalk and followed a dirt path worn into the grass. Within a few minutes they reached the south edge of town, where the country opened up into grassland with hills in the distance. The sun was going down. A crosswind blew from the west, and puffs of dust rose in the fading light.

"You seem quiet today," she said.

"I have a lot to think about, and I haven't gotten anything done today. Just waiting."

"I understand. It's just one thing after another. First Mr. Mercer, then Jack, and then this thing yesterday. I feel so sorry for your hired man."

"He'll be all right, but it's not the type of thing that's good for anyone at any age. All that would be bad enough, but I can't help feeling it was my fault. I have no doubt that the bullet was meant for me."

"You don't think they were just trying to scare you?"

"I've considered that. I'm sure someone wants me off the ranch, but I don't think they'll be satisfied with scaring me away. Not after what they've done so far. Like I've told you, I'm convinced it's not just the property. They want to get anyone who might know something and get in their way."

"And you think that's why they got Jack."

"Yes, I do, and I feel it's my fault, at least in part." Archer had been walking with his hat tipped into the wind. He held onto it as he turned to look behind. They were a good hundred yards beyond the edge of town. "We'd better turn around," he said.

He switched places so that the wind was on his left and Kate was on his right. When they were even again, Kate spoke.

"Don't take it all on yourself. It's not your fault."

"Some of it is."

"Well, you know more about it than I do, but I'll say this. Look out for yourself. Try to wait it out until this thing is over. Why don't you stay in town longer?"

"For one thing, there's horses to feed. We got out of there in a hurry before noon yesterday, and assuming that Whitmore is able to travel tomorrow, it'll be well after noon when we get back."

"You could send someone. Boot, for example."

Archer took a deep breath. "I need to go at that angle a little later."

"You don't think he has anything to do with it, do you?"

"Oh, no, of course not. But he's working for someone that I think does. I'd better leave it at that for right now."

"Oh. Knowledge is danger, you're saying."

"Seems to be."

"Like Jack."

Archer paused. He had a fleeting image of Rosanna, and a twist of anguish rose from the pit of his stomach. "Yes," he said. "Like Jack. And the other reason we need to go back is so we don't abandon the ranch. Whether that was their purpose or not, we can't just let them move on in."

"Well, I can see it's got you wound up more than before. I can't tell you what to do, and you know what you have to do, or what you think you have to do. So I'll just ask you to be careful. Don't go out very far."

He recalled the shadowy form of Jenks, beard and pistol, in the barn. "I'll be careful," he said.

They walked on in silence. The raw feeling of sorrow came back, accompanied by more of a sense than a picture of Rosanna. A woman he had been close to, in body, had disappeared and most likely had suffered harm. If he had helped cause Doolin's death, he might have caused Rosanna's as well. His intimacy with her was coincidental, but his sense of guilt was a complicated, unfamiliar feeling all the same.

At gut level, he knew this was no time to tell Kate about Rosanna — not about her disappearance and not about her relation to Jack, which of course would mean her relation to Kate. That knowledge could wait. As for the other part, the strange twist of feeling that came from his own relation with Rosanna, he couldn't see where anything could be gained by sharing that knowledge.

Back in town, Archer and Kate walked along the sidewalk until they came to her cross street. Night was falling as they headed west and then turned into the alley that led to the Fentons' house.

"The wind's not as strong here in town," he said. "You can talk without getting grains of dirt in your teeth."

"It's nice to hear you say something cheerful again."

"I'm not so sure that I feel cheerful yet.

But I have an idea of what it might take."
He gave her a sidelong glance.

"More than a passage of melancholy poetry?"

"Is that what does it for you?"

She smiled. "It lifts me up."

They stopped at the steps leading to the back porch. The moon had not risen yet, but he could see the shine of her eyes. As he put his arms around her waist, he said, "I'm sorry I'm so gloomy."

"I understand," she said with a soft smile. "We'll get through it. Just be careful."

"I will." He closed his eyes as he met her in a kiss. For the moment all tension floated away.

When they drew apart, she said, "You leave tomorrow, then."

"I think so."

"And when will you be back to see your bonny sweetheart?"

"You tell me."

"When the robin sings, and the peasants dance for joy."

He laughed. "Where I'm going, I'm afraid it's the magpie that sings."

"Is he a gallows bird?"

"It does cheer you up, doesn't it?"

"No harm, I hope." Her eyes were shining as she put her arms around his neck. "You come back to me safe, and don't let any of this come between us."

"I won't." He settled his arms around her waist again, and he closed his eyes as he kissed her. He kept the image of her brown eyes and her rich, dark hair.

Archer pulled the horses to a stop in front of the cook shack. He had driven slow for Whitmore's sake, and the sun was slipping in the west. Shadows were reaching out from the ridge that looked like a dinosaur's back, and the air in the ranch yard felt as cool as it did when a man walked through the bottom of a draw at the end of the day.

After helping Whitmore climb down from the wagon, Archer and Oscar walked with him to the door. Archer left the cook in charge and began carrying in the blankets, the men's personal effects, and the provisions he had gotten in town. Dusk was drawing in as he climbed back up to the seat and took the reins.

He turned the wagon around and brought it to a stop in front of the barn, where he could unbuckle the harness in the fading light. He made short work of unhitching the team, and as he turned the horses into the corral he counted all six.

Back at the wagon, he climbed into the

box to round up the axes and the crosscut saw, which he had not taken the time to unload before. As he did so, he saw that the .25-caliber rifle still lay beneath the seat, wrapped in canvas. He leaned forward, and as he did so he caught motion out of the corner of his left eye. The barn door had opened a crack.

He dove for the floor of the wagon box, flattened out, and lay still. He could not tell if he heard a small movement or if he imagined it. He twisted around, felt inside the canvas, laid his hand on the stock of the rifle, and pulled the gun out.

Thoughts came fast. If he stayed put, he was a sitting duck. If he rose up and looked around, he gave a target. He needed to get out of the box. He took off his hat, shifted onto his left side, and got ready.

With the rifle in his right hand, he pushed up and lunged to the far side of the wagon, laid his left hand on the sideboard, and vaulted over. Four gunshots blasted, and splinters of wood flew over him. He rushed to the front of the wagon and raised up enough to see a large grey shape moving around the rear of the box. He ducked, sidestepped over the tongue, and moved past the right wheel. The grey figure was taking slow steps to the opposite corner.

Archer shifted position and crouched behind the wheel. He tried to decide what to do first — lever in a shell or take aim. Noise or motion — either one would help the other man place him. Archer rose up to peer over the wheel.

The man crept along the opposite side of the wagon. It was Peavey. Archer knew it was Peavey. The man was a tall, grey hulk with hair that looked like rat fur in the last dim light of evening.

Archer settled to a crouch and kept a lookout through the spokes of the wheel. He would know when Peavey came around the corner.

The shape came into view — slower now, and bent forward. Archer used his last two fingers to work the lever, and a shell eased up out of the magazine. Peavey took a step, and a holler came from the direction of the cook shack. Archer clicked the shell forward into the chamber, and a blast of gunfire erupted as a spray of dirt came up by his right knee.

In one motion he rose up and stepped into view, then brought the gun to waist level and pulled the trigger.

Peavey folded as his midsection went back and his shoulders slumped forward. Archer levered in another shell and fired again as

Peavey began to straighten up. The grey shape flinched, turned, and fell away.

Hollering came again from the cook shack. "For God's sake, are you out there, Russ?"

Archer waited a couple of seconds to make sure Peavey wasn't moving. Then he called, "I'm here. Come on out."

Oscar came on a slow run, bare-headed and pale. He was breathing hard when he came to a stop. "By God, it's Peavey," he said. "Isn't it?"

"Yeah, it's him. Why didn't you holler earlier?"

"I didn't know what was going on, and the gun was still in the wagon." Oscar raised his glance. "I see you got him with it. Why didn't you use your six-gun?"

"Too easy to shoot wild with it, especially in the dark. That's what he did."

"Well, you sure got him. I'm glad of it. The dirty son of a bitch."

Archer gazed down at the grey figure, dead as a giant rat that had been shot in a grain bin. "I'd like to be glad, too, but whoever sent him isn't done yet."

CHAPTER FOURTEEN

Archer walked out of the sheriff's office and nearly ran into Boot Beckett coming down the sidewalk on his left.

"Whoa," said Beckett. "You're movin' like a bull with his head down. You goin' somewhere?"

Archer drew himself up straight. "Whoa yourself. What are you doing in town?"

"Got a little time off."

"Really? What's going on with the icehouse?"

"We got the walls all covered and then we set the rafters in place, but we can't put the roof on until we fill the walls. So we're waitin' on sawdust."

"I see. How long have you been off?"

Beckett shifted the toothpick he had in his mouth. "Just today. The boss said I could tend to some of my own things while he sent Peavey up to Newcastle for a load of sawdust. They've got a couple of sawmills

318

there, you know."

"I've heard that. And so the boss said Peavey went up there?"

"That's right. He left yesterday."

"Let's go this way," said Archer. He motioned backwards with his head.

The two of them walked to the corner, crossed the side street, and walked halfway down the next block. Archer signaled for them to sit on the edge of the sidewalk in front of an empty lot. So they sat like two kids looking out on the street.

"You must have somethin' pretty good," said Beckett, "seein' as how you came out of the sheriff's office the way you did."

"I might. I can start by telling you what I told the sheriff. Peavey's not in Newcastle. He's lying dead in the barn out at the Bar M."

Beckett's eyes opened wide as the toothpick dangled. "The hell."

"That's right. He was layin' for me, right at sundown. Oscar and Whitmore were in the cook shack, and I was puttin' the horses and some other things away. He opened up on me, and I had the good luck to get in a better shot."

Beckett gave a low whistle. "What's the sheriff say to that?"

"He said that dead men showed up in my

319

presence too often to be normal. I said the last two shouldn't be any surprise, as I'd already told him I had my suspicions about 'em. Did you know Whitmore got shot?"

"I just heard it today. How is he?"

"He's all right. Just not moving very fast. I told the sheriff I thought Peavey had done it, but he said he needed proof, since Peavey had an alibi. Now he does the same thing when I tell him who I think is behind it all."

"You don't think Peavey was actin' on his own."

"No. Not any more than he went to fetch sawdust. But rather than go out and ask questions, the sheriff says he'll wait for his man to bring in Peavey's body. Then he'll have Tuesday come into town, and he'll talk to him then."

Beckett gave him a close look. "You think he's afraid to go out there?"

"I think he wants to play it safe."

"So what are you going to do?"

Archer kept his voice low. "There are a few options. I could go back to the ranch and hope no one comes after me, I could hole up in a hotel room here in town and hope nothing ever happens, or I could go out to Tuesday's and ask some questions myself. I think I should do the last one. I've had enough of lettin' things come to me, but I was kind of hesitatin' to go out there by myself. Now that I ran into you —"

Beckett's eyes widened again. "Now wait a minute. You think this fella's payin' other men to do his dirty work, and you want to ride right into his place and ask him some questions about it?"

"I think he'll be surprised to see me, but I doubt that he'll do anything in front of you. He's probably wondering where Peavey is, but I don't think he'll tip his hand."

Beckett had an amused expression on his face as he shook his head. "You've got a lot of nerve, Russ."

"I've got to do something. I can't just sit and wait for things to take their course."

"What kind of questions are you goin' to ask him?"

Archer frowned. "I'm not sure yet. I think I'll have to feel things out. But I don't plan to tip my hand, either. Are you going with me?"

"Oh, I don't know." Beckett took the toothpick from his mouth and stared at the dirt in the street.

"It would make a big difference," said Archer. "Take all the danger out of it."

Beckett pushed back the corners of his mouth. "I can see that." After a couple of seconds of silence he tossed the toothpick in the dirt and said, "Oh, I guess so. But I'd like to stop at my place on the way."

As they rode out on the old stage route toward the Hat Creek Breaks, Archer filled in Beckett on the whole story as he acquired it from Doolin — how Peavey was hoping to take the Bar M from Mercer and sell it to someone else, and how that other person might be convinced that a cache of gold was buried somewhere on the Bar M holdings.

Beckett seemed to be more interested in the plunder than in the killings and attempted killings. "That's something to think about," he said. "We might have rode right over the spot at one time or another."

Archer said, "The thing that's got me is how little someone else's life means to a fella like that. I've heard of other men who were that way. They just don't have any feelings. They seem normal on the surface, but below that, someone else's suffering means nothing to 'em. Of course, that's the kind of person that ends up in prison, and if that's where he heard about this buried treasure, it might fit."

"The money part sure makes sense," said Beckett. "Otherwise, it would be a hell of a lot of trouble to go to, just for the land."

"I'd think so. And even with bigger stakes, he might have thought it was going to be easier than it turned out. Then he got in a little deeper with each step."

Beckett seemed to be still thinking on his own track. "You figger he's been to prison, then."

"That's the way things fit together for me. I know when we first met him, he didn't look as if he had seen much sun for quite a while. Do you remember that?"

Beckett laughed. "I remember we talked about his hands. And even now, he's not weathered and sunburned like your normal cattleman. And he just about never talks about where he's been and what he's done. It's as if he doesn't want anyone addin' two and two to see if his story holds together."

"I've sure wondered about him," said Archer. "I wouldn't be surprised if Tuesday is a summer name. Once you know someone isn't what he seems, anything is possible."

"And you're sure you know it — that is, that he's not what he seems."

"I don't know every last bit, but when he says Peavey went to Newcastle for a load of sawdust and Peavey ends up at the Bar M tryin' to put a bullet through my gizzard, a lot of things become surer, for me at least. I think it's one of those deals where once you see things one way, you can't see 'em the other way any more."

Beckett smiled and gave his head a shake. "I can follow your whole line of thinkin', and it matches with some of what I've seen, but I haven't gotten to the point where I can see him only in the new way and not at all in the old way. My idea of a hardened criminal is someone with a jail-dock who's got a mean streak in him that keeps him from gettin' along with folks in any normal way. It's all there to see."

"With the type I was talkin' about, some of them hide their mean streak. They're the kind that have a good word and a handshake for everyone but leave a body buried everywhere they go."

"If he's what you say, he leaves his bodies where others can find 'em."

"We're not done with him," said Archer. "Then again, I might be wrong. I might be a little ways off on one small thing or another, or I might be dead wrong. But I don't think I am."

"Well, we'll see what kind of an impression he gives us in a little while."

They rode through the Hat Creek Breaks and onto the side trail without speaking. As the horses trotted into the yard at Beckett's place, he called out. He held the bay horse still for a minute, then nudged it to go around back. Only the dun stood in the corral.

"Her horse is gone," said Beckett. "She rides that grey roan. And all the chickens are put up. So I'd say she went some place."

"Any idea where?"

"Not right off. But I'd imagine she'll be back before we are." Beckett looked at the sky. "We might as well get goin' so we can get back before dark." He turned the bay around and rode out of the yard.

Archer followed on the smoke-colored horse and came up even with him when they hit the trail.

The ride across country did not take long. The day was neither hot nor cold, and only the slightest breeze came out of the northwest. The ranch headquarters came into view just as they did on Archer's earlier visit, except that this time he saw the rafters of the new building in back of the ranch house and bunkhouse.

"That's Sadie's horse," Beckett said. "Hell, she's here."

The grey roan was tied in front of the bunkhouse, while Sadie and Tuesday sat in chairs up against the building. Archer had not seen them right away because of the shade.

Tuesday lifted a hand in greeting as the

two riders came into the yard. They swung down, led their horses forward, and tied them to the rail next to Sadie's.

"Good afternoon," said Tuesday. "Looks like everyone's out for a ride."

Archer nodded to him and touched his hat as he dipped his head in Sadie's direction. He did not know what to make of the expression on her face, but it didn't look like surprise at having been caught at something.

She turned her eyes toward Boot. "I thought you were here."

Unruffled as always, Boot said, "Jim gave me some time off, so I went into town to take care of a few things. I guess I could have stopped by, but I figured I'd be back soon enough. Then I ran into Russ in town."

Both Tuesday and Sadie turned toward Archer.

"I heard you'd been killed," she said. "I came to tell Boot."

A combination of numbness and chill went through Archer's upper body. He shook it off and said, "Who did you hear that from?"

"A man who stopped by to water his horse. He said he heard it in town."

"Well, he heard more than I did. I'm glad he was wrong."

Tuesday's voice was calm and friendly. "I'm sure we all are."

Archer turned his head to take in all three. "Thanks," he said. "It's an odd thing to hear. I don't know why someone would say it."

Tuesday made a small backward wave with his hand. "He was probably just repeating what he heard."

"Then I wonder why someone would have said it to him."

Tuesday gave a light shrug and said nothing.

Sadie spoke up. "Well, I'm glad to see you're all right."

"Thank you, Sadie. And thanks for taking the trouble to come and tell Boot." Archer brought his eyes back to Tuesday. "And how's the building coming along?"

"Oh, all right. As I'm sure Boot told you, we're waiting on sawdust. Once we start getting the walls filled, it won't take long to finish."

"Mind if I take a look? I'm always interested in these things."

"Go ahead. Boot can show you. He's done almost all the work on it."

Archer tipped a nod toward Tuesday and Sadie, then followed Boot around back of the two older buildings.

As Beckett had said, the walls were boarded up on both sides of the upright poles, and the bare rafters were mounted on the top. They gave the building a skeletal look. Archer's gaze returned a couple of times to the stone floor.

Beckett said, "We ran the rafters up so that as soon as we get a wall filled we can start putting on the roof and keep from gettin' any water inside the walls or inside the house."

"I see. When you get one wall done, you can start on the roof on that side. Meanwhile, someone goes for more sawdust."

"That's right." Beckett had his head lifted as he surveyed the top part of the building.

Archer took a last glance at the floor and turned away to walk back out front. When he got there, he said to Tuesday, "Looks like it's shaping up all right. How long do you think it'll take to haul a load of sawdust?"

"At least a couple of days each way. Probably three."

"It'll keep Mr. Peavey busy."

Tuesday gave a forced laugh. "I imagine so." After a short pause he said, "I realize the two of you have some disagreements over the property settlement."

"I don't know that we've actually talked about it."

"Well, I don't mean to be butting in where I don't belong, but I've gathered from him that he thinks he has a right to the property that belonged to his cousin. I think I've convinced him, though, that he doesn't have to go to the lengths of a lawsuit."

"Is that right?"

"Yes. I think I've persuaded him to drop it."

Archer took a short but full impression of Tuesday. The man was neat and clean as always, with his brown frock coat and matching hat, white shirt, and dark brown pants. His coat was buttoned so that only the tip of his pistol holster showed. His face was clean-shaven and light-complexioned, and his hands were neither weathered nor roughened.

Archer said, "I think Mr. Peavey might be beyond persuasion."

Tuesday's face hardened, and in that instant, Archer thought it even more probable than before that the man had been in prison and that Tuesday was a made-up name.

As if he caught himself revealing too much, Tuesday smiled. "That's all right, too," he said. "I don't think that either way will keep us from being country neighbors. Boot tells me that your place is just over the hill a ways."

"That's true."

"So we ought to meet more often and keep on conversational terms."

"Nothing wrong with that."

Tuesday gave him a casual glance. "Is there anything you wanted to mention today?"

"Oh, no. I just came over here with Boot to see if we could find Sadie."

"Well, I'm glad all that worked out all right." Tuesday turned and smiled at Sadie. "Sorry if you got a scare there, girl."

Sadie raised her eyebrows in a calm expression. "I'm fine. Like you said, it was probably just someone repeating what he heard." She turned her light blue eyes toward Boot. "I guess we ought to be heading home, then."

" 'Magine," said Boot. He had a new toothpick in his mouth, and he rolled it from one side to another.

"Come back any time," said Tuesday. "And Boot, I'll let you know when we're ready to start up again. Shouldn't be long." As Sadie rose from her chair, Tuesday did the same, but he did not shake hands with anybody.

Boot waited until Sadie was mounted on the grey roan, and then he stepped up onto the bay. Archer had led the smoke-colored horse away a few steps, and as soon as the others were in the saddle he swung aboard and caught up with them.

When they were a good half-mile from the ranch headquarters, Boot said, "Did you get to ask him the questions you wanted?"

"Huh. With the way things took a turn, I didn't have to go about it that way. But I got my impressions anyway."

"You think he's what you said?"

Archer nodded. "As much as before. How about you?"

"He didn't like what you said about Peavey."

"No, and that's the one point where I might have gone too far."

"Tipped your hand, you mean?"

"Yeah. I didn't want to do that, but I guess I couldn't resist it."

Beckett shrugged. "Won't make but a day's difference anyway."

"A lot can happen in a day." Archer called across to Sadie, who was riding on the other side of Boot. "Tell me, Sadie, what did that fellow look like? The one that told you I was killed."

"Pretty average. Dark-haired, like you. A little older. About your height. Rode a sorrel horse, about fifteen hands, narrow blaze, white socks in back."

Archer found amusement in her having more specific details about the horse than about the man, but he kept to the topic. "Which way did he go when he left?"

"He went back to town. That struck me as funny, but I had my mind on what he'd told me."

"I can imagine. Are you sure he came from town?"

"No, not really. I was inside when he showed up."

"Probably doesn't matter. He could easily have ridden a ways around, especially if he knew he was doing something devious."

"You think you'll try to find him?" asked Boot.

"Not right away. When we get to the main road, I think I'll double-back around and take a look — see what Tuesday's up to next."

"You need someone to go along?"

"Not now. If I do, I'll let you know."

The cool of the evening began to settle in as Archer kept his lookout. He sat in the shade of the hills almost a mile west of the ranch. At that distance he had little trouble picking out the individual buildings, but he couldn't see much detail. From this side, the icehouse was in front of the other two. The new lumber had a dull shine in the fading daylight, and the rib-like rafters were interspersed with shadows. Having seen the structure up close, Archer could fill in features that he could not see from where he sat — the hollowness of the walls, the silence of the stone floor.

Archer tipped his head to one side. The stone floor. Now that he could not see it, he felt as if he saw something about it that he could not see when he was looking at it. A shiver went through him.

He tensed his arms, shoulders, and chest as a way of generating warmth. He figured he had been sitting for about an hour. Tuesday had not appeared during that time, and it was the hour of the day when people did their chores. No smoke came from the stovepipe of either house. All three mute buildings cast their shadows while the skeletal rafters showed in the light.

A few more minutes passed until the next realization went through him. Tuesday was not at home. He would have waited to give his visitors a head start, and he was probably on his way to town when Archer was circling around to the north.

Archer stood up. He felt like a fool. He might as well have been watching a block of wood, and now he had lost a good two hours.

The dusky horse came alert with the tug on his reins. Archer walked him out a few yards, patted him on the neck, and mounted up. The long shadows stretched out on the grassland as he got the horse moving in a lope toward the Hat Creek Breaks.

The moon had not yet risen when Archer rode up the trail through the breaks and over the pine ridge. The smoke-colored horse was beginning to tire, and for good reason. It had been a long day with a push at the end. Archer let the horse walk. The road went mostly downhill from the ridge to town, and although night had fallen, the hour was not that late.

The horse was still picking up its feet when Archer rode into the main street of town. A few windows had light showing, and piano music drifted through the open doorway of a saloon. It was a familiar sensation to come in off the dark and lonely range to find the town awake and the night young. The moon was rising now, an uneven shape that he could see through the gaps between the buildings. *Calm,* he told himself. *Don't do anything rash.*

Light was visible through the window of

Fenton's store. Archer decided that if the door was open, he would try there first rather than go around to the back and knock on the door.

He tied his horse to the rail and checked once again to make sure his six-gun was in place. His hand went right to the handle.

He took a soft step up onto the sidewalk, then three more to the door. As he tried the handle and found it unlocked, he looked through the glass. Straight down the aisle, Fenton had his head bent downward toward the counter.

The bell tinkled as Archer opened the door, walked in, and closed the door behind him. Fenton looked up with an open expression, and then his face hardened.

"Good evening, Mr. Archer," he said in a loud voice. "I'm just closing up. Is there something I can help you with?"

Archer walked the rest of the way forward, his spurs making light jingles as his heels sounded on the wood floor. He came to a stop about a yard from the counter. "I'd like to speak with Kate if I could."

The storekeeper's beady eyes wavered and then settled on Archer. He had the air of someone who had been caught peeking through a keyhole and was summoning up his dignity in defense. "I'm afraid she's not available."

Archer frowned. "Is she not here?"

"I believe she's gone out for the evening."

Archer's pulse jumped, and he spoke on impulse. "Where?"

Fenton had his composure now. "I don't believe I need to tell you."

"Well, I'll tell you. I want to know where she is."

The storekeeper's eyes glinted behind his glasses. "Don't get truculent with me in my own store. I tell you, I don't need to tell you a thing."

Archer's mouth was dry, and he made an effort to keep his anger down. "Maybe you already did."

Fenton's bristly mustache moved before he spoke. "What do you mean?"

"Where's your pal Tuesday?"

"I don't know what you mean." The beady eyes wavered as before.

A floorboard creaked, accompanied by the sound of a footstep and shifting weight. A voice came through the doorway that led to the back of the store.

"It's all right. We can talk." Tuesday stepped into view with a .45 in his right hand. He gave a pull with his left, and Kate appeared in front of him. As she came to an abrupt stop, she jerked to keep her balance.

"Russ!" she said. "He told me you were hurt."

"Earlier in the day, he had someone say I was killed."

"News gets out ahead of time," said Tuesday.

Kate's eyes narrowed. "What does that mean?" she asked.

Tuesday smiled and pointed his gun at Archer. "You tell her."

"I think he was trying to roil things up, muddy the waters. But someone caught a fish anyway."

Kate gave a puzzled look.

"He sent Peavey out to kill me. Then he wanted to create a distraction to send Boot to town and from there out to the Bar M, to give Peavey an extra day to get back from Newcastle. So he had someone spread the news. Trouble is, Peavey didn't get his part done, and he's laid out like a block of ice."

Tuesday poked the tip of his pistol into Kate's ribs. "Enough smart talk, Archer. Put your gun on the counter."

"What for?"

"We're all three going for a ride."

"Now see here," said Fenton. "You don't need to take the girl now. You've got him."

Tuesday's voice was sharp as he spoke to the storekeeper. "Don't be stupid. She's got

337

a big mouth, and she knows too much."

Fenton's eyes became hard little beads. "If you do anything to her —"

"Oh, shut up. Someone could walk in here any minute. Go lock the door." With the pistol still pointed at Kate, Tuesday flicked a glance around at Archer. When he came back to Fenton, the storekeeper spoke.

"Not until I know what you intend to do. This girl works for me and lives under my roof. I'm not going to let some —"

"Shut up and go lock the door. Don't make me have to take you along, too."

The storekeeper's eyes opened, but the dark beads stayed fixed. "You're not taking me anywhere. Or her."

Tuesday pointed the shiny revolver at Fenton. "I don't think you understand me."

"I understand enough. If you're going to do something, you might as well do it here. You'll have a dozen people on your neck in a minute."

"That does it," said Tuesday, waving the .45 to take in Fenton and Archer both. "We're all going."

Fenton stood in place as his lower jaw moved side to side.

Archer spoke up. "You'd better do as he says. He's already got one person buried beneath his stone floor."

Tuesday's face became a mask of hatred as he swung the pistol straight at Archer. His voice was icy as he said, "I should kill you right now."

The front door burst open, and as the bell tinkled, a cheery voice called out, "Hey, how about a —"

Archer dove to his left to put the counter between him and Tuesday. As he did, the .45 roared and a gunshot split the air overhead. Broken glass made jangling music, followed by the sound of scuffing and scrambling on the wooden floor.

Archer moved a couple of more feet to his left and came up with his six-shooter ready. He did not have a clear target, though. Fenton had his hands on the ears of a twenty-pound sack of potatoes and was swinging it at Tuesday, who had his left arm up to block the object and had his gun pointed at Fenton's green apron. Kate was out of the picture and must have gotten away. Tuesday's gun blasted, but the report was not long as he plugged Fenton at a distance of three feet.

As the sack of potatoes fell and the storekeeper slumped back, Tuesday whirled to find his next target. Archer shot him in the middle of the white shirt, where a red flower blossomed. Tuesday fired one last shot by reflex. His gun was pointed low and off to the side, and the bullet tore open a burlap sack of beans. A handful spilled on the floor as Tuesday landed, sitting up. He tried to raise the pistol again, but his arm sagged and the gun tumbled to the floor. His eyes were blank and staring as his features relaxed. He fell over to his right side and lay still.

Shrill voices and screaming came from the living quarters in back. Fenton was squirming on the floor and groaning. Archer went to the open doorway and hollered to Kate that the shooting was over. After that, he walked into the store itself and stood with his back to the counter.

"Are you all right?" he called. "It's safe to come out."

"Who are you?" came a voice from the cross aisles in the front part of the store.

"I'm Russ Archer. The storekeeper's been shot, but the man who did it is out of business. If you can run for the doctor, that would help."

Movement sounded, and Archer barely got a look at the man as he held onto his hat and bolted for the door.

Kate arrived as the doctor was cutting open Fenton's shirt. A mess of blood showed on the shirt and undershirt as well as on the apron, which had been untied at the waist and flung aside but still hung around the storekeeper's neck.

"Is he going to make it?" Kate asked. "His wife wants to know."

"We'll see," said the doctor from where he knelt. "Just stand back for right now."

Kate moved out from behind the counter and stood by Archer. "That was terrible," she said. "The man was so cold-blooded, like a reptile."

"Well, he's done now."

Her chest went up and down as her breath steadied. Her eyes flickered in the direction of Tuesday's body, and she said, "There are some things I don't understand."

"I know. I'll explain them when we have a little time."

Kate hesitated. "There's one thing I've got to ask right now."

Archer cast a quick glance in the direction of the doctor, who was still kneeling and working. He brought his eyes back to Kate and said, "Go ahead."

"You said he had someone buried under a stone floor. Who is it?"

Archer took a steady breath. "Jack Doolin's other daughter."

CHAPTER FIFTEEN

Archer poured himself a cup of coffee and handed the pot to Whitmore. The older man winced as he turned in his chair and reached. In the week's time since the shooting, he had become adept at using only his left hand, and he made it a point of pride to do as much as he could for himself.

Oscar set a tin plate of hot biscuits in the center of the table, turned away, and came back with a crockery jar of plum jam. "That's all there is for dessert," he said.

"Fine with me," said Whitmore. He set the coffee pot down and reached in his stiff manner.

Archer waited and then took a biscuit, cut it in half, and spread some jam onto it. "I'm going to miss your cooking," he said.

Oscar raised his eyebrows and gave a sideways glance. "Maybe for a while."

Archer thought the cook was going to say something suggestive, but silence hung over the table. Then in an offhand tone, Oscar spoke again.

"As for our part, we'll miss the help. But I imagine we'll get along all right. Keep the mice from takin' over."

Whitmore had trapped his biscuit and cut it in two, and he now reached for the crockery jar. "Once you get settled in your next place, don't be a stranger. Drop by and see us, and tell us where to find you."

"Oh, I will. I feel bad about leavin', but I want to be there when they open up that tract of land, and I'd like to have a look at it before that."

"You've done more than enough here," said Whitmore. "You saw this place through the winter, not to mention all the problems. It's time for you to do somethin' for yourself."

Archer tipped a glance and said, "Thanks."

"If I was you, though, I'd be for tryin' to get more out of what you did here. After all, he was supposed to make you a partner."

"I'm all square, and I'm fine. I got wages for the whole time, plus another horse for myself. Any more than that, and I'd feel as if I got something I shouldn't have."

Whitmore shrugged. "You know best. It's your business."

Oscar came back to the table and sat down. "Even if you wanted to get more, it would be like tryin' to get blood out of a turnip." His saucy expression returned as he said, "There's better things to squeeze."

When the midday meal was over, Archer packed his gear on the buckskin, saddled the smoke-colored horse, and led the two animals into the middle of the yard. He took a last look around at the bunkhouse he had helped build, the corral he had repaired, the house where Lidge had died, and the barn where he himself could have died. He brushed away the crowding emotions and swung into the saddle.

With the lead rope in his left hand, he raised his right and said, "So long, boys."

"So long, Russ."

"Good luck. Come and see us."

The sun was warm in his face as he rode out of the headquarters of the Bar M.

Kate held onto Archer's arm as they walked away from the graveyard. "It's so much better for them to be together," she said.

"It's too bad either of them ended up here so soon."

Kate sniffed. "Especially her. Young enough to get another chance, and then to

344

be cut short. She couldn't have been all that bad."

Archer nodded. "I barely met her in passing, just that once in the saloon. Say what people will, a girl like that has her honesty. She works her way through life, and it's not easy."

Tears formed in Kate's eyes. "I would have liked to know her. You say she looked like Jack."

"There was a resemblance, as I thought back on it."

"I drew a picture of him," she said.

"You did?"

"Yes. Would you like to see it?"

"Of course."

She raised her bag, opened the drawstring, and took out a pasteboard packet. She stopped. "I should have thought of this while we were at their graves." She untied the string and opened the packet.

A fair likeness of Jack Doolin looked up from a common sheet of paper. Archer studied it for a few seconds.

"It looks like him, and I think there's a similarity to her. Maybe the longness of the face, something about the eyes."

Kate gave a sigh as she folded the packet together. "It's all so sad, to have had a father you didn't really know, and a sister you never met. Even the word is strange. Sister. And she's gone before she ever had a chance to live her life."

As they resumed walking, Archer said, "I'm glad we were able to get her a decent burial and pay our respects to them both. I feel right about that, as if things are in their proper place."

"Oh, yes. I do, too. It's not poetic and sad and beautiful, like in the poem, but as you say, there's a decent feeling about it. Yet still it seems so . . . unjust." She sniffed. "Let's do talk about something else. We'll talk about this again some other time. Were you sad to leave the ranch?"

"A little bit. I had invested some of myself in that place, but I knew I had to get away from it."

"And the new owners?"

"Cunningham the lawyer located some of Lidge's relations in Missouri, so the place will go to someone. Until they decide what to do with it, and they'll probably sell it, Oscar and Whitmore can take care of it. Cunningham, of course, controls the money. And if they need another hand, Boot Beckett is about as close as someone here in town."

Kate smiled. "He's a good one. I'm glad to know they've got him to call on." After a moment of walking in silence, she said, "Do you think anyone will find the gold?"

"Huh. I wouldn't be surprised if nobody ever did. There was a short while when I thought it was too bad that Tuesday took the knowledge with him. Same with any details about where he came from, what he did earlier in life, and whether Tuesday was even his real name. But once the idea settled in that he was dead and gone, I figured there was no point in wishing that some things had been different. You take it all together."

"It doesn't seem as if the idea of the gold ever excited you very much."

"Well, no, I guess not. By the time I heard the story, I had already decided I didn't want, or shouldn't have, the Bar M. Even if I had a claim on it, it was tainted, like I've said before. The idea of the gold had some of the same feeling. Even if it didn't belong to anyone anymore, it came from a dishonest beginning, and the work of finding it wouldn't have felt right. So I'm glad not to have it get into my blood. I wouldn't want to be always on the lookout for the place where it was buried. I can imagine spending all my waking hours looking for likely spots and digging holes. I'm better off not wanting it."

"So you don't care about it?"

"Well, it's not mine anyway, and to the extent that it's tempted me, I've made myself not care. You know, Lidge Mercer was good to me. He had his failings, but he had good intentions as far as wanting to do something for me. But if I learned anything out of all of this, it was to not want something I hadn't earned for myself."

"Not everyone would look at it that way."

"Oh, no," he said. "You take Boot for example. He would see it as an opportunity. From the few comments he's made, I've already gathered that he wouldn't have — how shall I put it — the same scruples. Not that he doesn't have any — they just wouldn't get in the way with something like this."

Kate smiled. "I can imagine that."

"It'll likely come up in conversation. We have to go see them, you know."

"That's true. I feel that I should have gone out there sooner. I know Sadie wanted me to. It's important for a girl to have her own house, her own hearth and home."

Kate and Archer visited Boot and Sadie the next day, arriving in the early afternoon. The day was warm, and the short-cropped grass near the house was showing green.

The red and brown chickens were scratching the ground and did not spook at the horse and buggy.

Sadie came out of the house and waved, then stood shading her eyes with her hand. As Archer brought the buggy to a stop, she walked forward.

"Well, look who's here," she said.

Archer climbed down and helped Kate to the ground.

Kate's eyes were glistening. "Oh, Sadie," she said, taking her hands, "I'm so happy to see you in your own place. And I hope you forgive me for not coming sooner."

"You come when you can. I'm glad you're here." Sadie took a kiss on her cheek and with a soft smile withdrew her hands. She put them on her hips and motioned with her head. "Boot's in back, showin' a horse to a buyer."

"You can show us your place," Kate said.

"Sure. We'll start with my critters." She waved her hand. "Chickens, of course. Can't have too many eggs. There's always someone who'll buy 'em." Sadie had her authority back.

Kate and Archer fell in beside her as the three of them walked around back. Boot had the dun on a long rope tied to the halter, and he was making the horse trot in a circle. A heavyset man in a derby hat and a sackcloth coat was smoking a cigar and observing. Sadie directed her guests out of the way and brought them to a small corral.

"This is my milk cow. She's a Jersey. I make butter. You can always sell it, too. And the whey —" She led them to another pen. It had lower sides with planks running around the bottom. Inside lay a dirty white pig with its pink skin showing through the hair. "What little whey there is, this fella takes care of it."

"He's a cute one," said Kate.

Sadie gave a clever smile. "He'll grow up to be ham and bacon in the fall. Just don't tell him."

Archer said, "Will you have Boot do that?"

"I may have to have it done. You know Boot. He doesn't always get things done when I need it. And I don't know how to make ham and bacon myself. I know how to render the lard, though."

The little pig flinched and grunted in its sleep.

"I hope he fattens up for you," said Archer.

"So do I. But one thing you learn. You do a little of everything, so you don't depend on just one thing to make or break you. Like farming. If all you have is your wheat crop and you lose it, you lose everything. But like this, if one thing fails, you have the others."

"Do you think you'll get any other animals?"

"Sheep. Boot hates 'em, or he says he does, but he knows I can raise a couple of them and do all right. There's people in town that eat lamb."

"And potatoes?" said Kate. "People raise potatoes here, don't they?"

"You bet. I just need Boot to dig me up a patch. If he doesn't, I'll have to. But new ground is hard to turn." Sadie pursed her little mouth as if she was intent on a thought. "I need to remember to get punkin seeds."

Kate took her hand again. "I'm just so happy for you, Sadie. You get to do all of these things on your own. And you know how to do them all."

Sadie pushed out her lower lip but did not take her hand away. "Got to keep at it. Not many windfalls in this country."

Boot's voice rose on the air in the tone of a person who was winding up a conversation. The man with the cigar said a couple of words in a gravelly voice. Boot led the dun horse to the corral and put him in while the other man went to his own horse and untied it. Sadie stood with her head up as she waited for Boot to join the group.

He had his thumbs in his belt loops as he came ambling up. He tossed a glance at the man riding away and said, "That's the third one that tried to cut my price in two. I fed this horse all winter, and I don't have to give him away now." He tossed his head and said, "What news?"

"Came out to visit," said Archer.

"How are things at the ranch?"

"Pretty steady, I think. I'm done there."

"Oh. When do these new people take over?"

"A far as ownership, probably pretty soon. But I don't think they'll do much other than put it up for sale and hope they get an offer."

Boot gave a half-smile. "Are the two old boys still there?"

"Oscar and Whitmore? Oh, yeah. But they're not doin' much more than makin' sure the place doesn't blow away. If they get in a tight and need some help, they might call on you."

"Be glad to help. Stay on neighborly terms." Beckett arched his eyebrows and poked his cheek out with his tongue. "I'm not workin' for anyone else right now anyway. I could even go check on 'em."

Archer smiled. "And keep your eyes open."

"Why not? With ownership bein' up in the air, there prob'ly won't be many folks lookin' to run me off if I was to go out and poke around a little." He looked at Sadie with a jaunty expression, as if to say, "What do you think?"

She had retrieved her hand. "How big is that ranch?" she said.

Boot wagged his head. "About thirty-two hundred acres."

"My God, you could be there the rest of your days."

Boot shrugged. "Somethin' to do."

Sadie's eyes grew wide as she put her hands on her hips.

"You could come along," he said, still breezy.

Sadie pushed out her mouth and shook her head. "No," she said. "I'll just let you go out there and grub around in the sagebrush and rattlesnakes until you get tired of it."

"Well, it's an idea," he said. He turned to Archer. "Are you two stayin' for supper?"

"No, I think we'll move along in a little while here."

"Back to town?"

"Actually, we're on our way north. I want

to take a look at some land that's coming up, and I want to be there to file as soon as it's open."

"North, huh?"

"Yep. On the other side of the Cheyenne River."

"North of where we went that time."

"That's right."

Boot glanced at the buggy. "Well, you've got some more travelin' to do today, then."

"We'll stop on the way back, make sure we get here for dinner."

"You do that." Boot's eyes traveled to Kate. "I hope you enjoy the trip. It's nice country."

"I'm sure I'll like it."

Archer and Kate said their goodbyes and climbed into the buggy. As they rolled along the trail toward the main road, Kate took a deep breath and said, "Do you think there really is a cache somewhere?"

Archer shrugged. "There might be, but it's not the first story I've heard like that."

"Nor I. I've heard stories, too. Not about stagecoaches but about banks and trains. The same idea, though. A big hoard of money, waiting to be found." After a few seconds she added, "I'm glad you can just walk away from it."

"Like I said, I don't like the idea of wearing myself out, fretting over it. You can dig a lot of holes in just one acre, let alone thirty-two hundred."

"Do you think Boot will get the fever?"

"Oh, he's got a fever of his own, to be always changing things. This idea might get a hold of him, and he might not ever give it up for good, but it won't wear at him like it would at me. He's able to see a little joke in it."

They came to the old stage route that was the main road, and Archer followed it north. The buggy rolled out into the great rangeland in the warmth of the spring afternoon. Archer put his hand in Kate's as they went on their way to find a piece of land of their own across the Cheyenne River.

ABOUT THE AUTHOR

John D. Nesbitt lives in the plains country of Wyoming, where he teaches English and Spanish at Eastern Wyoming College. His published work includes more than thirty books of traditional western, contemporary, mystery, and retro/noir fiction. John has won many awards for his work, including two awards from the Wyoming State Historical Society (for fiction), two awards from Wyoming Writers for encouragement of other writers and service to the organization, two Wyoming Arts Council literary fellowships, a Western Writers of America Spur finalist award for his western novel *Raven Springs,* and the Spur award itself for his noir short story "At the End of the Orchard" and for his western novels *Trouble at the Redstone* and *Stranger in Thunder Basin.* See his website at www.johndnesbitt.com.